Gide

shifting fog.

A shapely female in her early twenties emerged from the hazy shadows of trees and underbrush. Her long hair caught in the sparkling sunlight and danced like red-and-gold flames. She wore brown, trim fitting breeches that accentuated the shapely curve of her hips and a white shirt that molded itself provocatively to her full breasts.

Honest to goodness, Gideon had never seen a woman so captivating and alluring in all his thirty-two years of vast and varied experience. If there *were* angels sent down from above, he'd like to think this was what an angel looked like. Either that or she was one of the Native American spirit guides he'd heard described by his Osage mother.

And yet, a quiet voice inside his head whispered, *Here comes trouble,* and the cynic he'd become paid close attention.

* * *

Lady Renegade
Harlequin® Historical #1017—November 2010

Praise for
Carol Finch

"Carol Finch is known for her lightning-fast, roller-coaster-ride adventure romances that are brimming over with a large cast of characters and dozens of perilous escapades."
—*RT Book Reviews*

The Kansas Lawman's Proposal
"Fast-paced, sensual… One of the genre's top-notch Western writers delivers the expected in a tale that's as classic as they come."
—*RT Book Reviews*

Texas Ranger, Runaway Heiress
"Finch offers another heartwarming Western romance full of suspense, humor and strong characters… It's hard to put this one down."
—*RT Book Reviews*

McCavett's Bride
"For wild adventures, humor and Western atmosphere, Finch can't be beat. She fires off her quick-paced novels with the crack of a rifle and creates the atmosphere of the Wild West through laugh-out-loud dialogue and escapades that keep you smiling."
—*RT Book Reviews*

The Ranger's Woman
"Finch delivers her signature humor, along with a big dose of colorful Texas history, in a love and laughter romp."
—*RT Book Reviews*

Lone Wolf's Woman
"As always, Finch provides frying-pan-into-the-fire action that keeps the pages flying, then spices up her story with not one, but two romances, sensuality and strong emotions."
—*RT Book Reviews*

CAROL FINCH

LADY RENEGADE

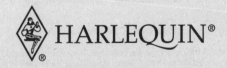

HARLEQUIN®

TORONTO • NEW YORK • LONDON
AMSTERDAM • PARIS • SYDNEY • HAMBURG
STOCKHOLM • ATHENS • TOKYO • MILAN • MADRID
PRAGUE • WARSAW • BUDAPEST • AUCKLAND

Recycling programs
for this product may
not exist in your area.

ISBN-13: 978-0-373-29617-0

LADY RENEGADE

Copyright © 2010 by Connie Feddersen

This edition published by arrangement with Harlequin Books S.A.

For questions and comments about the quality of this book please contact us at Customer_eCare@Harlequin.ca.

® and TM are trademarks of the publisher. Trademarks indicated with ® are registered in the United States Patent and Trademark Office, the Canadian Trade Marks Office and in other countries.

www.eHarlequin.com

Printed in U.S.A.

This book is dedicated to my husband, Ed, and our children, Kurt, Shawnna, Jill, Jon, Christie and Durk. And to our grandchildren, Livia, Harleigh, Blake, Kennedy, Dillon and Brooklynn. And to Kurt and Shawnna's children, whenever they may be. Hugs and kisses!

Chapter One

Osage Nation, Indian Territory
Early 1880s

Lorelei Russell halted her strawberry roan gelding in the copse of trees overlooking Burgess Ranch and Stage Station. A well-manicured two-story clapboard house, a stage station, three wooden sheds and an oversize barn sat in the lush valley. The spring sunset cast filtered light and shadows in the trees, giving the Osage Hills a fanciful quality.

Dismounting, Lorelei patted her horse, Drifter, affectionately then received a nudge from him on her elbow in response. Hiking off, she reread the note she'd received from Anthony Rogers, foreman at Burgess Ranch.

She had meant to stop by earlier in the day, but she and her father had been busy unloading the delivery wagon that had arrived at their trading post and ferry on Winding River. Then she had made a delivery to a homebound customer before stopping by to see Anthony.

Lorelei had hoped to return home by dark, but Russell's Trading Post was ten miles south of the station on the stagecoach route. Although the territory had become a refuge for outlaws that holed up in thickly timbered hills and rocky gorges, Lorelei had lived the last decade of her twenty-three years in the area. Her father, a former military officer, had made certain she could take care of herself. She was very familiar with the tree-choked hillsides of the Osage reservation and she could protect herself with a variety of weapons.

Her wandering thoughts trailed off when she glanced at Anthony's note again. The honest truth was she had procrastinated in stopping by to see Anthony. He had been courting her for over three months but her feelings for him hadn't progressed past the friendship stage. Unfortunately, she had the impression that Anthony had developed the kind of affection for her that she couldn't return. It wasn't that he wasn't attractive, with his sandy-blond hair, thick-lashed blue eyes and lean physique. He just wasn't…

She sighed heavily. She wasn't sure what love was, but she didn't think this was it.

"Thank goodness you're here." Anthony suddenly appeared from the deepening shadows to envelop her in a hug. "I was getting worried, sweetheart."

"Papa and I have been busy with inventory and customers," she explained as she backed from his embrace.

He nodded and smiled. "I should have come to the trading post since we're running low on a few supplies, but I've had dozens of last-minute chores to wrap up here."

"Last-minute?" she repeated curiously.

He reached out to trail his forefinger over her cheek. "I have a confession, Lori," he murmured as he stared deeply into her eyes. "Every hour I've spent with you leaves me wanting to spend even more."

Lori smiled weakly, but she didn't have the heart to lead Tony on by saying that she felt the same. When he clutched both of her hands in his own, she tensed. He looked so serious, almost impatient to spew out the words she didn't want to hear.

To her dismay, he went down on one knee and stared up at her with a hopeful smile. "I'm in love with you, Lori. I want you to marry me and come away with me so we can make a clean break and a fresh start. We can go wherever your heart desires. Colorado, California, Montana. Anyplace you say."

Her jaw sagged but she couldn't formulate a sentence when her mind was whirling like a cyclone. He wanted her to elope with him? Leave the territory abruptly? *Why?*

Tony never spoke much about his past and now she wondered why. Was he a wanted man? Was the law about to catch up with him? Did he feel the desperate need to run for his life?

She knew that Judge Isaac Parker in Fort Smith had sent out several dozen Deputy U.S. Marshals to apprehend outlaws that fled into the territory in hopes of outrunning their crimes. Had someone recognized Tony from a Wanted poster and turned him in?

"Lori? Sweetheart?" Tony squeezed her hand. "Will you do me the honor of marrying me? We can be off tonight so we can begin our new life together and leave this place far behind."

Lori pulled Tony to his feet. "Why do you want to leave the territory in such a rush?" she questioned intently.

Tony glanced this way and that, provoking more questions she wanted answered. "I hadn't meant to fall in love with you, Lori, but it just happened. You fascinate me. I want you to come with me. We can leave tonight. Right now. I have money saved up for our trip."

He certainly avoided her questions, leaving her to suspect that he *was* a fugitive of justice. Her concern escalated when he kept glancing every which way, as if he anticipated trouble.

"Will you?" he persisted. "I promise I'll take good care of you, Lori."

Lori didn't need a man to take care of her. Her father had spent years ensuring his only surviving child could handle herself with a pistol, rifle and knife and manage several hand-to-hand combat maneuvers. She'd perfected those skills while dealing with several unsavory characters that stopped at the trading post and used the ferry that transported passengers, wagons, stagecoaches and horses across the river.

"I'm sorry, Tony," she said as gently as she knew how. "You are a dear friend and you know I treasure your companionship. But—"

"But you don't feel the same way I do," he interrupted in disappointment. His broad shoulders slumped but he nodded acceptance. "You can't blame a man for asking. I know I'm not your first proposal."

"None of them have been as flattering and tempting as yours," she replied honestly.

"At least I have that. I'll miss you like crazy, sweetheart."

When he eased closer to kiss her goodbye Lori sincerely wished she could feel something besides a lukewarm reaction to his embrace. Nevertheless, her heart knew what it felt and there was no convincing it otherwise. She tried to be honest, especially with herself. She couldn't give Tony what he wanted. She refused to consider marriage until she discovered that unique feeling her father claimed he had shared with her mother, even years after she and her young son had succumbed to diphtheria.

Her wandering thoughts broke off and she snapped to attention when she heard a crackling of twigs in the underbrush. Heavy shadows enveloped the trees, concealing whoever or whatever lurked in the near distance. Tony muttered a curse when a gunshot rang out in the gathering darkness. Lori heard a bullet whistle past her head before it plugged into a tree beside them. She tried to object when Tony tucked her protectively behind him. She tugged on his arm to bustle both of them behind a tree for protection, but another gunshot erupted before they reached cover.

She knew the instant the bullet found its mark. Tony staggered against her, gasping for breath. When another shot ripped through the trees, Lori grabbed one of the pistols in Tony's double holster and returned fire. She heard the thrashing in the underbrush and thud of horses' hooves. But her focus was on Tony, who crumpled to the ground.

"Sweet mercy," she whispered when she saw the bloodstains spreading quickly across the left side of Tony's shirt.

She dropped to her knees beside him when he lifted his hand to her.

"I'm sorry," he gasped. "I didn't mean to drag you into this. But I do love you. Now run! Get out of here before it's too late."

His apology baffled her. Why did she need to escape? Was she considered guilty by association? Escape from whom? Who was after him? A bounty hunter who had discovered Anthony Rogers's true identity and tracked him down? What had Tony done that earned him a bushwhacking?

"Go...now..." He panted for breath as he clutched his chest.

"No, I want to help you," she insisted, using his kerchief to stem the flow of blood oozing from his wound.

Almost frantic now, Tony shoved at her hands, but she could tell he was losing strength with each passing second.

"Go, damn it. Get out of here! If you care anything about me at all, you'll do as I say and flee for your own safety!"

Stumbling to her feet, Lori looked around, wondering if Maggie Burgess, the widowed owner of the station and ranch or one of the hired hands had heard the shots. Where was the help Tony desperately needed?

A moment later, she saw Maggie appear from the corner of the station where stagecoach travelers took their meals.

"Over here!" Lori yelled. "We need help!"

Maggie clutched the front of her skirts and raced across the lawn toward the copse of trees.

"Damn it, get out of here!" Tony mumbled weakly. "Please, sweetheart. It's the last thing I'll ever ask of you. Go…"

When his lashes fluttered shut and he sagged lifelessly on the ground Lori backed up four paces. Frantic, confused and uncertain where the sniper lurked, she wheeled toward her horse, Tony's pistol still clutched in her fist.

"Oh, my God!" Maggie Burgess wailed as she raced toward Tony's unmoving form. She glared at the gun in Lori's hand and then at Tony. "You killed him! *Why?* Because you chased after him and he wanted nothing to do with you? You little tramp!"

"I didn't kill him," Lori protested as she scanned the darkness, in case the killer was waiting to dispose of all of them. "We need to take cover before more shots are fired."

"You're a liar!" the brunette railed as she dropped down beside Tony. "Now what am I to do? I've lost my husband

and now you've murdered my foreman. Who will help me run my business? How will I survive?"

When Maggie grabbed the spare pistol, Lori was certain the grief-crazed widow intended to shoot her for the crime she falsely presumed Lori had committed. As Maggie clutched the pistol in both hands and raised it to fire, Lori darted behind the nearest tree. The shot zinged past her, compelling her to run for her life.

"Whore!" Maggie screeched, then fired off another shot. "Murderess! Sonny! Teddy! Come quickly. The killer is trying to get away! Hurry!"

Lori sprinted toward her horse, grateful she was wearing her usual attire of breeches and shirt so she could move swiftly and agilely.

On her best days, Lori couldn't compete with Maggie Burgess's stylish clothing. But then, Maggie didn't have to vault onto a horse and race into the night to avoid capture.

"What happened, Mizz Burgess?"

Lori glanced back to see the silhouettes of Sonny Hathaway and Teddy Collins, two of the hired hands, racing uphill toward Maggie.

"Lorelei Russell just killed Tony!" Maggie wailed. "Stop her before she circles back to the trading post to seek her father's protection!"

Maggie's command sealed Lori's escape route, forcing her to ride toward the wild tumble of timbered hills so she wouldn't drag her father into this horrible misunderstanding. She hoped when Maggie had time to calm down and review the situation she'd realize that Lori hadn't fired the fatal shot.

Lori nudged Drifter in the flanks and he took off like a shot, zigzagging through the trees to put more distance between her and the two hired hands sent to pursue her.

She swore she could still hear Maggie screeching like
a banshee, but Lori didn't look back. She held on to the
saddle horn and curled over Drifter's neck to make certain
a low-hanging tree limb didn't knock her off the galloping
horse.

She allowed herself to spill the tears that had clouded
her eyes when she'd realized Tony was beyond help. Now
she could cry for her lost friend and curse herself for reject-
ing his marriage proposal. It broke her heart, knowing
Tony had offered his love and she'd turned him down—the
moment before the fatal gunshot ended his life at the young
age of thirty.

In addition, Maggie Burgess was so beside herself with
grief and fury that she'd shot at Lori. She felt sorry for the
young widow who was only six or seven years older than
Lori.

Maggie had married Hubert Burgess who was sixteen
years her senior. Two months ago, Hub's horse had bucked
him off while he was chasing cattle rustlers and he'd died
instantly. Maggie had yet to recover from her anguish, and
now someone had shot and killed her ranch foreman, leaving her grief-stricken, desperate and feeling abandoned and
overwhelmed.

Lori's thoughts scattered in the wind when she heard the
thunder of hoofbeats behind her. The report of a rifle shattered the silence. Lori plastered herself against Drifter's
neck and urged the gelding into his fastest pace as he
scrambled uphill. The flare from a discharging rifle caught
her attention and she frowned, bemused. The shot came
from the west, not the south where Sonny and Teddy rode
in hot pursuit.

Was the bushwhacker who had killed Tony after her,
too? A cold chill slithered down her spine when she remembered Tony had stepped in front of her like a shield to take

the fatal shot. By all rights, *she* should be dead right now. She would have been the innocent victim struck by the killer's careless shot in the darkness. Whatever Tony had done in his past to draw gunfire, he'd committed a selfless act. He didn't deserve to die! she thought remorsefully.

Lori muffled a sniff and tried to block out the awful scene that kept replaying itself in her mind. She couldn't allow herself to be distracted while racing to safety with two hired hands chasing her, as well as the sniper, who evidently had circled to the west to shoot at her.

Guided by the light of the moon, Lori headed toward the wild, broken Osage Hills where deep gulches and rock-and-timber hilltops offered protection. She cringed, knowing the grief-stricken widow and the hired hands believed the worst about her. They planned to take the law into their own hands to see her pay for a crime she didn't commit.

Glancing uneasily around her, she held on as Drifter scrabbled uphill, weaving his way around oversize boulders and trees. She knew bears and panthers roamed the area, not to mention vagabond outlaws. Not counting the two-man posse and the mysterious sniper who had killed Tony.

She squeezed her eyes shut and choked on a sob. She hoped that wherever Anthony Rogers was—and no matter what he'd done in his secretive past—he could hear her silent apology and he'd forgive her for turning him down. The thought of never seeing Tony again tormented her to no end, especially when she'd sent him off to the Hereafter with her rejection echoing around him.

Five days later

Deputy U.S. Marshal Gideon Fox scrunched down in the bushes, watching the outlaw known as Pecos Clem

Murphy build his morning campfire in the valley between two steep embankments in the Osage Hills. Despite the thick fog that cloaked the valley, Gideon hadn't had trouble tracking Pecos Clem—thanks to the man's cohorts. They had been all too happy to offer Gideon directions—after he'd applied some *un*friendly persuasion.

Clem whistled while he worked. The former Texas cowboy and his brigands had turned to cattle rustling and horse thieving and had been hiding out in Indian Territory for several months. But very soon, Clem would rejoin his two friends, who were sitting in the jail wagon at marshal headquarters.

Gideon crept closer to the stubble-faced, scraggly-haired outlaw. When Gideon noticed the trip wire six inches in front of his boot, he stopped dead in his tracks. He glanced speculatively from the wire to Clem. No wonder the wily outlaw was lounging by the campfire, looking carefree and unconcerned while he brewed his morning coffee. The sneaky bastard was *inviting* Gideon to come closer and fall into a trap.

Giving Clem more credit than he did previously, Gideon stepped over the booby trap and surveyed the area. If he were Clem, he'd set another trip wire. Sure enough, partially concealed by fallen leaves and twigs, another trip wire awaited Gideon. But he carefully avoided it.

He'd seen all kinds of schemes and traps during his years as a member of the Osage Reservation Police Force and then as a commissioned deputy marshal serving the federal court in Fort Smith. Dealing with Clem served to remind Gideon of his motto: Don't believe everything you hear or see. And don't trust anyone but yourself and your own family.

Gideon had seen too many men die with stunned expressions on their faces. He didn't plan to join the ranks of the departed.

Crouching in the underbrush near a tree, Gideon grabbed his dagger from his boot then hurled it into the tree stump where Clem sat. Wheeling quickly, Clem fired off three shots that sailed ten feet over Gideon's hiding place. Then Gideon tossed a broken tree limb to his left and watched Clem fire off two more shots. The outlaw was lightning-quick with his pistol.

"Show yourself!" Clem barked. "Only cowards crawl and slither on their bellies in the grass."

Gideon had been taunted, ridiculed and baited scores of times and he really didn't give a damn about an outlaw's opinion of him. Clem could call him The Devil Himself and it wouldn't faze Gideon. His objective was to rid his people's land of the thieves and murderers that invaded the territory to escape the law from neighboring states.

"You gonna show yourself, yellow-belly?" Clem taunted.

Gideon didn't reply, just surveyed the campsite once again. Since Clem wore double hostlers on his hips, Gideon figured the outlaw had seven shots left in his six-shooters. Plus, he had access to Gideon's dagger—and perhaps a dagger of his own. Also, there was an empty scabbard on the saddle Clem had used as his pillow for sleeping. Gideon predicted there was also a rifle tucked under the pallet.

"Friend or foe?" Clem demanded impatiently. "Coffee's ready. You coming in or not?"

Gideon glanced overhead then grabbed another broken limb to hurl upward.

"Hell!" Clem growled when he heard the clatter in the tree above him.

Since Clem expected someone to drop down on him, Gideon took advantage of the distraction and charged forward. By the time Clem realized the threat was behind him, not above him, Gideon slammed into his back and knocked away the pistol. Clem went down with a grunt and groan then spewed profanity. Before Clem could roll away to grab a dagger or his pistol, Gideon snatched up his knife and pressed it into Clem's throat.

"Wanted dead or alive, according to Judge Parker," Gideon snarled threateningly. "You decide how you want to meet him. As for me, I'd just as soon toss your sorry carcass over the back of a horse and let the undertaker deal with you."

Clem glanced over his thick shoulder. "Who *are* you?"

"Deputy U.S. Marshal Gideon Fox." He manacled Clem's wrists then hauled him to his feet.

"Well damn," Clem muttered. "I ain't been in the territory too long but I've heard of you and none of it's good. A real bastard who'll chase a man to the gates of hell…and beyond, I'm told. A blue-eyed half-breed to boot. I never did care much for Injuns."

"Quit flattering me. It'll get you nowhere."

From Lori's hiding place behind a boulder on the hillside, she watched the tall, muscular man, wearing black breeches, a dark shirt, leather vest and boots move through the soupy fog like a shadow within a shadow to capture the outlaw. The man who claimed to be a Deputy U.S. Marshal was exceptionally quick on his feet and handy with weapons.

Although Lori had overheard the conversation, she was leery about approaching the lawman. But after holing up in caves for five days—and encountering one unsociable panther, while dodging Sonny Hathaway and Teddy Collins—she decided a lawman could offer legal protection.

She needed to tell her side of the story about the murder and clear her name. Plus, whoever had killed Tony was running loose, which meant she was still in danger.

Lori had grieved the loss of her friend as she had washed his blood from her shirt in a nearby stream.

Unfortunately, she hadn't been able to wash away the torturous memory of that tragic night.

Several of Tony's comments continued to baffle her. She welcomed a formal investigation that would give her the opportunity to make her statement and find the man who shot Tony. Whatever had been going on that fateful night, Lori owed her life to Tony, who'd taken the fatal bullet for her.

Her regretful thoughts trailed off and she came to attention after the lawman had captured the outlaw. Now was the time to pick her way down the rugged hillside to introduce herself to the lawman. Mentally rehearsing what she intended to say, Lori led Drifter around the trees and boulders, then tethered him. She could only hope the Deputy U.S. Marshal would offer protection and agree to accompany her back to Russell Trading Post to clear her name and reassure her father that she was alive.

Gideon pushed Clem ahead of him, just in case there was another booby trap strategically situated between Clem and his stolen horse. When Clem halted, trying to lure Gideon into taking the lead and dragging him forward to spring the trap, Gideon stayed put.

"We can still do this the easy way," Gideon breathed down Clem's neck. "I can shove you into the trip wire and you can shoot yourself. You'll be as dead as a man can get. Not me. I'll be around to collect your bounty and the reward."

"You're all heart, Fox," Clem said and scowled.

"I hear that a lot… *Now move.*"

Muttering, Clem stepped over the booby trap.

"Where'd you learn to set traps?" Gideon asked conversationally as he quick-marched Clem to his stolen horse— the evidence needed to stick him in Judge Parker's jail, awaiting a prison sentence.

"I rode with Confederate raiders in Kansas during the war." Clem glanced back at Gideon and smirked disrespectfully. "Where'd you learn to *avoid* 'em? In Injun warrior training school?"

"Sure. I graduated at the head of my class," Gideon replied without missing a beat. "I get even better at it while dealing with former guerilla fighters like you. I have a lot of practical experience with sneaky, lying, cheating, thieving white men."

Swearing foully, Pecos Clem tugged on the rope Gideon had used to tie him to the tree. Although Clem called Gideon several rude, disrespectful names, he ignored them and saddled the gray stallion. According to the reports delivered to the marshals' mobile headquarters, Pecos Clem and his two cohorts had raided an Osage ranch and stolen several horses. The gray was the last one recovered.

"How'd you find me?" Clem sniped as Gideon hoisted him onto the horse then tied his feet to the stirrups. "Did my backstabbing friends squeal on me? Damn those rascals!"

"Nope, I smelled you two miles away," Gideon replied.

"*I'*m not the stinking Injun around here. *You* are," he muttered hatefully. "We ran off your redskin cousins in Texas and herded them into this territory. If it was up to me, you and your kind would be dead and gone."

Gideon's response was a snort. Clem could spout insults until he ran out of breath. Gideon was riding Indian reservations in the territory of white criminals and he was protecting *his* people from harm. That's what mattered.

"You hear what I said, Injun?" Clem ridiculed. "I—"

His voice trailed off at the same moment that Gideon noticed movement in the shifting fog. The sun broke free briefly, leaving a pocket of light shimmering on the hillside. A shapely female in her early twenties emerged from the hazy shadows of trees and underbrush. Her long curly hair caught in the sparkling sunlight and danced like red-and-gold flames.

She was tall—maybe five foot six inches, he guessed. Plus, she was all too alluring in brown, trim-fitting breeches that accentuated the shapely curve of her hips and the white shirt that molded itself provocatively to her full breasts.

He blinked twice, wondering if he was seeing a mirage or some sort of mystical apparition. The shifting fog and glittering spears of sunlight gave the woman an ethereal quality impossible to ignore. The world seemed eerily still and Gideon stood transfixed. Even Pecos Clem seemed too dazed to attempt escape while Gideon was hopelessly distracted.

Honest to goodness, Gideon had never seen a woman so captivating and alluring in all his thirty-two years of vast and varied experience. If there *were* white men's angels sent down from above, he'd like to think this was what an angel looked like. Either that or she was one of the Indian spirit guides he'd heard described by his Osage mother.

And yet, a quiet voice inside his head whispered, *Here comes trouble,* and the cynic he'd become paid close attention.

Chapter Two

"Gideon Fox?" Her voice floated toward him on the slightest hint of a breeze.

How'd she know my name? he asked himself, stunned.

Gideon spoke not a word while the woman moved gracefully toward him. When she came close enough for him to make out her facial features, which were surrounded by that shiny mass of flame-gold hair, the astonishing sight of her stole his breath right out of his lungs. Alert golden eyes, rimmed with a thick fringe of black lashes, focused intently on him. She had a creamy complexion, a pert nose and plump pink lips ripe for kissing.

Hell and damn! He couldn't recall another time in his life when he'd been so awed by the sight of a woman. He couldn't seem to look away, just stood there wondering if he had set off a trip wire, died and ended up on the spiritual pathway to the Osage Afterlife and didn't know it yet.

"Are you real?" Clem chirped, obviously as hypnotized

as Gideon by the unexplained appearance of the bewitching creature that had materialized out of nowhere.

She glanced at Clem for a half second then fixed those captivating golden eyes on Gideon and said, "My name is Lorelei Russell and I need your assistance, Marshal Fox."

The fairy-tale image shattered like broken glass. Gideon had heard that name the previous day in marshal camp. A messenger had arrived to alert the lawmen that a woman had murdered her lover then fled into the rugged Osage Hills. Apparently, she hadn't realized the network of information passed quickly among the roaming bands of deputy marshals who patrolled Indian Territory.

If she thought to attach herself to him, after cleverly making use of the fog and sunlight to bewitch him, then she thought wrong. No matter how lovely and captivating she was—and she definitely *was*—she wasn't getting her hooks into Gideon Fox. His hardscrabble life had taught him to be wary and suspicious. Dealing with ruthless criminals made him excessively cynical and cautious. Gideon wasn't falling into her trap, either.

To ensure Pecos Clem couldn't escape, Gideon double-checked the ropes that held the outlaw to the saddle. He'd be damned if he let himself be distracted by sinful temptation at its best—or worst, depending on how you looked at it. He did not intend to lose one prisoner while capturing another.

"What can I do for you, Miz Russell?" Gideon asked as nonchalantly as he knew how.

"I would like for you to escort me to my father's trading post near Winding River so I can clear up a misunderstanding and track down a murderer who killed my friend."

So she planned to use him as her protective shield, did she? He wasn't surprised. Half the people in this world expected him to do favors for them. With the exception of his two younger brothers and his sister-in-law, he amended. Then again, even they could become demanding on occasion.

The other half of the population tried to avoid him before he hauled them to Judge Parker's federal court.

"I'm in the middle of an arrest, Mizz Russell." He turned directly to face her—and wished he hadn't. The woman *looked* like she should be against the law and her effect on him was staggering. Gideon tried exceptionally hard to pretend indifference but it wasn't easy.

She shifted her weight from one booted foot to the other, drawing his unwilling attention to the curve of her hips and her long, shapely legs. "Couldn't you leave your prisoner with other marshals? I know your mobile headquarters and jail wagon must be around here somewhere."

"I could," he acknowledged. "But I'm nine miles west of headquarters."

She nodded pensively, causing a riot of red-gold curlicue strands of hair to bobble around her exquisite face. "I'll fetch my horse. After we drop off your prisoner we can head west."

Gideon had no reason to mistrust her intentions—and no reason not to. "I'll go with you to retrieve your mount," he insisted as he tethered the gray horse to a tree. "Clem isn't going anywhere until I get back."

Letting Lorelei lead the way wasn't such a good idea, Gideon decided a moment later. The seductive sway of her hips hypnotized him. Worse, he found himself speculating how this wicked, murdering angel looked naked.

He could picture that curly mane of flame-gold hair spilling over the grass as he settled himself exactly above her. He could imagine the feel of those well-proportioned legs hooked around his waist as he buried himself inside her and fell into the depths of those thick-lashed golden eyes. It would be like flying into the blistering heat of the sun….

The erotic thought blazed through his mind and scorched his body, leaving it sizzling with forbidden desire. Ruthlessly, Gideon ignored the tingling sensations and reminded himself that no matter how appealing this sinful angel was, she had murdered her lover.

The only reason he'd reacted so fiercely to her was that he'd been away from women too long. His forays to capture criminals in Indian Territory—that encompassed seventy thousand square miles—usually lasted six weeks. He'd been in the wilderness for *five* weeks. *Any* female would look good to him by now, he tried to convince himself.

Unfortunately, this particular woman possessed excessive feminine appeal. The fact that Lorelei had murdered her last lover and wanted Gideon to get her off, scot-free, should have repelled him. But it didn't, damn it.

"What are you doing out here alone?" Gideon asked as she hiked up the hillside.

"I'm hiding from the two men chasing after me."

An honest lady outlaw? Interesting. He wondered what her angle was. Everyone had an angle, after all. There was always a catch, always a trap. A man had to stay on his toes to avoid tripping himself up.

"Why are they chasing you?" he asked—as if he didn't know.

"Because they were ordered to do so by the person who mistakenly thought I committed a crime. Which I didn't," she said emphatically as she led the way up a rocky ridge.

"Uh-huh," he mumbled neutrally.

She approached the sturdy strawberry roan gelding that looked to be too high-spirited for a woman to handle. Apparently, Lorelei Russell could handle men and horses with the same degree of skill—and he better not let himself forget that. Instinct and intuition had warned him at first sight that she was trouble. Sure enough, he'd been right.

The instant she turned her back to reach for the horse's reins Gideon pounced. He snaked his arm around her waist and slammed her curvaceous body against his, entrapping her. Instant awareness shot through his body when she squirmed against him in a fierce effort to escape. He was doing a fine job of holding on to his alluring captive and controlling a flaming case of lust until she gouged her elbow into his chest with such force that he couldn't draw breath. Then she kicked him in the knee—and she would have landed a disabling blow to his crotch if he hadn't reacted instinctively by jackknifing his body and spinning away.

Growling, Gideon recoiled, then lunged at her when she squirmed from his arms and tried to leap onto her horse. He launched himself through the air and tackled her around the knees before she stuffed a booted foot in the stirrup. She yelped when he forced her facedown on the ground and crawled atop her. She spat out a mouthful of gravel and dirt and cursed him soundly as she tried to buck him off.

"So much for the angelic image you tried to project, hellion," he growled at the back of her curly head, while she wormed and wriggled ineffectively beneath him.

"What is the matter with you!" she yelled at him.

"There's a warrant out for your arrest and a price on your head. I'm arresting you for murder," he snapped as he rolled her to her back and pinned her wrists to the ground.

Wide amber eyes swept up as her full breasts heaved from exertion. Gideon noticed the second button on her shirt had come undone during their scuffle. Before his overly active imagination ran away with itself—again—he retrieved the spare set of handcuffs that hung on his double holster.

"How did you know about that already?" Lori panted as he snapped the metal bracelets in place.

"I'm a Deputy U.S. Marshal and I'm half Osage. I know all and see all. I can sure as hell see you for what you are," he muttered as he hauled her abruptly to her feet.

This could not be happening! Lori thought in dismay. She had come to Gideon Fox for help and he had turned on her without giving away the fact that he knew who she was. He had been waiting to pounce on her, damn him.

"Nice horse," he complimented as he picked her up and tossed her onto the saddle. "Did you steal it?"

"No, Drifter is mine. A gift from my father, in fact."

She glowered at the brawny marshal whose stubbled beard and collar-length raven hair gave him the appearance of the dark angel of doom. His vivid blue eyes missed nothing as he looked her up and down while he retrieved a coil of rope from his back pocket to lash her foot to the stirrup. She was poised to gouge Drifter the instant Gideon circled to restrain her other foot.

"Don't try it, honey," he ordered. "You're wanted dead or alive, just like Pecos Clem Murphy. Apparently you know what it's like to shoot somebody so you know it's messy business. I don't want to have to do that to you unless necessary."

"You'd shoot an innocent woman?"

His long, thick lashes framed his steady gaze. He focused on her while he secured her foot. "I have before. The innocent part was up for debate." He stared pointedly at her. "It is now, too."

This was *not* the kind of man Lori had hoped to contact to help her clear up the horrible misunderstanding that left her running for her life—and now captured. She needed sympathy and compassion. She needed a man with an open-minded attitude.

Instead, she had tangled with this hard-edged, stone-hearted lawman of mixed heritage. The part of him that carried Indian blood probably resented all white intruders on tribal property. She doubted he cared one whit that she and her father had a special trader's license to sell goods and transport travelers across the river.

In addition, Gideon Fox had taken one cynical look at her and judged her guilty of the charges mistakenly leveled against her. But then, who was she to criticize? she asked herself. She'd only known him fifteen minutes and she disliked him already. Not because he had his booted feet in two separate civilizations. Not because he was rough around the edges, abrupt mannered and didn't look the least bit sophisticated or dignified. But because he had wrongly misjudged her and he cared only about the reward he could collect when he hauled her and Clem to Fort Smith for trial.

When Gideon bounded up behind her in the saddle, she stiffened. He was whipcord muscle and imposing strength and she resented the feeling of helpless frustration riveting her. She forgot to breathe when he tucked his chin on her shoulder and wrapped both swarthy arms around her to hold her manacled hands to the pommel of the saddle.

He must have sensed her discomfort because he said, "Easy, honey. I'm only making double damn sure you don't gouge me in the chest and emasculate me with a blow to the crotch. What little virtue you have left is safe with me."

"I am not now, nor will I ever be your *honey*," she snapped, unsettled and annoyed by the betraying sensation of pleasure that having him wrapped around her provoked.

"Nothing but a careless endearment, I assure you," he

breathed against the side of her neck, setting off another round of tingles that had no business whatsoever assailing her when she so disliked this heartless lawman.

"Would you prefer that I call you *witch* or *hellion* instead of *honey?*"

"I would prefer that you release me." She shifted restlessly in the circle of his sinewy arms. "Get your own horse, Marshal. Drifter doesn't like having you riding him and I'm not fond of it, either."

"You don't want me riding you?" he asked with entirely too much teasing amusement in his rich baritone voice.

Lori was grateful that he couldn't see the beet-red blush that worked its way up her neck to splash across her face. "Certainly not!"

His rumbling chuckle reverberated through his broad chest and vibrated against her back, increasing her awareness of him to the extreme. "But if you and I *rode* together, you would expect me to favor you with a quick release from your handcuffs so you could dash off again. Just so you know, I don't like to be propositioned by lady outlaws."

"That was as far from a proposition as it could get!" she huffed as she nudged him—hard—with her shoulder. "Give me some space, Fox. I don't like any man crowding me."

"Is that why you shot your former lover?"

"I didn't shoot Tony!" she all but yelled at the infuriating man. "He was bushwhacked and I was nearly a victim caught in the cross fire. In fact, I think maybe *you* gunned him down to collect a reward."

"*Me?* Hell and damn, woman. I was nowhere near the west side of Osage reservation. I've been tracking Pecos Clem."

"Well then, if not you specifically, then another glorified

executioner for hire whose only concern is the price on a person's head."

So there, she thought spitefully as they approached Pecos Clem, who had been secured so effectively he couldn't have gotten loose if his life depended on it. Now Gideon knew what she thought of bounty hunters wearing the sanctioned labels of Deputy U.S. Marshal. Maybe the marshals who patrolled the territory were the unsung heroes who tried to enforce law and order. But some of them—like Gideon Fox, obviously—were only interested in collecting bounties and relying on decrees of *dead or alive* to make their job easier.

"If you think I'll sit here and endure a lecture from a feisty, smart-mouthed murderess then you're wrong," he growled in her ear. "You can tell your story to Judge Parker. I'm not the least bit interested in what you have to say. My job is to bring you in. Nothing more. Nothing less."

"But I need to return to the trading post to reassure my father that I'm all right," she protested hotly. "That is the very least you can do."

"I'll send him a note…if I get around to it."

"That will not suffice," she snapped at him. "The real murderer is running loose. He might have killed Tony for the bounty on his head."

"Your former lover was an outlaw? Why am I not surprised."

"I don't know if he was or not," she muttered, exasperated. "Tony was secretive about his past and I've been wondering if he'd had a brush with the law and hid out in the territory. He might have been using an alias, for all I know. But what I *do* know is that he was nice to me. It's up to you to find out the truth. And for your information, he wasn't my lover. He wanted to marry me and I—"

Lori dragged in a steadying breath. The awful scene

exploded in her mind's eye and the horrid memory of watching Tony collapse after the sniper shot him, while trying to shield her from harm, bombarded her with killing force. She choked back a sob, refusing to dissolve into tears in front of this hard-hearted marshal.

No doubt, he'd think she was putting on an act to milk his sympathy. As if he had a sympathetic bone in his powerful body—one that he pressed up against her as if he were her own shadow.

"He wanted to marry you so you shot him?" he remarked caustically. "You could have just said *no*."

"Damn it, Fox. You are an ass!" she sniped furiously and blinked back the tormenting tears that threatened to destroy her crumbling composure.

"And you are a cold-blooded killer," he said in a steely voice. "If there's such a thing as a femme fatale, *you*'re it."

"You are going to be eternally sorry when you discover that I'm telling the truth. I lost a dear friend to an unknown assailant."

"Right," he said, and smirked.

It was pure torment for Gideon to use his body to surround his alluring captive. With each movement of the horse beneath him, he could feel Lori's rounded rump brushing provocatively against his crotch. He could smell the appetizing scent of her body and it threatened to cloud his senses the same way the fog clogged the Osage Hills.

The sooner he delivered this sinfully seductive siren and Pecos Clem, the horse thief, to headquarters the happier he'd be. She could spout her lies nonstop, but Gideon wouldn't fall prey to them—or her. He'd heard hundreds of convoluted claims in his day. The jail in Fort Smith was teeming with inmates who shouted their innocence to high heaven. They lied through their teeth—anything to ensure they could escape justice.

Gideon glanced at Clem, who was still secured to the horse and the tree. He veered right and breathed a gigantic sigh of relief when he reached the spot where he'd left his horse, Pirate. The black-and-white pinto-and-Appaloosa crossbreed had a patch of black around his right eye— hence the name. Gideon was exceptionally fond of his well-trained, reliable mount. Like himself, Pirate was of mixed breeding. The spirited stud was part of the prize herd Gideon and his brothers, Galen and Glenn, raised on their combined properties near Heartstrings River.

Ignoring his thoughts, Gideon dismounted Lori's horse but kept a firm grip on the reins in case she tried to thunder off and force him to chase her down. He suspected she was skilled at losing herself in the wild tumble of mountains and rock-filled ravines in the Osage Hills.

Which is why the two-man posse chasing her had no luck overtaking her, he reminded himself.

However, Gideon had grown up in the Osage Hills and he'd tracked hundreds of outlaws across Indian Territory. He was damn good at his job, even if he did say so himself. His reputation preceded him. It provided him with an edge because most outlaws thought twice about crossing him. Of course, there were those—most of them dead and buried—who challenged him to back up his threats.

That wasn't to say Gideon hadn't been shot up, shot down and knifed on occasion—especially when the odds were stacked against him. Yet, by the grace of God and the Indian deities that were part of his culture, he was still alive and kicking.

"Nice horse," Lori said when Gideon grabbed Pirate's reins. "Did you steal him?"

"Very funny, hellion," he muttered when she threw his sarcastic comment back in his face.

"Did you take the stallion as a trophy of war from a dead man, perhaps?" she asked flippantly.

Gideon slung his leg over the saddle then moved Pirate beside Drifter so he could check Lori's saddlebag. "Wha'd ya know," he drawled as he retrieved the pistol stashed in the leather pouch. He spun the cylinder to find one cartridge missing. "You must be a fair shot if you plugged your former lover with one bullet. I'll remember that."

"For the last time, I did not shoot Anthony Rogers," she growled at him, her golden eyes flashing like hot sparks. "And yes, I am a skilled markswoman. Hand me the pistol and I'll show you how accurate I am when provoked—"

He arched a brow and smiled wryly when she slammed her mouth shut so fast she nearly bit off her tongue. "That's as good as a confession in my book, honey."

When she sputtered furiously, he smothered a grin. He had to hand it to this fiery minx. She had spirit galore. Gideon appreciated that in his horse. He hadn't thought he'd appreciate it quite so much in a woman. But he did, even though he really didn't want to admire *any* qualities in this particular female. He was unwillingly attracted to her already.

That was more than enough to shatter his peace of mind.

He'd wrestled her to the ground, sprawled on top of her luscious body and shared a horse with her while she sat between his legs and in the circle of his arms. Being close to her had a disturbingly arousing effect on all his senses. His sixth sense included—the one that had helped him cheat death on several occasions. Now it warned him that this woman was a serious threat to him so he'd better watch out.

Leading Lori behind him—and checking over his shoulder at irregular intervals, just in case—he trotted over to retrieve Pecos Clem. The outlaw was overly distracted. Clem was staring blatantly at Lori's enchanting face and her arresting feminine assets. For the life of him, Gideon didn't know why Clem's devouring gaze annoyed him. Gideon took up a position between his two prisoners so Clem couldn't ogle Lori constantly.

"What's your crime, sugar?" Clem drawled as he leaned around Gideon to give Lori the once-over again. "Being too damn pretty for your own good?"

To Lori's credit, she met Clem's leering gaze and said, "No, I was accused of killing the last man who looked at me the wrong way."

Gideon concealed his laughter behind a cough when Clem shot her a glare and resettled himself in the saddle.

"I'd like a private word with you, Marshal, when we stop for a break," she requested.

"I don't schedule breaks." He picked up the pace. "Camp is two hours away...if we set a fast clip."

She scowled at him, but he ignored her as he trotted across the meadow and headed for the rugged hills.

Lori silently cursed Gideon for the next two hours. From time to time, she glared at the scraggly-haired, bewhiskered outlaw with a beak of a nose and close-set hazel eyes. The man leered at her every chance he got. She'd dealt with his kind on numerous occasions when travelers and stagecoach passengers passed by the trading post and ferry. She had been propositioned so many times in the past six years that she swore she had heard every line a man could dream up.

If Pecos Clem thought he could shock or impress her with his comments, he was sadly mistaken. Besides, he couldn't leave much of an impression on her because the brawny marshal rode between them, partially blocking her view of Clem.

Of course, Lori didn't have time to pay any mind to Clem because she'd focused all her anger and frustration on Gideon.

Restlessly she twisted her hands. The cuffs were rubbing her wrists raw. If she'd known then what she knew now, she would have accepted Tony's surprising proposal and ridden off with him before the bushwhacker aimed and fired.

Instead, she'd tried to be fair and honest with Tony. And what good did that do? He'd been killed and a hard-nosed marshal who saw her as a dollar sign had captured her. He refused to listen to her side of the story, damn him.

When they reached the rise of ground above the marshals' encampment, which sat halfway up a hill, Lori realized that she would soon be housed in a jail wagon with six male prisoners. Frustration and disgust seized her, making her shiver apprehensively.

"I want to see to my needs before I find myself without the slightest privacy," she blurted out.

She met Gideon's speculative stare without batting an eye. No doubt, he was trying to figure out if this was an escape attempt, before he caged her like a wild animal.

After a long-suffering sigh, he nodded his raven head. "Okay, we'll stop for a moment." He glanced sternly at Clem. "What about you? You need to relieve yourself?"

"I'd like to relieve myself of my half-breed captor, if that's what you're asking," Clem retorted.

Lori gauged Gideon's reaction to the racist comment. He didn't change expression, just tethered Clem and his mount to a nearby tree. Then he turned those intense blue eyes on her.

"Come on, hellion. Make it fast," he murmured as he led her away from Clem.

To her outrage, he used a coil of rope like a leash so she couldn't get more than ten feet away from him. "At least grant me minimal modesty and turn your head," she grumbled as she circled behind the nearest bush.

He didn't honor her request, just looked over her head while she struggled to tug down her breeches with her hands bound together.

"When you wind up in hell, Fox, I hope you're forced to listen to stories from all the tormented souls you sent there *by mistake*."

His gaze dropped to hers. "A lot of men have wished me in hell," he replied nonchalantly.

"Be sure to add my name to that list," she retaliated, and watched the makings of a smile twitch the sensuous curve of his lips.

Gideon Fox might enjoy watching her face turn candy-apple red from embarrassment because he wouldn't grant her privacy, but somehow, someday, she vowed to have the last laugh. He could apologize until he lost his voice for refusing to believe she was innocent but she wouldn't forgive him for putting her through this humiliation.

That is, *if* Judge Parker didn't sentence her to hang from the gallows before she located the man who really committed this awful crime against Tony.

With what little dignity Gideon allowed, Lori fastened herself up. She nearly tripped when he tugged on her leash unexpectedly. She glowered at him and said, "Shall I come to heel or sit up like a trick dog? Or is this humiliation enough to satisfy you for the time being?"

"It's not my job to pamper you," he assured her tartly.

"Gee, and I thought you were such a nice, accommodating fellow when I first met you," she sassed him.

She wished she'd kept the comment to herself when he stepped toward her, eclipsing the sun that had finally fought its way through the fog. The same unwanted sensations of awareness and attraction that had been hounding her all day assailed her again.

She'd been unnerved when he sprawled on top of her and then encircled her in his sinewy arms while they rocked together suggestively on Drifter's back. Even now, when she was as irritated with him as she could get, those shocking feelings of sexual excitement bombarded her.

She tilted her head to compensate for the difference between her and his six-foot-four-inch, rock-hard masculine body. A jolt of awareness zapped her again—much to her baffled amazement.

The man was practically standing on top of her, his powerful male body inches away from hers. He reminded her of the predatory panthers that roamed the Osage Hills. A lithe, powerful creature that called no one master. The ridiculous impulse to reach out to measure the breadth of his chest assailed her. How was it possible to dislike a man so much and still be physically attracted to him?

Clearly, witnessing Tony's senseless death and running for her life had destroyed her sanity.

"Hellion," he said as he leaned down to stick his ruggedly handsome face in hers, "I've tolerated your snippy comments long enough. I've reached my limit so hush up."

"If you've reached your supposed limit, why didn't you backhand Clem and send him cartwheeling off his horse after he made those disgusting, racist comments about your mixed heritage? *I* wanted to slap him for you and *I* don't even like you very much myself."

He arched a thick black brow and studied her intently

with those piercing blue eyes of his. "You don't share Clem's low opinion of my people?"

"My father taught me to live and let live," she insisted. "I have nothing against the people we serve at the trading post. Indian or white, doesn't matter. There's an overabundance of cads and scoundrels from every race, creed and color, as far as I can tell."

"Live and let live?" he repeated caustically while he stared at her lips, making her wonder what it would be like to kiss him. *"Except* for former lovers who test your temper, you mean?"

The taunt ignited her fury in one second flat and made her wonder why she speculated about his kisses. Before she realized what she'd done, she plowed her manacled fists into his belly, forcing him to double over and gasp for breath. When he reflexively lowered his head to protect himself, she upraised her bound hands and smacked his chin. His head snapped back as he stumbled and fell into a graceless sprawl.

Chapter Three

Lori wheeled around to escape from the infuriating marshal who tormented and humiliated her to no end. She yanked on the leash, hoping he'd lose his grasp, but he held on tightly. She yelped when he jerked hard, pulling her off balance. Before she hit the ground, he was looming over her, looking as fierce and deadly as any four-legged predator she'd ever encountered.

"Don't try to escape because you'll never win," he growled harshly.

"If I hadn't been half-starved these past few days, I'd have had the strength to put up a better fight," she blurted before she could bite back the remark.

"It was fight enough, hellion. But it damn well better be the last because I won't go this easy on you next time."

"You call this going easy?" She gave an unladylike sniff and glared in defiance.

"If you get on my bad side, *honey,* I guarantee that I will make your life miserable," he said menacingly.

"I suspect that all your sides are bad sides," she countered before good sense warned her to shut her mouth.

Curse it, her knee-jerk reaction was to sass him. It was like asking to die. She couldn't understand why she couldn't restrain her rebelliousness when he looked so ominous.

"I just gave you a test and you failed it."

She grumbled under her breath. She should've known he'd purposely provoked her. And she was too sensitive to everything he said and did. Consequently, her temper got the better of her and she'd reacted the same way she did to men's unwanted advances. She fought back. It was a natural reflex.

"Not only are you willing but also quite *capable* of violence," he told her as he eased down on her hips to restrict her movement.

"You *provoked* me to retaliate," she muttered begrudgingly. "You bring out the worst in me."

"I'm left to wonder if your former lover *refused* to marry you and *that's* why you shot him."

"That is not what happened and I don't like you at all, Gideon Fox," she said with a spiteful hiss.

"I can live with that." He stared intently at her. "Are you carrying his child and he rejected you?"

His suspicion outraged her. "No, I'm not!"

To her further frustration, having Gideon sitting on her in such a suggestive manner left her thoughts galloping off in the most improper direction. She could not possibly be attracted to this maddening marshal…could she? He taunted her, provoked her, tested her…and *still* she lay here wondering how she would respond if he leaned down and kissed her, despite the stubble of his five o'clock shadow that had progressed past the shadow stage days earlier.

She'd gone insane. That was the only logical explanation.

Her emotions were in the worst possible turmoil. An unknown assailant had shot at her accidentally. Tony had died tragically. Two hired hands from the stage station—and maybe the killer himself—were chasing after her. She'd gone to Gideon Fox for protection and he had arrested her.

Fool that she was, she'd looked to him for comfort and support and he believed her to be guilty—without bothering to open an investigation.

Her thoughts scattered when his raven head moved deliberately toward hers. The air practically popped and crackled between them as he settled his sensuous lips over hers. The scrape of his whiskers was in direct contrast to the surprisingly gentle manner that he stole the breath right out of her lungs. His tongue glided into her mouth and he breathed new life into her.

Lori closed her eyes involuntarily. When he settled suggestively on top of her, the tension melted from her body and she instinctively shifted beneath him, unsure what she wanted or needed, but she definitely needed something his mind-boggling kisses only hinted at.

This man—her sworn enemy who believed the worst about her—was not supposed to taste like heaven or make her feel these warm, throbbing sensations that left no part of her body untouched. But he did.

Before she realized what she'd done, she looped her bound hands over his head and emulated his arousing technique. Suddenly she was ravishing his mouth as he'd ravaged hers. She matched him, kiss for impatient kiss, using everything he had unknowingly taught her. She hoped he felt half as devastated as she did while they were chest-to-chest, hip-to-hip and kiss-to-breathless-kiss.

She shifted restlessly as he nudged his knee between

her legs. The erotic sensations he incited took on a life of
their own as she breathed him in, tasted him, teased him
as he teased her with tantalizing kisses that seemed to go
on forever.

His hands moved over the fabric covering her breasts
and she arched helplessly into him when the fire of desire
burned brighter, more intense. She forgot to breathe when
his hand settled between her legs, touching her in that
secret place where she burned for him the most.

Then, while she lay breathless, yielding and starving
for something she couldn't name, he reared back, nearly
jerking her arms from her shoulder sockets. Scowling, he
grabbed her wrists and pulled her bound arms over his
head. He stared at her with the strangest expression, as if
she had somehow betrayed him. Though why he would
think any such thing made no sense to her. Honestly, *nothing* about the last few minutes made any sense to her.

"I suppose I just failed another of your mysterious tests,
Marshal Fox," she said, her voice nowhere near as steady as
she'd hoped. "I consider it very unfair that you don't give
me time to study for these spur-of-the-moment tests."

His expression transformed into a scowl as he hauled her
to her feet and set her away from him. He said not one word
as he shepherded her back to where Clem was tethered to
his horse and the tree, then tossed her unceremoniously on
Drifter's back. Then he tied her hands and feet in place.

While they rode toward camp, with Clem in tow, Lori
forcefully discarded the memory of kissing Gideon Hard-
Hearted Fox for all she was worth and of him kissing her
back with the same wild, reckless desperation. She fixed
her attention on the three marshals guarding the wagon
where five outlaws sat cross-legged in a six-by-eight-foot
jail cage.

"This is what the first level of my private hell looks like," she murmured to herself as they approached camp.

It's what she deserved for kissing Gideon Fox…and liking it so much.

Gideon cursed himself up one side and down the other for his unprofessional mishandling of Lori's escape attempt and the subsequent embrace. Damn the woman! She'd stunned him by knocking the air out of him. If she'd hit him harder with her doubled fists she could've broken his jaw, but she knew how much pressure to apply without maiming. Her double-fisted uppercut had jarred him. And embarrassed the hell out of him.

So naturally, he'd punished her by kissing her—and inadvertently punished himself to the extreme.

Hell and damn! Was he out of his mind? Must be. There was no other reasonable explanation for his inexcusable behavior. Unless you counted being bewitched by a wicked siren that lured him into the depths of forbidden desire and left him drowning in erotic pleasure.

Gideon was thoroughly ashamed of kissing her—and yearning for another taste of her. He'd tested her temper on purpose and he'd provoked her to retaliate. Unfortunately, he'd also discovered that no matter how mad she made him, he couldn't resist kissing her lush pink lips, sinking into her soft body and skimming his hands over her tantalizing curves and swells.

Gideon decided he was more than ready for a mental and physical break from the grueling demands of chasing fugitives, sleeping with one eye open and standing at the ready to fight for his life. Dealing with criminals who'd just as soon kill him as look at him was wearing him down. Hence, his absurd reaction to the lady renegade he toted to camp.

When he reached camp, every pair of male eyes zeroed in on Lori. Her trim-fitting clothing called entirely too much attention to her tempting body. Fellow marshals and outlaws alike drooled and fantasized about doing the same thing he'd done several minutes earlier.

He had no reason whatsoever to feel protective or possessive, just because he'd impulsively kissed this seductive woman who was wanted for murder.

You'd think the charges against her would be deterrent enough. But no, he'd ignored common sense in his reckless desire to taste her and touch her.

Gideon shifted his attention to Pecos Clem, who was glaring hot pokers at his two cohorts—the men Gideon had forcefully persuaded to give up their leader's hiding place.

"Nice work, Fox," Deputy U.S. Marshal Stephen Wilson remarked while he made a close inspection of Lori's feminine assets—and she had plenty of them, damn it. Then Phen dragged his eyes off her long enough to glance questioningly at Gideon. "Who is she, and does she have a few sisters who look just like her?"

The other men snickered at Phen's question...until Gideon said, "This is Lorelei Russell. Remember the name?"

The three marshals studied her speculatively then frowned. A moment later Deputy U.S. Marshal Noel Perkins strode over to untie Pecos Clem's feet from the stirrups then hauled him to the ground. "Your friends have been missing you, Clem. Glad you can join them."

Dismounting, Gideon walked over to untie Lori's feet. Instead of pulling her none too gently from the saddle, as Perkins had done to Clem, he clamped his hands on her narrow waist...and wished the hell he hadn't. Touching her again, no matter how inadvertently or innocently, sparked fiery sensations and memories of their scorching-hot kisses. The minute her feet touched the ground he set her away from him, as if he'd been burned—because that's exactly how he felt.

While she stared up at him, her golden eyes smoldering with anger and resentment, he turned away. He gestured to the three marshals who waited introduction.

"Lorelei Russell, these are my compatriots. Phen Wilson, Noel Perkins and Mitch Hines. They ride for Parker, same as I do." He gestured toward the jail wagon. "Two of the men in the cage are with Pecos Clem. The other three are Chester Felding, Leland Bates and Ambrose Thomas. They are wanted in Missouri for bank robbery and assault."

Lori surveyed the scruffy men in the metal cage, then inwardly cringed at the prospect of being stuffed in the mobile jail with them. Felding, who had a square face, bulky shoulders and a missing front tooth, leered at her as if she were standing naked. Thomas, a frizzy red-haired, overweight prisoner with arms and legs like tree stumps, licked his lips as if she were his next meal.

Bates reminded her of a rat with his pointy nose, dark, beady eyes and scarecrow-thin features. His leer made the hair on the back of her neck stand on end.

Clem's two cohorts were no better. The scraggly scoundrels ogled her unblinkingly, making her squirm uncomfortably.

Repulsed, she shifted her attention to the three deputy marshals who scrutinized her closely. *Better the devil I know,* she thought, glancing sideways at Gideon. Then again, she might find compassion in one of the other lawmen.

She hadn't found it in Gideon Tough-As-Nails-Fox.

Lori tossed around a polite smile to Phen Wilson, the lanky, blond-haired marshal with pale blue eyes, high cheekbones and a cleft in his chin. He looked to be thirty-five or thereabouts.

Noel Perkins was about the same age as Phen Wilson. He had straight brown hair and hazel eyes. He was thick-chested, stocky and not as tall as Gideon, who towered over everyone.

Mitch Hines had a friendly smile and Lori hoped she could count on him for the simplest of necessities during her captivity. She nodded a greeting to Mitch, whose gray eyes swept over her in careful assessment a second time. His sandy blond head was a little too big for his narrow shoulders, but she predicted he was quick of foot and as agile as a cat.

She wouldn't want to get into a footrace with him during an escape attempt—if and when she could manage one.

The impulse to flee suddenly assailed her and she shifted restlessly from one scuffed boot to the other.

"Don't even think about it," Gideon murmured, as if he'd read her mind, damn him. "The odds are not in your favor. There isn't an incompetent lawman in the bunch."

"The odds are against me no matter where I go," she grumbled. "You refuse to listen to my side of the story and you won't accompany me home to investigate."

When he infuriated her by tugging on the rope leash still attached to her metal bracelets, she glared holes in his broad back. Lori had never felt so outraged and powerless and she never wanted to feel this way again. It was humiliating and exasperating and she blamed all her woes on Gideon Fox.

He was so blasted mistrusting and cynical…and it incensed her to no end this bullheaded marshal physically appealed to her. She thought she had better taste in men!

"What are you going to do with her?" Phen Wilson

asked. "We can't cage her with those men and you damn well know it."

Gideon glanced this way and that. "We'll stake her out under a shade tree," he suggested.

Perkins glanced over at Lori and frowned. "That sounds a little harsh. She's a woman."

"A woman wanted for murder," Gideon reminded him. "She didn't show her last lover much sympathy."

Lori stamped her foot in frustration. "He was not my lover," she protested. "He was my friend and I didn't kill him. For all I know my friend was hiding out in the territory, like your prisoners, and a bounty hunter identified him, shot him and claimed the reward for Tony after I left. I might have been cleared of this disastrous mistake—" she doubted it, but there was an outside chance "—but Marshal Fox refuses to take me back to find out for certain!"

As the other three marshals stared pensively at her she kept talking, hoping to sway them into being lenient and volunteering to check out her story. "Please consider that I'm upset about Tony's death. It's bad enough that he proposed and I turned him down right before someone ambushed him and very nearly shot me in the process. There are questions that need to be answered!"

"Why'd you turn him down?" Mitch Hines asked curiously.

She stared into his pale gray eyes and said, "Because I didn't love him and he wanted me to elope to anywhere, as long as it was out of the territory. Which made me wonder if he felt the need to run from the law. Tony was likable and he was kind to me but he was very secretive about his past."

Just when she thought she might be making headway with the other marshals a shout erupted in the distance. Lori glanced over her shoulder to see a man in his mid-twenties—with raven hair and a bronzed complexion that resembled Gideon's—galloping toward them, riding an Appaloosa gelding.

Gideon tugged on her leash as he headed toward the new arrival, forcing her to scurry to catch up with his long, urgent strides.

"What's wrong, Glenn?" Gideon demanded as he reached out to grab the Appaloosa's reins.

"Galen was shot in the arm last night when two horse thieves swooped down to steal our horses," Glenn reported gruffly. "You have to come, Gid. Sarah and I have tried to keep Galen down so he can heal, but he's determined to find our prize horses...."

His voice trailed off when he glanced past Gideon to appraise Lori with his dark eyes. "Ma'am," he greeted politely. "A pleasure to meet you."

Gideon rolled his eyes and said, "Lorelei Russell, this is my youngest brother, Glenn."

"Hello, Glenn." She flashed him a smile as she stepped up beside Gideon. "I'd shake your hand but your big brother has mistakenly tied me up."

"She's wanted for murder."

Glenn's dark eyes popped and his jaw sagged against his chest. "She's your prisoner?" he chirped incredulously.

"I'm not guilty but your mule-headed brother refuses to listen to reason," Lori inserted.

Gideon glanced at her in annoyance then looked over his shoulder at the men in the cage. "How many of you are innocent?" he called out to the prisoners.

All the outlaws gave a shout while Gideon stared pointedly at Lori. "You can see why your proclamations fall on deaf ears. Everyone around here is misunderstood, just like you, hellion."

"Well, she doesn't look guilty to me," Glenn said as he

gave her the once-over again, paying particular attention to Lori's alluring curves and swells.

"Looks can be deceiving and don't you forget it, Glenn."

Hell and damn, thought Gideon. His twenty-six-year-old brother wasn't immune to Lori's charms, either. Just what he needed, a love-starved little brother taking Lori's side.

"Are you coming?" Glenn asked anxiously. "Sarah is upset."

"Who's Sarah?" Lori inquired.

"Galen's wife. She's afraid he'll take off while I'm fetching Gideon and she can't chase after him because she's five months pregnant."

Gideon pivoted toward his horse. "I'll be back as soon as I can," he called to the other marshals.

"What about the woman?" Phen Wilson questioned as he glanced from the cage of men to Gideon.

Gideon blew out a frustrated breath. As much as he wanted to get this sassy spitfire out from underfoot—because he'd proved he couldn't trust himself with the forbidden temptation she presented—he didn't feel comfortable leaving her in camp, either. It wasn't that he didn't expect the other marshals to treat her humanely. It was just that she was...

He scowled at himself. It was just that she fascinated him and he didn't want to leave her here indefinitely to captivate one of the other lawmen to the point that he stole a few kisses and caresses from her. Plus, he didn't want her to work her wiles on the other lawmen who might accompany her cross-country. There was no telling what might happen while she and one of his fellow marshals were alone.

"I must be out of my mind," he growled to himself as

he scooped up Lori and plunked her down on Drifter's saddle.

All three marshals waggled their eyebrows and grinned speculatively. Gideon hated what they were thinking. But he couldn't leave her behind. He felt so conflicted he wanted to swear two blue streaks. Nevertheless, he clamped down on his tongue, ignored the taunting stares and mounted Pirate.

While Glenn took the lead, and Gideon held the reins to Lori's strawberry roan gelding, the procession headed north. Twenty minutes later, Glenn dug into his saddle-bag and leaned over to offer Lori a slice of home-cooked bread and a stick of beef jerky. She smiled gratefully as she accepted the food with her bound hands.

"Thank you, Glenn. Truth is that I'm famished. I've been living in a cave for several days with little nourishment."

Gideon shifted uncomfortably in the saddle when Glenn stared disapprovingly at him. However, in his defense, Gideon had been busy interrogating Pecos Clem's cohorts and tracking down the dangerous fugitive. Then he'd spent the day trying to ignore a woman who posed so much temptation that he'd broken his rule about becoming involved with any prisoner—especially a woman prisoner—and stopped just short of burying himself in her lush body in a weak, mindless, lusty moment.

Sweet mercy! What had he been thinking?

"Surely you don't think she's guilty of anything except being too beautiful for her own good," Glenn murmured for his ears only.

"I have a good deal more experience with fugitives and their melodramatics than you do," Gideon said confidentially. "You start believing every sad tale someone tells and you could wind up shot, stabbed or knocked unconscious, while your fugitive makes a fast getaway and leaves you for dead."

Glenn glanced over at Lori and smiled longingly. Gideon had to admit that she looked exceptionally fetching with her flame-gold hair dancing in the breeze and the sun spotlighting her beguiling figure. He knew from personal experience that staring into her alluring features and getting lost in those entrancing golden eyes could make a man believe what she wanted him to believe.

Clearly, Glenn had made a snap judgment. Thanks to encouragement from his lusty male body, he'd decided Lorelei Russell was a victim of circumstances beyond her control. Certainly not a murderess with a hefty reward on her head.

A lot the kid knew, Gideon mused sourly.

"What can you tell me about the horse thieves?" Gideon asked, hoping to distract his moon-eyed brother.

"Not much to tell," Glenn replied then bit into Sarah's mouthwatering bread. "It happened last night. We heard the horses stamping around in the corral and we dashed outside to check on them. The thieves wore bandannas over their faces and they started shooting. Unfortunately, Galen was in the direct line of fire."

"What kind of horses were they riding?" Gideon asked. "Did you notice any brands?"

Glenn shook his head, munched on his food and frowned thoughtfully. "Just brown horses, I guess. It was dark and foggy, but I didn't see any brands…. More bread, ma'am?"

Gideon sighed in exasperation while Glenn smiled and extended more food to Lori. She graced Glenn—the smitten fool—with a dazzling smile that practically outshone the sun.

"Thank you, Glenn. It's very generous of you to share your food with me. I appreciate it."

My, she was pouring on the charm, wasn't she? If Gideon had to listen to much more of this sticky sweetness he'd have a toothache. And Glenn had an idiotically happy expression on his face that made him look about twelve.

"No trouble, ma'am. Shame on Gid for not offering you food until now."

"Please call me Lori," she insisted, casting him another dimpled smile.

Glenn bowed from the saddle, looking as charming and rakish as Gideon had ever seen him. "Lori it is. Where do you hail from?"

Gideon thought he was going to be sick. Nonetheless, he remained silent while Lori filled Glenn in on her life story. The cynic in Gideon wondered how much truth there was to it. He tried to pretend he wasn't listening and didn't give a damn, but he was curious about her.

"My father was a lieutenant colonel in the army and we moved from one post to another for years. I was eleven when I lost my mother and younger brother to a diphtheria epidemic. Papa said he couldn't be around military posts without the memories of Mama breaking his heart. He acquired a special trader's license and we opened a trading post in the Osage Nation. When the number of travelers increased and the stage company wanted to provide service in the Pawnee Nation to the south we staked the river to provide ferry service."

She smiled at Glenn again and ignored Gideon as if he were invisible. "What about you and your family, Glenn?"

"Our father was a French trapper," he replied. "Our mother was full-blood Osage. I was twelve when someone killed our father and stole his furs while he was on his way to Rendezvous."

"I'm sorry," Lori commiserated. "It's difficult to lose a loved one."

"Yes, it is," Glenn murmured. "Out of loneliness and desperation, my mother remarried two years later."

"Unfortunately, the abusive bastard played the role of the attentive suitor convincingly…until he got what he wanted. A place to stay and rapport with our people so he could cheat us all," Gideon added bitterly.

"I'm sorry about that, too," Lori murmured.

"He was the one who was sorry," Glenn remarked. "He shoved our mother during one of his mean drunks. When she hit her head and collapsed, he left her to die. Gideon went after him. He'd been working with the Osage Police to support our family and he tracked down our stepfather. The fool tried to shoot Gideon out of the saddle."

Lori glanced curiously at Gideon. "Were you injured?"

He nodded. "I took a gunshot in the thigh."

"But he put our stepfather down and the bastard didn't get up again," Glenn said grimly. "Gideon became brother, mother and father to Galen and me after that."

Lori wondered if Gideon's abusive stepfather was the first fatality of his job as a law enforcement officer. But she didn't ask. Both men lapsed into silence for several minutes after telling the grim tale.

When she glanced at Glenn, he was staring at her with masculine appreciation. Even if his cynical older brother didn't trust her, Glenn seemed willing to give her the benefit of the doubt. Too bad he wasn't a marshal who'd listen to her story and agree to open an investigation.

"What do you do these days, Glenn?" she inquired as she resettled herself more comfortably in the saddle.

"I help Galen with the horses and other livestock. I do most of the field work while he's on police duty on the reservation." He glanced quickly at Gideon then looked away. "I want to serve with the Osage Police like Galen, and like Gideon did before Judge Parker recruited him to be a Deputy U.S. Marshal."

"So why haven't you?" she questioned.

He hitched his thumb toward Gideon. "Because my big brother says having two brothers being shot at on a daily basis is enough. But it turns out I'm as good a shot as Gid, not that it matters to him."

Gideon barked a laugh. "Not even on your good day, kid. When you can hit a target, backward and blindfolded, we'll talk."

Glenn's broad chest puffed up like an offended toad's. "I'm twenty-six years old, damn it... Excuse my language, Lori. I can do whatever I want, if I want. You aren't my boss anymore."

While Glenn and Gideon exchanged teasing taunts, Lori smiled to herself. She missed having a brother. For years, it had been only Lori and her father, working together to establish the trading post to feed, supply and transport travelers.

After hearing about Gideon's dealings with his scheming, abusive stepfather, she understood why he was wary of believing strangers' stories. She knew he felt the burden of responsibility to care for and protect his family. She wondered how it would feel to have him protect *her* rather than distrust her motives and spew his cynicism at her.

Come to think of it, why had he brought her along when he could've foisted her off on his fellow marshals and be done with her? That's what she'd expected, but he'd surprised her.

She couldn't help but ask him about it.

He shifted awkwardly on the striking Pinto-and-Appaloosa stallion. For a moment, she didn't think he planned to answer. He didn't bother to do her the courtesy of glancing in her direction when he finally spoke.

"You're my prisoner and I'm collecting my bounty money."

The comment cut her to the core. She told herself she suspected as much. It wasn't because he didn't trust the other marshals to keep her captive. It wasn't because he thought she might come to harm while caged with known outlaws who might maul her or molest her during the trek to Fort Smith.

No, it was about the money he'd collect when he delivered her to trial.

"At least you're honest," she mumbled.

"One of us should be."

Lori gnashed her teeth. "I'm really beginning to dislike you *intensely,* Marshal Fox."

"It's not my duty to win friends, Miz Russell."

"Good thing. You'd fail miserably. You have the charm and disposition of a rattlesnake."

Glenn chuckled at the unflattering exchange. "Too bad Galen isn't here to enjoy this. Very few people dare to talk back to my big brother."

She figured the only reason Gideon allowed her to get away with it was because he didn't want to shoot her or strangle her while his youngest brother was an eyewitness.

Chapter Four

"Ah, home at last," Gideon declared three hours later.

Lori stared into the lush valley, admiring the rock-and-timber home butted up against the north hillside to block off cold winter winds. The ranch boasted one of the most panoramic settings she'd seen for miles. A spring-fed creek meandered through the meadow to flow into the nearby river. It passed close to the two-story home and oversize barn similar to the one at Burgess Ranch and Stage Station.

There were a half-dozen large sheds equipped with stalls for cattle and horses. Dozens of horses grazed in the pasture. But apparently, someone had stolen the prized breeding stock. Considering the fine quality of broodmares and colts on the ranch, the top breeding stock must be something extraordinary.

So this was where Gideon and his brothers had grown up, she mused as she cast him a discreet glance. She predicted the men had built the spacious home and outbuildings with their own hands. Lori wondered how Sarah Fox dealt with the three brothers who came and went from the ranch. She sincerely hoped Gideon treated his sister-in-law with more trust and respect than he did Lori. Otherwise, the woman should seriously consider whacking Gideon's hard head and knocking some manners into him.

As the threesome rode downhill a petite woman with shiny black hair, expressive brown eyes and olive complexion—that hinted at her Osage and white ancestry—stepped onto the covered porch. She wore a calico gown that modestly concealed her rounded belly.

The instant Gideon dismounted Sarah flew into his arms. "Thank goodness, Glenn found you!" she gushed as she hugged the stuffing out of Gideon. "I can't keep that mule-headed brother of yours down without resorting to every Indian remedy of a sedative. He wakes up and swears he's going to hunt down those thieves. You have to do something with that crazed brother of yours, Gid!"

No doubt, the whole family expected the eldest brother to resolve all problems they encountered. Being unflappable, self-reliant and more than capable, Gideon quietly reassured Sarah that he would take care of Galen. Then he strode toward the porch. He stopped abruptly then lurched around to glance at Lori. As if he wasn't sure what to do with her.

She shouldn't feel offended because she was his afterthought. *You are a fool to expect anything from that hard-nosed marshal,* she reminded herself sensibly. She was one of his many duties and she was nothing more than a dollar sign in his eyes. What did she care what he thought of her? She didn't, she told herself fiercely. As far as she was concerned, Gideon Fox was a pain in the ass, the gigantic obstacle standing between her and freedom and exoneration.

He was also her first shocking experience with irrational

lust. She still couldn't fathom why Gideon intrigued her. She knew he wouldn't blink an eye at shooting her down if she attempted escape. At most, she was nothing but a convenient warm body to him. Someone to wrestle around in the grass and kiss because there wasn't another available female for miles—with the exception of his pretty sister-in-law.

Well, *she* had a grand suggestion as to what he should do with her, she thought huffily. He could release her and she would promise never, *ever* to bother him again.

"Glenn, do something with Lori," he requested as Sarah grasped his hand and tugged him up the steps.

"Come on, Lori," Glenn said, jostling her from her contemplations.

To her surprise, Glenn untied her feet from the stirrups and discarded the infuriating leash attached to her manacled wrists. With courteous care—something Gideon Hard-Hearted-Fox knew absolutely nothing about—Glenn scooped her from Drifter's saddle and set her on the ground. She noticed Glenn took his sweet time setting her on her feet and releasing her. His body brushed against her, but to Lori's frustration, she didn't feel the same tingles of awareness that Gideon set off.

She wished she had. Glenn was arrestingly handsome, with a muscular build, thick raven hair and twinkling black eyes. Plus, he was only a few years older than her and he didn't treat her with such wary distrust.

"I'm sorry I can't do anything about the cuffs," he murmured without backing away. "I would if I could. But I'd have to answer to my big brother."

"It's all right, Glenn. I appreciate your consideration."

To her surprise, he slid his arm around her waist and shepherded her up the steps into the house. When they stepped into the spacious parlor and dining area, she heard gruff voices wafting down the hallway.

"Sit down, you idiot!" Gideon boomed like thunder.

"Get the hell out of my way!" came another deep, agitated voice that she presumed belonged to Galen Fox.

Glenn shuttled her down the hall and they paused in the doorway. Lori assessed the dark-haired, bare-chested patient who had a bloodstained bandage wrapped around his upper right arm. Galen, who looked to be a couple of years younger than Gideon, thrashed wildly on the bed while Gideon tried to shove his head against the pillow. Galen attempted to backhand Gideon while Sarah scolded her partially sedated husband for tearing the stitches and defying his older brother's orders.

"See what I mean, Gid?" Sarah fussed. "None of the remedies to sedate him are as effective as they should be."

"That's because you can't sedate *stubborn*," said Gideon.

When Sarah realized Lori lurked in the doorway, her dark-eyed gaze dropped to the metal cuffs. She frowned, bemused, as she glanced between Lori and Gideon.

"I'm sorry you have to observe this family squabble." She reached out to thump Galen on his good shoulder. "Behave yourself, Galen. We have a visitor."

Gideon whirled around to stare disapprovingly at Glenn. "I told you to do something with her," he said gruffly.

Galen stopped struggling then glanced around Gideon's broad shoulders. His dull green eyes widened as he looked Lori over thoroughly then peered questioningly at Gideon. Lori could tell Galen was under the influence of some sort of home remedy because his eyelids drooped noticeably and his movements were sluggish—too sluggish to effectively battle his brawny brother.

"Since when do you go around cuffing beautiful women?" Galen slurred out, and then smiled devilishly. "Is that the only way you can convince one to spend the night with you?"

"Galen! Hush up," Sarah admonished.

"She's a fugitive," Gideon grumbled. "She killed her boyfriend and if you don't lie still I'll hand her my pistol and turn her loose on you. Now stop fighting me, damn it!"

When Sarah's wide-eyed gaze swung to her, Lori thrust out her chin and squared her shoulders. "I did not shoot anyone. It's a misunderstanding that I came to Gideon to clear up, but he won't listen to reason," she protested. "And it is nice to make your acquaintance, Galen, Sarah. My name is Lorelei Russell. If you'll kindly hand me your weapon I'll turn it on Gideon. That should put him out of your misery. And mine."

Galen managed a goofy-looking grin as his gaze slid back and forth between Lori and Gideon. "I like her. She has sass and gumption."

"You like anyone who defies me like you do," Gideon muttered. "Now lie the hell down and shut the hell up! You won't do anyone around here any good if infection sets in or you bleed to death because you refused to take time off to recover from injury."

"Thank you," Sarah said with a gusty sigh. "Now listen to our brother, Galen. He only wants what is best for you."

"No, he doesn't. He just likes to boss me around because he was the firstborn. Doesn't make him smarter, just older."

"Mind your manners in front of our guest," Sarah reprimanded as she eased down beside her husband.

"Prisoner," Gideon corrected, tossing Lori a sideways glance that sought to intimidate. He wasted his time.

"Seriously, Galen, toss me a gun and I'll shoot the tyrant for you," Lori persisted, tongue in cheek. "He'll never boss you around again."

Another lopsided grin touched Galen's lips as he relaxed on the bed for the first time. Sarah bit back a smile as her gaze leapfrogged back and forth between Lori and Gideon, who scowled darkly.

"I hope you can back up that snippy mouth, hellion," Gideon grumbled at Lori.

"With guns or knives," she sassed him. "Take your pick."

Gnashing his teeth, Gideon stalked over to grab hold of her elbow then nudged Glenn out of his way. *"You* stay away from Lori." He glared at Glenn then pinned Galen with a hard stare. "And *you* stay in bed." He focused icy blue eyes on Lori. *"You* are coming with me, hellion."

"I'd love to, since you asked so nicely," she retorted, wondering why she couldn't guard her tongue when it came to dealing with Gideon.

Swear to God, he *did* bring out the worst in her.

The instant they were out of sight and walking down the hall Gideon leaned close and said, "If you don't stop undermining my authority with my family I'll—"

"You'll what?" she shot back when he paused to take a breath. "Give me fifty lashes? Hang me high? Shoot me down? I am *not* a criminal, even if you prefer to think I am. If you can't treat me with the slightest courtesy in front of your family then do not speak to me at all."

"Just shut up for once," he growled as he loomed over her like a thundercloud.

"No, you're insulting and mistrusting. You make me furious and I—"

His mouth came down hard on hers, effectively shutting her up. Lori cursed herself a dozen times over for responding to him rather than gouging him in the groin and making a run for it. Honestly! How could she react so fiercely to his kisses when most of the time she wanted to strangle him? It just wasn't fair. No man had ever held this kind of power over her and Gideon Fox was the last man on earth she wanted to have it. It was infuriating, humiliating, baffling.

"Hell and damn, woman, see what you made me do?" Gideon whispered against her lips. "I don't want to like you." He kissed her again, negating his gruff comment.

"I don't want to like you, either," she said when he allowed her to come up for air. "In fact, I *don't* like you. You possess all the annoying qualities that don't appeal to me. You make me say things I wouldn't say to anyone else. You make me just plain crazy."

"I prefer sweet-tempered, docile women who don't defy me at every turn," he said, then kissed her again—and she let him.

"That's why you have to pay by the hour for devoted attention," she couldn't resist saying.

He lifted his raven head a fraction then stared down at her from beneath half-mast lashes. His ruggedly handsome face was a hairbreadth from hers. Surprisingly, a smile twitched his sensuous lips.

"How much will it cost for you to be nice to me for a full hour?"

"You couldn't afford it, Marshal Fox."

"Ah, so you're a high-class courtesan," he taunted. "Is that what you and Anthony Rogers were arguing about? Your exorbitant fee? Now the truth comes out."

She went for his throat. He'd gone too far with his tormenting ridicule. He'd brought Tony's name into it when she was feeling guilty and grieving his loss.

He grabbed her bound wrists, forcing them down in front of her, as if she was no more than a weak child. Curse him! He was as strong and powerful as he looked and she hated being dominated, especially when she was angry and frustrated with herself for being so attracted to this infuriating man.

"One day I hope you find yourself protesting your innocence and no one will listen to you. Then you'll know how exasperating it is to face mockery and scorn when you know in your heart and soul that you have done nothing to deserve unfair accusations and demeaning treatment."

Growling, Gideon quick-marched her out the front door, down the steps and bustled her toward the barn. He tethered her to a pole and left her beside two milk cows, a pen of sheep and two strapping paint horses.

"And stay there," he snapped before he spun on his heels. "Prisoners are not allowed special privileges in my book."

"You can go to hell, Gideon Fox," she called after him.

"Been there. It's everything it's cracked up to be." He shot her a narrowed glance over his shoulder and added, "By the way, the devil sends you his regards, *hell*ion."

When he disappeared from sight, leaving her tied up like an animal, days of tormenting emotion bubbled up inside her then erupted like molten lava. Lori cried her eyes out. She cried for Tony, for the injustice her life had become, for the worry her father must be experiencing. And most of all she bawled her head off because of Gideon Fox. That cynical, blue-eyed, cantankerous rascal of a deputy marshal made her feel sensations she wanted to share with anyone else in the world but him!

* * *

On his way back to the house, Gideon stopped to draw water from the well then washed his face so he could cool off—physically and emotionally. It was a crime what that high-spirited female did to him. She disrupted his logical thought processes. When he came within five feet of her, desire and wariness warred inside him.

The damnable truth was that he wanted that golden-eyed virago more than he'd wanted any other woman in his life. Yet, he didn't want to want her because she represented the kind of individual he was sworn to apprehend.

In addition, he refused to make the kind of disastrous mistake his mother made when she fell for her second husband's manipulative lies.

If Lori knew how many twisted, treacherous lies and proclamations he'd heard from outlaws—men and women alike—she would have tried a different tack with him. Gideon had heard and seen the worst humanity could do to each other and he'd lost faith. Time and time again, people had looked him right in the eye and lied through their teeth to protect themselves.

Scrubbing his hands over his face, Gideon forcefully set aside his frustrating inability to deal professionally with Lori. Instead, he focused on his family. He'd been the head of the household for so long that he considered it his duty to make certain everything ran smoothly. He'd rather take a bullet himself than to see Galen suffer. Especially since it upset his pregnant wife to such extremes. Sarah was so deeply and completely in love with Galen that it still amazed Gideon to watch her interact with his middle brother.

Gideon had lived with that ornery Galen and impulsive Glenn for years. He didn't consider them exceptionally lovable. Perhaps the fact that ruthless raiders had killed

Sarah's family five years earlier made her cling so fiercely
to her new husband and family. After Gideon tracked down
every last one of the three men and then watched Judge
Parker send them to the gallows, Sarah had sworn eternal
gratitude.

"He's at it again," Sarah said as she breezed onto the
porch. "Galen insisted he can mount a horse to begin a
search for our horses. I swear you'll have to tie him to
the bedposts. Glenn is trying to do just that, but he needs
help."

Shaking himself like a duck to shed water, Gideon strode
into the house. He could hear Galen swearing a blue steak,
long before he witnessed the struggle between Galen and
Glenn.

Gideon walked over to press his palm to Galen's fore-
head, noting his high fever and forcing his brother down
while Glenn secured his good arm to the iron headboard.
"Stop resisting. You're a sick man and you're worse than
a belligerent prisoner." Like the one he'd tethered in his
barn. "You're hurt and you need rest," he added tersely.
"Do us all a favor and calm down."

"You have your own problems," Galen panted, completely out of breath. "Can't expect you to take time off
to hunt down our horses. They'll be miles away if I don't
track them."

"I will track them down. Count on it," Gideon guaranteed. "The other marshals can handle the jail wagon and
still round up fugitives before we head to Fort Smith."

"What about the woman?" Galen's green-eyed gaze
zeroed in on him. "What are you going to do about her?"

"I think you should let her go." Glenn spoke up. "She
looks innocent to me."

Galen and Gideon exchanged glances before staring at
their younger brother. Gideon said, "So is a delicate rose…

until you grab hold of it and suffer the painful prick of its thorn. Looks are deceiving, little brother. It's time you learned that."

Glenn gestured toward Sarah. "Lori is pretty like Sarah."

"Thank you," Sarah murmured.

"I think Lori also has a kind heart and generous nature," Glenn continued. "You should give her the benefit of the doubt."

"I did more than that," Gideon replied. "I tested her and she attacked me."

"*Tested* her?" Glenn smiled wryly. "How?"

"I provoked her temper."

"I can see why she might've attacked you." Glenn crossed his arms over his chest and studied Gideon all too closely. "I never knew you were so rude to women."

The comment caused Galen and Sarah to arch their eyebrows and study Gideon speculatively.

"Sparring with each other, were they?" Galen asked.

"Stay out of this. You're injured," Gideon snapped.

"Nothing wrong with my mind, except when my lovely wife overdoses me with that foul-tasting sedative."

"Everything's wrong with your mind," Gideon said, and smirked. "When you're sedated you think you can fly and your judgment is skewered."

"He's not that bad," Sarah put in defensively. "And I must say I'm surprised by your attitude toward Lori. In fact, I'm on my way out to offer her food and make amends."

"Just be careful that she doesn't bite the hand that feeds her," Gideon warned.

Sarah scoffed as she exited the room, provoking Gideon to mutter under his breath. He wasn't accustomed to his family ganging up against him. All because of that feisty female prisoner who went around shooting former lovers for proposing to her. If that wasn't the dumbest excuse he'd ever heard, he didn't know what was.

Furthermore, his family should trust his instincts.

Gideon lashed Galen's leg to the bedpost—just in case he became rowdy again.

Galen cursed him sourly. "That isn't necessary, you—"

"—tyrant," Glenn teased, borrowing Lori's description.

Gideon's arm shot toward the door, as if his annoying little brother was too dense to know where it was. "Leave. Go with Sarah to make sure Lori doesn't try to escape while taking her meal."

"Where is she?" Glenn inquired.

"Tied to a post beside the sheep pen in the barn."

"Tied to a post?" Glenn howled in outrage.

"She's a prisoner, not a princess," Gideon reminded him caustically. "I'm not going to book her a room at the hotel in the Osage Capitol at Pawhuska for safekeeping."

Flashing Gideon a disapproving glance, Glenn hastened from the room.

Galen smiled wryly. "We both seem to be upsetting the family today."

Gideon plunked down in the chair next to the bed. "I'm cranky from lack of sleep. I've been tracking fugitives for five weeks. You're irritable because you've been shot, sedated and restrained. We're destined to upset a few people along the way... Now tell me about the horse theft."

Galen yawned broadly then shrugged his good shoulder. "Not much to tell. I heard the broodmares and Appaloosa stud stamping around and banging against the corral railing. They were nickering uneasily so I went to investigate and called to Glenn on my way out the door."

"What time was this?"

"Before eleven. I was late in returning from police head-quarters in Pawhuska. I'd had to investigate a domestic quarrel between John Running Bear and his wife, Leta."

Gideon nodded. "Those two were going at each other while I was an officer with the Osage Police. As I recall, Leta constantly accused John of cheating on her."

Galen nodded. "Not much has changed. They still go on the warpath and take after one another. Their neighbors heard them raising a ruckus from a quarter of a mile down the road."

"So you came home late," Gideon prompted to get his brother back on track.

Galen blinked owlishly then shook his dark head to clear his thoughts. "Sarah fixed me something to eat. Glenn had already gone upstairs to his room. When I heard the horses nickering, I hurried outside. Like I said, I called to Glenn and grabbed my pistol on the way out the door. I figured a panther or bear was lurking around, disturbing the horses.

"The light was behind me so I couldn't see much more than two silhouettes on horseback, trying to open the corral gate. The men had on hats and kerchiefs to conceal their faces. I shouted at them and fired a warning shot as Glenn barreled out the front door. One of the men shot me in the arm."

He glanced down at the stained bandage then scowled. "Glenn was determined to chase the bastards, but I refused to let him, for fear he'd wind up shot, too. Or worse. Besides, someone has to be here to do the chores while I'm patrolling my district of the reservation. I don't want Sarah doing any heavy lifting. She works hard enough around here."

Gideon smiled faintly. "You won't let Sarah overdo it, even when she insists on pitching in to help any way she can. She's a good woman, Galen. Still don't know what the hell she sees in you."

Galen flashed a lopsided grin. "I have a lot of hidden charm."

"*Well* hidden," Gideon teased. "It's escaped my notice for years."

Galen's smiled faded. "So tell me the whole story about Lorelei Russell."

"I don't know the whole story. A messenger arrived in camp before I went looking for Pecos Clem Murphy. The foreman at Burgess Stage Station and Ranch had been shot by a jealous woman who might be headed our direction. The widow who owns the place witnessed the incident then put up a reward for the capture of the woman who killed her foreman and left her understaffed."

Galen frowned drowsily. "What does Lori have to say in her own defense?"

"She claims the foreman was her friend. He supposedly proposed and she turned him down. According to her, a shot rang out from the underbrush and her would-be husband collapsed."

"So she ran for her life," Galen mumbled. "Is that it?"

Gideon shifted restlessly, knowing he'd been too wary of Lori to ask for details. He didn't want to hear more of her lies and he was afraid he'd be swayed because of his personal desire for her. He should've left her at marshal camp, but they'd likely take her side, just because of her compelling beauty and irrepressible spirit.

"I didn't ask for the specifics. I had just captured Pecos Clem when she walked out of the fog. I took her captive when I realized who she was, then headed for camp. Then Glenn showed up and here I am."

"I think you need more details," Galen insisted.

"Thank you so much for telling me how to do my job."

Galen yawned again. "You're welcome. Always glad to return the favor, big brother."

Gideon rolled his eyes ceilingward and expelled an audible sigh. "You think I'm a tyrant, too?"

"She said it. I didn't."

"Always nice to have family support and appreciation," Gideon grumbled sarcastically as he rose from the chair. "I cared for you and our reckless little brother for years after we lost our parents. This is the thanks I get."

"Thanks," Galen said dutifully.

"Thank me by staying in bed until the fever breaks. I'll scout the area to see if I can pick up the horse thieves' trail."

"I'd appreciate it, Gid. Those horses are our future. *All* of our futures. One day we can resign our commission in law enforcement and live comfortably here."

"I'm looking forward to it," Gideon admitted as he walked away.

He'd spent too many years battling the elements and outlaws, while living like a predator in the wilds. But a marshal's salary and collected bounties paid the bills and made it possible to purchase exceptional broodmares and stallions. Gideon and his family had made money selling livestock to stage stations for years, but they were making a name for themselves with Appaloosa and pinto crossbreeds. Horses like Pirate were in great demand and brought high prices because of their flashy color, unique markings, speed and powerfully built bodies.

Speaking of Pirate, Gideon had left the stallion tied to the hitching post. The horse was his most reliable friend and constant companion. He needed attention and a bucket of grain.

Striding down the hall, Gideon glanced up then skidded to a halt when he saw Lori sitting at the dining table with

Glenn and Sarah. Like old friends making up for lost time, they were talking quietly.

He would not let that female weasel her way into Gideon's family and turn everyone against him. "What's going on?" he growled, making the threesome flinch in surprise. "My prisoner is to remain tied outside in the barn."

Glenn squared his shoulders and met Gideon's condemning frown. "She's a woman and she deserves better treatment. I watched Mother be mistreated and knocked around, as if she counted for nothing. I won't have Lori tied up with the sheep while she's at my ranch."

"*Our* ranch." Gideon was quick to correct him.

"I'm here more than you are," Glenn pointed out. "So... you want something to eat or not?"

Gideon muttered under his breath when Lori glanced up at him briefly. He could tell she'd been crying by the redness and swelling around her golden eyes. Probably crocodile tears to draw Sarah and Glenn's sympathy. These two were younger and more trusting than Galen and Gideon, whose rough-and-tumble profession made them jaded and cautious.

While Lori ignored him completely, Gideon took a seat and ate the tasty stew in silence. Lori posed questions to Sarah and Glenn, who were gracious hosts and were eager to share their life stories. No harm in that, Gideon supposed. However, he wasn't going to soften toward the flame-haired siren who played hell with his iron-willed self-discipline until he had all the facts.

If he decided to open an investigation rather than carting her back to the marshals' mobile headquarters.

He refused to listen to Lori's side of the story. If he investigated, he wanted to hear what the Widow Burgess had to say about the incident. But first and foremost, he needed to recover the stolen horses so Galen could relax and recuperate.

Swallowing down the meal in haste, Gideon came to his feet. Then he reached over to grab Lori's arm and hoisted her up. "Let's go."

"She's not finished eating," Sarah protested.

Gideon propelled Lori toward the front door. "That will tide her over for now."

"I'll bring out bread and cheese later," Glenn volunteered.

"No, you won't," Gideon called over his shoulder. "You keep your distance and tend to the ranch chores while I'm tracking the thieves."

"When will you be back?" Glenn asked.

Gideon smiled astutely. "I'll be back when I get here, so if you're planning to grant Lori more privileges, don't. I don't want to run you in for obstructing justice, Glenn. Then Sarah won't have any help around the ranch because you'll be locked up."

"My, you are such a ray of sunshine," Lori said in a caustic tone—for his ears only. "Is there no end to the special privileges of being one of your family members?"

Was he that hard on his kin? he wondered. He was accustomed to being in charge. Plus, his profession made him authoritative and decisive. Lori had him questioning himself.

That hadn't happened before.

He stared into her thick-lashed amber eyes and noticed they were twinkling with mischief. He suspected she was messing with his mind, the same way he'd messed with hers while he battled the lusty temptation that clawed at his defenses.

"I need to find you a muzzle," he grumbled. "Surely we have one stashed around here somewhere."

Lori sighed audibly when Gideon tied on her leash then secured it to the post.

"I'll check on you after I scout for tracks and figure out what direction the thieves took."

She batted her long lashes at him and drawled, "I'll miss you while you're gone, Marshal Fox. Please hurry back."

Gideon loomed over her, taking advantage of his towering height. He crowded her against the post, telling himself not to react to the suggestive brush of his body against her luscious contours.

"Do not take advantage of my family's kindness and generosity," he warned. "You can torment me all you want, but don't use them for your devilish purposes. Do you understand me, Lorelei?"

"I don't understand you at all," she said, squirming against him, making him wonder if she was trying to avoid him or arouse him—and she was definitely doing that, damn it. "Now go away. I've enjoyed you as much as I can stand for one day."

"That goes triple for me." He wheeled around to retrieve his horse.

Chapter Five

"Honestly," Lori muttered at herself. "What makes you so defiant toward that man?"

She flopped back on the padding of straw and quilt Glenn and Sarah had graciously provided. She stared up at the barn loft, as if it held all the answers to her problems. Earlier in the day, Gideon had provoked her to attack him, to rebel against his abrupt orders.

That exercise in frustration had led to heated kisses and caresses that never should have passed between them.

Lori expelled a frustrated sigh as darkness closed in on the panoramic valley Gideon called home. He'd been gone for hours and she appreciated the reprieve. Thankfully, Glenn and Sarah had come by to check on her. Their companionship made her captivity somewhat bearable. But nothing changed the fact that the past several days had been a frustrating nightmare. Cowering in a cave during the daylight hours to avoid the two-man posse sent to overtake her, and being kept on a leash by Gideon, made her wish for the activity and freedom she'd taken for granted.

The prospect of spending years in jail—or worse—for being convicted of killing Tony made her shiver with apprehension. She wondered how many innocent people remained behind bars, insisting they spoke the truth, while guilty criminals ran around scot-free.

Lori rolled to her side, watching the sheep mill around the stall beside her. She wondered if counting them would help her fall asleep. She doubted it. She had too much on her mind.

Being wanted for murder frustrated her to no end. She'd never had to fight so hard to be believed before. Her word of honor and her character had never been questioned—until now.

She thought of her father and wondered if he believed the awful story circulating about her. Hopefully, he still had faith in her character.

Lori was anxious to return to the scene of the crime so she could personally investigate. Only *she* knew where the sniper had stationed himself in the underbrush to take those shots. There might be empty shell casings and other evidence in the bushes that no one would think to check.

Unfortunately, convincing Gideon Stone-Hearted Fox to investigate seemed impossible.

She supposed she was going to have to alter her behavior toward him if there was a chance of persuading him to listen. *Kill him with kindness,* so to speak. Lori wrinkled her nose, wondering how she'd manage to hold her tongue while that blue-eyed devil continued to mistrust and taunt her. It would require great patience and firm resolve on her part. She wasn't sure she was up to the task because he could ignite her emotions—all of them—in nothing flat.

On the other hand, she supposed she might try her luck at seducing him. If she offered favors, she could expect a few in return. Desperate situations demanded desperate measures, after all.

Lori blew out an exasperated breath and asked herself how she could pull off a successful seduction when she had no skills or practice at it. She spent most of her time *resisting* men's advances, not *inviting* them.

She wondered how many female prisoners had tried to use their wiles on Gideon Fox and how many had failed.

She calculated the number at one hundred percent.

With a weary sigh, Lori closed her eyes and begged for sleep. She suspected that only divine intervention would free her from the charges against her. Before she nodded off, she wondered if God himself dared to go up against Gideon Fox.

Maggie Burgess waited impatiently for the stagecoach passengers to climb from the coach. The coach was two hours behind schedule and she'd had to hold the evening meal until the travelers finally arrived. Damnation, her life had become hell since Tony died and she'd sent Sonny Hathaway and Teddy Collins to hunt down Lorelei. So far, she had heard nothing from her missing hired hands. The bounty she'd offered for Lori's return hadn't produced results. Besides that, she was shorthanded on the ranch and the stage station. Only Sylvester Jenkins was still around to work with the livestock, exchange the teams of horses and check the coaches when they arrived.

Her thoughts trailed off when the passengers strode beneath the lamppost that illuminated the dark compound in front of the stage station. She nodded a greeting to a young couple then focused her full attention on the tall, swarthy man who lit his cigar, causing golden light to flare against his angular features. She stared at the well-used pistols in the double holsters that hung low on his lean hips.

She lifted her gaze to survey his dark hat, dark hair and dark jacket. He had the look of a hard-edged lawman or bounty hunter whose attention shifted constantly to study his surroundings and scout for trouble before it pounced on him. Either that or the man was an ex-soldier, she mused. Then again, he might be an outlaw.

In this territory, you never knew for certain.

Maggie had watched her fair share of passengers come and go. She had listened to her husband and foreman speculate on the occupations of travelers. Oh, yes, this man looked a mite dangerous and very confident of his abilities. She'd wager he was handy with a variety of weapons.

Since Sonny and Teddy had no luck tracking Lorelei, it was time to take matters into her own hands and hire a professional to bring Lorelei to justice for her crime. That woman was going to pay for what she had done to Tony, Maggie vowed fiercely. That witch had worked her wiles on Tony for three months and now he was dead because of her.

"A moment of your time, sir," Maggie insisted, blocking the stranger's path before he entered the station.

He took a puff on his cigar then gave her the once-over. His steely gaze made her wonder if she had been too hasty in trying to charm him into accepting her proposition.

"What can I do for you, ma'am?" he drawled.

She flashed her best smile and reminded herself that it was up to her to see Lorelei pay dearly. "I am in need of a gun for hire to track down the female outlaw who shot my foreman. I wondered if you might be interested in the job. I have posted a reward. Plus, I'm offering the uncollected salary owed to him."

The stranger blew a lazy halo of smoke into the air then

stared at her with chilling silver-gray eyes that made her shift uneasily. "A woman, you say?"

Maggie nodded and gave Lorelei's name and detailed description before conveying the incident that left Tony dead.

"Did Miz Russell admit she shot your foreman?"

"No, she tried to convince me that someone ambushed Tony from the bushes, but I didn't see anyone. I think she was simply trying to throw suspicion on someone else."

He stared intently at her. "Did she claim she actually *saw* the shooter and could identify him?"

Maggie frowned, bemused. The man was intent on knowing the unnecessary details. But Maggie refused to be sidetracked. She wanted Lorelei tracked down and punished severely.

"She didn't offer a description of the shooter and I doubt there was one. Why else would she thunder off on horseback if she wasn't guilty?"

He squinted at her through a curl of smoke that drifted around his head. "And you are thoroughly convinced the lady outlaw acted alone?"

"She was standing over him with one of his pistols in her hand," Maggie insisted. "She has to be hiding out in the hills and I want her punished for her crime."

The stranger stared at her for a long moment then extended his callused hand. "All right, we have a deal. If you'll pay the unclaimed salary to me now to cover my expenses and furnish me with a reliable horse, I'll bring her back. Then I'll pick up the bounty money as my bonus."

Maggie was so delighted that he accepted that she pumped his hand enthusiastically. "Have a seat inside and I'll bring you a double helping of your meal. While you're eating I'll gather the money." She glanced at him expec-

tantly. "Thank you, Mister…?" She waited for him to fill
in the blank.

He tilted his dark head back and blew another smoke ring
in the air. "Reece McCree," he murmured before he sauntered into the stage station to join the other passengers.

Maggie blinked, stunned. She'd heard that name mentioned several times the past year. McCree had developed
a reputation as a bounty hunter who prowled the Territory
and the Southwest to apprehend the most dangerous criminals who carried the highest prices on their heads.

A delighted smile pursed her lips as she scurried off
to serve supper. Now she would get results, she assured
herself excitedly. McCree would track down that devious
woman and Maggie would have her vindication. Then she
would sell this station and ranch and move east as she had
longed to do, though Hubert had refused to pull up stakes
and leave this godforsaken territory. Now there was nothing to keep Maggie here in this uncivilized wilderness.
Nothing but the capture of Lorelei Russell for making her
life miserable.

"She will pay," Maggie murmured spitefully before she
manufactured a smile and served up supper.

Gideon returned home long after dark. He had stopped
at the stream to bathe then halted Pirate beside the barn. He
debated about torturing himself by confronting his prisoner
again. He should leave her alone until morning.

But that was the easy way out, he reminded himself.

Heaving a weary sigh, he dismounted, then led his horse
into the barn. It wasn't like him to avoid a prisoner. Then
again, he'd never dealt with one like Lorelei Russell, who
lambasted his emotions on so many levels that he didn't
know which one to fight first.

"Who's there?" she called out in the darkness.

"Who are you expecting?"

"Oh, it's you. I was hoping you'd gotten lost."

Even now, that sassy mouth of hers annoyed and amused him at once. Gideon halted and frowned disapprovingly when he discovered that Glenn or Sarah—or both—had opened the window to provide moonlight and fresh air. The moon was bright enough to illuminate the stall and he could see Lori's shapely body all too clearly.

There was a bed of straw, a quilt and a pillow. He wouldn't be surprised to learn that his infatuated little brother and his bleeding heart of a sister-in-law had taken the quilt and pillow off Gideon's bed. For spite.

As if Lori hadn't been offered enough comforts, he noticed she was wearing a skirt and blouse that had belonged to Sarah before her waistline expanded. The scoop-necked blouse displayed Lori's full bosom to its best advantage, he noted. Plus, she'd combed her thick, lustrous hair….

He frowned when it dawned on him that she couldn't have changed clothing without someone unlocking her cuffs.

Anger roiled inside him at the thought of his family defying his instructions. Galen would have a key because he carried cuffs while on duty. Therefore, Glenn or Sarah must have borrowed them—with or without Galen's permission.

He stared accusingly at Lori. "Did you manipulate my little brother or sister-in-law into providing you with a change of clothes and talk them into unlocking your cuffs?" he demanded gruffly.

"No, they are far more considerate and humane than you are." She sat up cross-legged on the padded pallet. "They allowed me to take a bath, with Sarah standing watch at the door and Glenn guarding the window to make sure I didn't try to escape."

He had bathed in the creek on his way home but his princess-of-a-prisoner had attendants!

When Lori rose gracefully to her feet, the moon and starlight sparkled in her red-gold hair. He noticed she'd pinned it up on her head, leaving the elegant column of her neck exposed. She approached him and halted at the end of her tether.

"Did you find the men who stole your valuable horses?" she surprised him by asking.

"No, but I located the tracks leading away from here and I know which direction they are headed. I also found the campsite they used to bed down last night."

"Are you going after the men tomorrow?"

He cocked his head, unwillingly admiring her curvaceous figure and bewitching face. No doubt about it, Lorelei Russell was a beautiful, intriguing woman. He could understand why men became captivated—including his knot-headed little brother, who had judged her by her temptingly attractive appearance and found her innocent of any and all crimes.

Before he did something stupid, like help himself to another taste of those luscious pink lips, Gideon wheeled around to unsaddle Pirate. He gave his horse a treat then placed him in a spacious stall. A moment later, he strolled past Lori's meager accommodations to see that she was still standing there staring at him.

He paused, cursing his betraying gaze, even as his eyes wandered over the enticing curve of her neck to the voluptuous swells of her breasts. His attention wandered to the trim indentation of her waist and the exposed portion of her legs that indicated the skirt was too short for her.

Gideon wasn't sure which was worse—this alluring

feminine attire or those trim-fitting breeches and shirt that accentuated all her tantalizing assets. He had the uneasy feeling that she could dress in a burlap sack and he would still find her impossibly attractive.

Lust hit him like a brick as his gaze roamed over her again. Damn it all, why did he have to be the one who captured her? Why couldn't she be someone else's problem? Why not one of his fellow marshals? Every blasted time he got close to her he was vividly reminded of how long it had been since he'd touched or tasted a soft, yielding female and had an opportunity to ease his basic needs.

"I want you to let me go, Gideon," she murmured. "I'll even promise to meet you in Fort Smith at whatever time and place you designate. You have my word."

"Right." He scoffed at her. "Now what's a murderess's word worth? I forget."

She flashed him a glare and muttered something he didn't dare ask her to repeat. Then she said, "I need to reassure my father that I'm all right and figure out what happened that fateful evening at the stage station. I keep playing the incident over in my mind, going through it in slow motion, focusing on everything Tony said to me. Something isn't right. I can feel it. I'm not sure what it is but it's niggling at me and I have to go back."

He barked an incredulous laugh. "You have me mixed up with my tenderhearted family. I've sworn to uphold the law. It's Judge Parker's duty to decide if there is enough evidence to convict you or to open an official investigation."

She inhaled a deep breath that made his attention drop to the swells of her breasts. He wondered if she'd done it on purpose when she said, "What will it take to persuade you to show leniency? Money? Comfort? Pleasure? What's your price?"

Desire coiled into a painful knot south of his belt buckle. He gritted his teeth and said, "I can't be bought."

"Can you be convinced to look the other way while I leave?" Lori questioned as she strained against her leash. "Can you be persuaded to at least *consider* that I might be telling the truth?"

When he took a step toward her, Lori felt that now-familiar sensation of irrational lust sizzle through her body. It baffled her that something unexplainable inside her called out to him.

It was the damnedest feeling she'd ever experienced.

She'd only known this swarthy lawman a day. Yet, unruly desire assailed her when she caught his scent, felt his lean, muscled body brush familiarly against hers and tasted him. She simply couldn't ignore his dynamic presence, no matter how hard she tried. And she had tried, to no avail.

"What are you suggesting, hellion?" he asked in a husky voice as he reached out to trail his forefinger over her lower lip, then trace the line of her jaw.

Pleasure hummed through her as his hand drifted down her shoulder to skim over the scooped neckline of the borrowed peasant blouse. Burning heat flared inside her as she focused helplessly on his sensuous mouth. God help her, she craved his kiss, craved the feel of his masculine body gliding suggestively against hers.

Of all the men in this world, why did *he* have to be the one who made her ache to discard her inhibitions and taste forbidden desire?

"Take what you want from me, Gideon," she whispered as his knuckles brushed against her breast, making her arch wantonly toward him.

"My pleasure for your freedom?" he rasped. "That's the bargain you're offering me?"

"Temporary freedom," she clarified, her voice wobbling from the erotic effect his caress had on her. "I'll come back to you." And if he didn't kiss her quickly, she was going to burn into a pile of smoldering ashes.

When he angled his head toward hers, her eyes fluttered shut. She felt herself melt against him as his arm slid around her waist. She desperately wanted her hands free so she could rake her fingers through the damp raven hair that indicated that he, too, had taken the opportunity to bathe recently. Instead, her hands were imprisoned between them and she inwardly moaned when his lower body glided suggestively against her, assuring her that he was aroused.

He distrusted her and disliked her, but he lusted after her to the same irrational degree that she lusted after him. Knowing that made her bold and she brushed her bound hands against the hard ridge beneath the placket of his breeches. She was rewarded with his growl of pleasure as he tightened his grasp on her.

"You drive a hard bargain, vixen," he rasped before his scalding kisses trailed along the curve of her neck.

His freshly shaved cheek skimmed the swell of her breasts and another frisson of heat sizzled through her body. Lori swallowed a gasp when he tugged at the neckline to suckle her breast.

She swore her legs had turned to jelly when scorching sensation after scorching sensation blazed through her. Her head fell back against his shoulder as he flicked his tongue against one taut nipple and then the other. Suddenly he picked her up with no effort whatsoever and laid her down on the pallet. He pulled her cuffed hands over her head so she couldn't continue caressing the hard length of his arousal through the fabric of his breeches.

"Enough of that," he growled against her neck. "You're

setting me on fire already. I've no wish to burn down this barn. It took my brothers and me a long time to build it."

Lori gasped aloud when his hand cupped her bare breast and he plucked at her nipple with thumb and forefinger. She arched helplessly toward him, astonished by the sensations of pleasure that streaked through her. Then he flicked at her nipple with his teeth and tongue.

One wild sensation after another shot through her body as he taught her the meaning of lusty pleasure.

It amazed her that a man who had been gruff and unaccommodating all the livelong day could become so attentive and tender when he touched her body. Sweet mercy, he was such a contradiction that she swore she'd never figure him out. He could ignite her temper in nothing flat and inflame her forbidden desires in the space of one heartbeat.

Suddenly her precious freedom was the farthest thing from her mind. She was burning alive with the pleasure of his gentle touch and she wanted to know what other nerve-shattering sensations he could unleash inside her.

Wondered what wicked sensations she could arouse in him.

When his hand glided beneath her skirt to caress her from ankle to knee, she held her breath—or rather, what was left of her breath after he stole it from her lungs with his ravishing kiss. She waited in shameless anticipation as his brazen touch moved across her inner thigh then skimmed her hip. She didn't voice the slightest protest— couldn't have if her life depended on it—when he teased her mouth with the gliding penetration of his tongue. When he cupped her in his hand, Lori arched toward him. His thumb grazed her heated core, leaving her to sizzle and burn with the most erotic pleasure imaginable.

She found herself wanting more and more. She needed something to appease this wild throb of desire that threatened to overwhelm her with each tantalizing motion of his hand beneath her skirt. Then his fingertip slid inside her and she couldn't contain the wobbly groan of pleasure that tumbled from her lips.

"Gideon...please..."

"Please what?" he whispered as his warm lips skimmed the column of her throat. "Tell me what you want."

The feel of her moist heat bathing his fingertip had Gideon aching to such extremes that it was difficult to breathe, to think. He'd been afraid that if he touched this maddeningly alluring firebrand that he wouldn't be able to stop until he'd had his hands and lips all over her lush body.

Sure enough, he couldn't get enough of her quickly enough to satisfy this crazed yearning that left him hard, desperate, aching and irrational.

Earlier, when her hands had skimmed over his arousal he swore the top of his head was going to blow off. He hadn't dared to let her touch him like that again, for fear he would explode. As it was, her eager responses to his kisses and caresses pleased him to no end. He'd never given a thought to bending a woman to his will with his touch. But taming this spirited firebrand was challenging, fascinating. He watched her come alive in his arms and he wanted to hear her whisper his name in helpless surrender.

"Gideon..." she panted breathlessly.

"Mmm?" He marveled at the satisfaction he derived from stroking her intimately, repeatedly.

Gideon wanted nothing more than to be buried deep inside her, feeling those long sleek legs wrapped around him as he rocked against her, appeasing this insane need she ignited within him. When he glided two fingers inside her and then bent to suckle the pebbled peaks of her breasts, her bound arms slid over his head to hold him close. He could feel her body shivering against his fingertips as he withdrew then delved deeper again. He set a provocative cadence that left her gasping for breath and moving in rhythm with his intimate caresses.

When she shattered around his hand and held on to him for dear life he gritted his teeth and wished he had been there with her when she climaxed. Instead, he ached until hell wouldn't have it. Rather, hell *would* have it because he'd broken his hard-and-fast rule about becoming personally and emotionally involved with his captives.

None of his captives tempted him the way Lori did. Most were men, after all. The women who'd offered him favors had never tempted him past his self-disciplined control.

Yet, this woman did. He *wanted* her like hell blazing. He *desired* her to mindless extremes. He even considered bedding her and granting her the freedom she desperately wanted….

The thought reminded him that she'd offered her luscious body to him as bargaining power. Maybe her responses were a little too eager and enthusiastic—so much so that he'd be inclined to look the other way so she could escape.

Gideon recoiled, furious with himself for allowing this amber-eyed siren to use his reckless need for her to tempt him past his usual resistance. No doubt, she was an exceptional little actress who made him feel as if he held some unique power over her tantalizing body and her emotions. He had extreme contempt for fakery and hated being taken in by manipulation. It stung his pride that he'd fallen beneath her wicked spell and nearly succumbed to a fit of lust.

Swearing foully at himself, Gideon sat up then pulled down her high-riding skirt. Before this scheming siren could lure him in again, he bounded to his feet. She still lay there, her full breasts exposed from his kisses and caresses, staring up at him with slumberous golden eyes that cast a nearly impossible trance of seductive temptation.

"Cover yourself, hellion," he snapped then turned away from the arousing view that left him hard and aching all over again. If there were such things as witches who cast spells to bedevil men she was in a league with them.

His bitter thoughts scattered to the four winds when he heard someone approaching. Immediately on guard, wondering if the thieves had circled back to see what else they could steal while Galen was feverish and wounded, Gideon drew his pistol. When the intruder approached, he pounced. He clamped one arm around the man's neck and stuffed the pistol in his neck.

"Awk!"

A moment too late Gideon realized his little brother had come calling. "Hell and damn, boy, you should have announced yourself."

"I am not a boy and I didn't know you were back," Glenn squeaked as he shoved at Gideon's arm to grant himself breathing space.

Gideon stepped back to reholster his pistol. He spared Lori a glance, noting that she was huddled in the corner, her blouse modestly in place and her skirt settled over her legs. The look she flashed him indicated that she expected an answer to her proposition after their near tumble in the hay.

The very idea that she had offered herself to him in exchange for her freedom incensed him. Especially since *she* had found release and *he'd* deprived himself when he'd come to his senses in the nick of time.

"The answer is no," he snapped tersely. "But nice try."

She glowered flaming arrows at him, as if he had betrayed her. As if *he* had used and abused *her*. Damn it, it was the other way around—and didn't he know it! Scowling, he turned and walked off without looking back.

"Leave her be, Glenn," he demanded gruffly.

"I brought her fresh cakes that Sarah baked," Glenn explained.

"Fine, feed your pet then go to bed."

The comment drew Lori's outraged gasp, but still Gideon didn't glance over his shoulder. He suspected she was glaring murderously at him—as only a conniving murderess could.

"I found the thieves' tracks," Gideon went on to say. "You can come with me day after tomorrow to hunt down the men. I'm not leaving until I'm assured Galen is recovering."

On the wings of those remarks, Gideon exited the barn. He was looking forward to hunting down those horse thieves. Anything to take him away from that flame-haired, golden-eyed minx who had tempted him until he didn't recognize himself. She had destroyed the code he lived by the moment she materialized from the fog, looking like a misplaced angel.

"Not an angel," he corrected himself sourly as he stalked upstairs to his room. "She's the devil's sister."

Gideon muttered several profanities when he entered his room and realized that his quilt and pillow were gone, just as he thought they'd be.

Chapter Six

Lori was so humiliated and embarrassed she wanted to dig a hole, crawl into it and die of shame. Desperate, she'd tried to sell her body and soul to that callous devil but she was no closer to freedom than before. He'd toyed with her to prove his power over her traitorous body. He'd used her uncontrollable desire for him as a weapon against her, and she hated her weakness for him.

She'd come apart in Gideon's arms, reveling in his tantalizing caresses—and he'd pulled away abruptly. Then he'd looked at her as if she were his worst enemy. He'd spewed out a few snide comments that cut to the core.

How could she be so susceptible to someone who treated her with mistrust and disrespect? She'd become his pet on a leash!

Damn that coldhearted marshal!

Damn her for thinking she could bargain with the devil!

The mortifying situation took its toll on Lori's emotions.

Despite her valiant attempt to maintain her composure, she burst into tears and embarrassed herself again.

This time with Glenn as a witness.

"Aw, honey, don't cry," Glenn murmured as he dropped to his knees in front of her.

"Your big brother makes me so crazy I can't think straight!" she blubbered. "He refuses to believe I'm as much a victim as my friend who died. He treats me horribly and I'd like to—"

She clamped her trembling lips shut before she voiced a threat against Gideon that made her seem suspicious in Glenn's eyes.

"You'd like to shoot him?" Glenn finished for her. Then he reached over to rake his hand through her disheveled hair. "I know the feeling well. Gid has been lording over me for years, refusing to see that I've grown up and that he doesn't have to feel responsible for me these days. I swear, he looks at me and still thinks I'm twelve."

That was nothing, Lori thought to herself. When *Gideon* looked at *Lori,* he thought she was wicked to the bone and nothing she could say or do would convince that blockheaded marshal otherwise.

That helpless thought provoked more tears. Lori hated that Gideon had reduced her to blubbering sobs in front of Glenn. He was just as good-looking as Gideon and he was a lot nicer to her. He treated her as if she were human and female.

Gideon treated her as if she were the Origin Sin.

So why didn't she feel the same fierce attraction to Glenn?

When Glenn sank down beside her, pulling her close to comfort her, she cried harder. Sometimes life was so maddening and unfair. Glenn was offering her soothing words and compassion. Idiot that she was, she longed for

Gideon's shoulder to cry on. If that wasn't testimony to her lunacy, she didn't know what was.

"Tony and I were bushwhacked," she said on a panted breath, needing to tell someone who would listen to what really happened that fateful night. "Tony proposed and I turned him down as gently as I could. That's when we heard rustling in the underbrush then a gunshot. Tony stepped in front of me like a shield to protect me. He caught the second of the three bullets the sniper fired.

"Maggie Burgess, the widowed owner of the stage station, heard the shots and came running. She falsely assumed I'd shot Tony because I was holding the pistol I'd used to return gunfire. Tony told me to run for my life when he collapsed and Maggie was screaming at me and shouting for her hired hands to capture me. Like a dazed fool I ran."

She lifted her face to Glenn, imploring him to believe her. "I swear that I had nothing to do with Tony's death. Now the bushwhacker is running loose. I can only speculate as to why he wanted to dispose of Tony in the first place."

"I'm sorry you had to endure that ordeal," Glenn commiserated as he held her. "It's the same as Galen getting shot by horse thieves. It could just as easily have been *me*. It should have been," he added emphatically. "Having Galen shot upset Sarah and she's carrying a baby. She doesn't need that kind of torment right now."

Lori blotted her eyes on her sleeve and sniffled as she sat upright. She stared at the shackles that rubbed her wrists raw. "You better return to the house before Gideon rants at you for showing me the slightest kindness. I don't want to be the cause of conflict between you and your brother. He's already warned me against involving you in my problems."

Glenn climbed agilely to his feet. He stood over her for a long moment then turned away. "I'll see you in the morning."

"Don't bother," she insisted. "I'm serious, Glenn. I don't want to be the cause of trouble for you or Sarah."

Glenn shrugged a broad shoulder then walked away.

Lori inhaled a cathartic breath then expelled it slowly, struggling for hard-won composure. Her life had gone straight to hell and Gideon was her resident jailer. He pleasured her and tormented her to such extremes that she couldn't sort out her feelings for him. Instinct told her to run away from him, as far and as fast as she could, but shackles and a leash made that impossible.

Exhausted, frustrated, Lori flounced on her pallet and begged for sleep. An hour later, she finally nodded off.

The next day, Lori noted that Gideon avoided her like the plague. He only showed up to allow her to relieve herself and stretch her legs, but he spoke not a word and only glanced in her direction when necessary. His impassive stares and disinterest hurt her feelings but she would be damned if she let him know that his opinion of her mattered so much.

She'd heard his boisterous laughter outside the barn. She'd wished she could be the reason for that pleasant sound instead of the cause of his scowls. But someone in his family, not *her,* had provoked the delightful sound of amusement.

Glenn and Sarah checked on her at irregular intervals and brought meals. For that, Lori was grateful. If Gideon had supplied her food, she figured it would've ruined her appetite.

Late that evening Lori heard someone approach her improvised jail cell. *Please don't let it be Gideon.* She couldn't tolerate another round of emotional torture. To her relief, Glenn stepped into view. He carried the shirt and breeches that Sarah had washed for her. A canvas knapsack hung over his shoulder.

Lori gaped at him when he crouched down in front of her to display the key to the handcuffs. No doubt, he had confiscated it from Galen again, as he had when he had granted her a bath and change of clothing the previous day.

"I'm not going to let Gid take you to Fort Smith until you've had a chance to ask questions and search the scene for evidence that proves you're innocent," he murmured as he clicked open the cuffs.

Lori stared into his dark eyes with hope and amazement. "You're letting me go free?"

"Not exactly. Gideon would kill me if I did that. I'm going to escort you to Burgess Stage Station and Ranch to make sure you're safe and protected."

Lori shook her tousled red-gold locks. "The last man who tried to protect me died. I don't want you to come to harm."

He smiled reassuringly. "I might not be Gideon's caliber of a lawman yet, but I'm damn good with weapons. I'm going with you and that's that."

Lori threw her arms around his neck and hugged the stuffing out of him. "You are such a wonderful man, Glenn. You don't deserve to have Gideon for a brother or me as a troublesome friend—"

Her voice died beneath Glenn's quick, unexpected kiss, and she felt the same reaction to Glenn that she'd felt with Tony Rogers—brotherly affection. Hell and damn, she thought, unaware that she'd borrowed Gideon's favorite expression. Life truly wasn't fair.

"We better get moving before someone—like

Gid—discovers we're missing," he murmured as he rose to his feet and hoisted her up beside him. He scowled when he noticed the raw flesh left by her shackles. "Those are Gid's fault. He should have seen to your comfort and he's been entirely too hard on you."

"That's because he dislikes me and distrusts me," she replied as she changed clothes, while Glenn walked over to saddle the horses.

Glenn fastened Drifter's girth strap in place. "He's not always like this."

"Really? You could have fooled me. I guess we just bring out the worst in each other," she said as she crammed her feet into her boots.

He made a neutral sound that could have meant anything.

"I'd like to be around when he realizes that he's mistaken about me and feels the need to apologize. Not that I would accept his apology without letting him suffer first."

Glenn chuckled quietly. "I wouldn't mind seeing the mighty Fox eat crow myself, honey."

Lori decided that *honey* must be the Fox brothers' fallback endearment. She'd heard all three men use it. Galen and Glenn could call her honey any time they pleased, but she didn't want to hear it from Gideon.

She didn't take time to analyze why the casual endearment, coming from his lips, offended her. She just wanted to beat a hasty retreat from Fox Ranch before the fire-breathing dragon realized she had escaped. He didn't like her now. His opinion of her would deteriorate completely after she slipped her leash—literally—and was spirited away in the darkness.

She grabbed Drifter's reins and told herself if she never saw Gideon again that was fine and dandy with her.

"We'll use the shallow creek to cover our tracks," Glenn

whispered as he led the way to the barn door. He checked to ensure the coast was clear before slipping around the corner into the copse of trees. "Gideon is too blasted good at tracking and scouting. I'm sure he'll figure out where we're going, but maybe he won't be hot on our heels if we have a head start."

Lori cast one last glance at the spacious cabin illuminated by moonlight. She would have liked to take time to thank Sarah for her kindness, but she didn't dare risk encountering Gideon.

She left, knowing she'd never experience those wild, reckless sensations with another man. Yet, the one who stirred her desires wasn't the man she needed. Besides, she convinced herself, she didn't need any man in her life. She was strong-willed and independent and she could manage just fine on her own, thank you very much.

So fare-thee-well and good riddance to Gideon Fire-Breathing Fox.

Gideon groaned softly as he came awake to realize he'd slept in his own comfortable bed once again. The sense of security and his exhaustion must have combined to make him sleep soundly. He hadn't awakened until dawn and he swore he hadn't moved a muscle all night. He felt stiff, achy and groggy. Not to mention that he'd worn himself out the previous day, dashing from one chore to the next to keep his mind off that amber-eyed minx who was more addictive than whiskey.

Reluctantly, he threw his legs over the side of his bed and sat up. He raked his tousled hair away from his face and was reminded that he needed a haircut. He'd get one in Fort Smith, he promised himself. Standing, he worked the kinks from his back and legs. He wondered why he felt so listless. Overworked, he decided. He definitely needed a vacation from these tedious forays to capture fugitives.

Once he'd dressed, he tiptoed downstairs so he wouldn't disturb Galen and Sarah. He sliced off two pieces of bread to appease his growling stomach. On second thought, he cut a piece for Lori. It was the slightest of concessions on his part. But he wasn't going to bend over backward like his tenderhearted sister-in-law and his sappy little brother— who seemed too infatuated with Lori to show the kind of common sense Gideon had tried to pound into the kid's head for the last dozen years.

Gideon intended to set off early to track down the missing horses. Now that Galen was on the road to recovery and his fever had broken, Gideon felt comfortable leaving the ranch. He packed beef jerky in his saddlebags and filled his canteen. Stepping outside, Gideon inhaled a breath of fresh spring air then mentally prepared himself to face Lori before he rode away. He was still uncomfortable with the tryst two days ago and he was sexually frustrated as hell.

He blamed her for responding to him, damn her. She'd tried to use him to gain freedom, and he'd allowed himself to forget that indisputable truth during those mind-boggling moments when he was kissing and caressing her intimately.

Soon as he rounded up the horse thieves, he intended to return Lori to marshal camp and let the other lawmen deal with her—which he should have done in the first place. But the moment the other men in camp had leered at her, he'd felt possessive and protective. His mistake. He wouldn't let it happen again. Someone else could investigate her case. Or not. It wasn't going to be him.

He'd decided to take the outstanding warrants and track a few more fugitives before riding back to Fort Smith. Time and distance from that seductive temptress was exactly what he needed. The woman was nothing but trouble. He'd sensed that the instant she came walking from the fog. He should've run screaming in the opposite direction when he had the chance.

His thoughts evaporated when he walked into the barn to see that she wasn't in the stall. Her horse was gone. So was Glenn's. Furious, Gideon wheeled around to storm back to the house. He was so angry that he barged into Galen and Sarah's bedroom unannounced.

He skidded to a halt when he realized Sarah had clutched the sheet to her bare chest and Galen—injured though he was—had rolled sideways to retrieve the pistol he kept under his pillow—same as Gideon did.

"Damn it, Gid," Galen growled while he held his older brother at gunpoint. "What the hell are you doing in here?"

He glanced at Sarah, who had turned a half-dozen shades of red before she pulled the sheet completely over her head.

"Sorry, Sarah," Gideon mumbled.

Obviously, Galen's injury, and Sarah's delicate condition, hadn't prevented them from enjoying the pleasures Gideon had been doing without for more weeks than he cared to count.

"Close the door on your way out," Galen snapped as he discarded the pistol. "Let us get dressed." He glared at Gideon. "And do not ever do that again, even if you are a Deputy-goddamn-U.S. Marshal!"

See what that infuriating woman has reduced you to? Gideon snarled at himself as he shut the door then waited for the married couple to make themselves presentable.

"All right. We're decent," Galen called out a few minutes later. "Now what is so blasted important?"

Gideon burst back into the room to see Sarah unwrapping

the bandage on Galen's arm. He was still bare-chested, but he'd donned a pair of breeches.

"Your idiotic little brother stole the key to your cuffs again and turned my prisoner loose," Gideon reported tersely.

Galen leaned over to open the drawer to the bedside table. "You're right. He did."

Gideon's accusing gaze landed on his attractive sister-in-law, who looked everywhere except at him. "In addition, someone around here, as if I don't know who, uncuffed my prisoner the day before yesterday so she could bathe and change into a borrowed set of clothing."

Galen's lips twitched as he glanced at his wife. "Nice of you to be considerate of Lori."

"Thank you, dear," she murmured.

Gideon howled in outrage. "You are undermining my authority!"

Sarah pivoted to meet his accusing stare. "I couldn't very well let the poor woman wear the same clothes she had to use for several days, could I?" She glanced at Galen. "Your big brother didn't show her the slightest consideration."

"She's a prisoner!" Gideon shouted in frustration.

"I don't know what's come over you, Gid," Sarah chided, hands on hips. "As much as I love you, I want to rail at you for being so insensitive and purposely snide to that poor woman."

"That *poor woman* killed her former lover," he reminded her harshly.

"I don't believe that. I happen to like Lori and I've heard a few of the details that put her on the run."

"Of course you believe her," Gideon muttered sourly. "You're compassionate and Glenn is gullible. She did her damnedest to earn your trust. Believe me when I tell you that criminals will do and say whatever necessary to gain sympathy from anyone who will listen and help them escape."

Just look at how *he'd* stumbled and fallen two nights past when that alluring witch offered him whatever he wanted for her precious freedom. Damn it, he wasn't sure who made him more furious. Him or her. And he'd be damned to hell if he fell for that trick of seduction again. Once he recaptured her—and he would recapture her, he vowed fiercely—he would show no mercy whatsoever! Furthermore, she was never going to tempt him past his resistance again!

Sarah tilted her chin to a belligerent angle that reminded him a little too much of Lori. "I trust my intuition," she declared. "She is innocent."

Gideon rolled his eyes. "Spare me from female intuition."

"It is also the Osage's deep sense of knowing," she contended. "You would sense it, too, if you weren't so busy trying to convict Lori of wrongdoing without listening to the details of the incident."

He arched a dark brow. "Did she tell you the entire version of her story? Is that what convinced you?"

"No, she told it to Glenn who told it to me."

"Secondhand lies," he grumbled. "Glenn is infatuated with her. Of course, he's going to believe what she tells him." He tapped himself on the chest. "*I* have the necessary details. The Widow Burgess claims Lori shot and killed her lover. Then she ran. Fugitives don't usually run unless they've committed a serious crime and don't want to get caught. That's all *I* need to know and the rest is up to Judge Parker."

"How reliable is the witness?" Galen asked as Sarah placed a poultice and a clean bandage over his wound.

"Not you, too?" Gideon groaned in dismay. "You're a lawman. I expected you to side with me."

Galen glanced at Gideon then at Sarah. "Would you fetch me a drink, please, love?"

She smiled wryly. "Why don't you simply say that you'd like a private word with your brother?" She shot Gideon an annoyed glance as she passed him on her way to the door. "I have a few more words for you, too, Gid. None of them are very nice and all of them have to do with your inconsiderate treatment of a woman."

"For the last time, she's a prisoner!" Gideon crowed as Sarah walked away.

He huffed out a breath as Galen grinned and shook his ruffled head.

"Hell and damn, surely you've logged in enough years in law enforcement that you know better than to believe the absurd tale of a rejected marriage proposal and a bushwhacker in the underbrush. I checked her pistol. She fired a shot."

"And you can *prove* she killed her supposed lover with that bullet?" Galen challenged. "Not that she returned fire or hunted game while in hiding?"

"Circumstantial, I will admit," Gideon retorted. "But people don't usually end up with a sizable bounty on their heads and murder accusations following them around if they aren't *prime* suspects *seen* at the scene of a crime."

Galen settled himself against the headboard then regarded Gideon astutely. "You wanna know what I think?"

"Not particularly, but since you like to spout your opinions I'll probably have to listen to you anyway," Gideon said, and snorted.

Galen ignored the taunt. "I think that you don't want to believe Lori because you are extremely attracted to her and you aren't comfortable with that."

"Where the hell did that come from?" Gideon demanded indignantly, agitated to the extreme that his brother had hit too close to the truth.

Galen grinned broadly. "It's like Sarah said. Our tribe acquired a deep sense of knowing that has passed from generation to generation. You know what you sense and feel, Gid. You are fighting it."

"This is ridiculous," Gideon sputtered. "My instincts are shouting that she charmed Glenn into setting her free then convinced him to accompany her cross-country. She'll probably convince him to fight me when I catch up to them. Pitting brother against brother is the ultimate betrayal, in my book. That tells me that she's capable of anything."

Galen sighed audibly as he eased onto the edge of the bed. "I better go with you so you don't kill Glenn."

"You are staying here," Gideon insisted. "Sarah can't handle all the chores of chopping wood, herding livestock and cleaning barn stalls while you and Glenn are gone."

Galen staggered slightly then plopped back to the bed. His face turned white as salt. "Okay, so maybe I don't feel up to a long, fast ride across rugged terrain. For certain, I don't want to leave my wife alone." He stared intently at Gideon with narrowed green eyes. "But you have to promise me that you won't go off half-cocked and shoot Glenn for becoming Lori's knight in shining armor. *Swear* it to me, Gideon."

Gideon muttered and growled for a half minute then said begrudgingly, "I swear I won't shoot my foolish, love-smitten little brother for falling under that conniving witch's spell."

"And promise you won't shoot the lovely witch," Galen insisted, flashing another wry grin. "Also promise to be more sensitive or Sarah will come after you with a loaded gun."

"Fine," Gideon said, and scowled. "I'll treat her like the damn Queen of Sheba."

Galen chuckled as he stretched out on the bed. "I'd like to be there to see that." He flicked his wrist dismissively. "Better get going, Gid. I don't know when they left, but they might be way ahead of you by now."

Gideon pivoted on his heels. "Take it easy until I get back. I don't want to return to find your wound infected and you delirious with fever again."

"I'll do my best not to inconvenience you, dear brother," he teased as Gideon strode off.

Sarah was waiting beside the front door with extra food for Gideon's journey.

"For me? How thoughtful. I thought you considered me the enemy," he said as he accepted her generous offering.

Her lips twitched. "These are for Lori and Glenn. I know you are an experienced survivalist and you can take care of yourself." Her expression turned somber. "Treat her as you would treat me, Gideon."

Gideon dropped a kiss to her cheek. "Your expectations for me are too high, Sarah. You're just too kind to admit it."

"You look for the worst in people, Gid."

"And you always look for the best in people, even if there is no good to be found," he countered.

"I see the good in *you*," Sarah was quick to assure him. "This family would have had its home and property stolen out from under it by swindlers who constantly prey on our people, if not for your vigilance. I know you have a good heart, but dealing with hardened criminals, like the ones who destroyed my family, warped your perspective. I also think that you are afraid of trusting your feelings for Lori."

Gideon groaned in frustration, but Sarah followed him

when he tried to walk away. "Galen has told me how your
mother let herself fall for a man's poison words, only to
discover that he wasn't what he seemed when she married
him. You had to stand up to him when he tried to abuse
your mother and brothers. You also had to go after him
when he shoved aside your mother and let her die without
getting medical attention. I think you are afraid of making
the same mistake as your mother, but Lori is nothing like
your stepfather."

Gideon swore under his breath and kept right on walking. "Just take care of Galen and don't strain yourself trying
to work so Galen won't have to. I'll take care of everything
when I drag Glenn and my prisoner back home."

"Do not shoot your brother," she called after him as he
hurried off to saddle Pirate.

"Why does everyone think I'm capable of shooting my
idiotic little brother?" he asked the world at large.

Chapter Seven

Glenn kept glancing sideways at Lori at regular intervals. She presumed he was checking to see how well she was holding up while crossing the rugged terrain of rock-strewn and timbered hills.

"You don't have to worry about me keeping the pace. Remember, my father was in the military," she reminded him. "He trained me to ride and to become self-reliant."

Glenn walked his horse through the shallow creek then paused to take a break. "All the same, I don't plan to be as inconsiderate of your needs as Gid."

"Could we speak of something more pleasant than Gideon?" she requested as she dismounted. Thoughts of her shameless surrender to Gideon's surprisingly gentle caresses kept assailing her when she let her guard down. She did not need to hear his name mentioned aloud.

"Whatever you wish, honey," Glenn said accommo-datingly.

"I'll see to my needs since we've stopped to rest."

"Don't wander off too far," Glenn cautioned. "This area is heavily populated with panthers."

"I became acquainted with one while I hid in a cave."

Lori walked into the bushes to grant herself privacy. She contemplated sneaking away from Glenn and forcing him to return home. He would speak the truth when he told Gideon that she'd run off. Perhaps Gideon wouldn't be too hard on Glenn and blame her since he had such a low opinion of her. Heavens, she seemed to be Gideon's favorite scapegoat.

He believed everything that went wrong was her fault.

Right there and then, Lori decided that she'd leave Glenn behind—for his own good. She would escape while he was hunting game for their next meal. Then, she'd hide out until he gave up and went home.

Or until Gideon came looking for him.

She winced at the unpleasant prospect.

"Lori? Are you okay?" Glenn called out anxiously. "You're still there, right?"

"I'm fine."

A moment later, she walked into the clearing and noticed Glenn's gaze roaming appreciatively over her. She had been the recipient of unflattering masculine stares on many occasions. Glenn's interest was respectful and flattering and he didn't make her uncomfortable. She sincerely hoped the handsome young Fox brother didn't have romantic inclinations toward her, just admired feminine scenery, as men were prone to do.

Kind and likable though he was, there was no magic, no irresistible attraction. Even if there were, the prospect of having Gideon as her brother-in-law didn't bear thinking about. In his eyes, she would never be worthy of Glenn's affection.

She noticed Glenn had glanced over his shoulder for the

umpteenth time. Though he insisted he wasn't concerned about confronting Gideon, she knew he must be apprehensive. And he had every right to be. Lori had seen Gideon in action when he sneaked up on Pecos Clem Murphy. Even the wily outlaw's clever trip wires and booby traps hadn't fazed Gideon in the least.

Sly as a damn fox, that's what he was, she mused. Nothing got past Gideon. He was exceptionally skilled at his profession. Honestly, she was more than a little surprised Glenn had been able to sneak her away from the barn.

She shrugged off the thought and decided the weariness of Gideon's tedious forays in the wilderness to capture fugitives had caught up with him. The reassurance of being home for the first time in weeks allowed him to sleep soundly.

Either that or the satisfaction of making her a slave to her forbidden desire for him had him sleeping like a baby.

Lori bit back a smirk. She tried to imagine that hard-edged lawman as an infant—and couldn't. She would've sworn wolves or rattlesnakes had raised him, if she hadn't met his family.

The unexpected sound of a horse's shrill whinny jerked her back to the present. Her horse pranced skittishly and Glenn's Appy gelding tossed its head uneasily. A wild scream pierced the air and Lori knew immediately that a panther was prowling nearby. Instinctively she bounded onto Drifter, urging him toward the sound, not away from it. She wanted to make sure an unsuspecting traveler didn't become the victim of attack.

"Lori, wait!" Glenn muttered as he raced behind her.

She paid him no heed. She guided Drifter through the trees then skidded to a halt. She looked over the cliff to see six spectacular Pinto and Appaloosa horses. They were staked beside a hastily constructed lean-to made of cottonwood striplings and rope. The makeshift cabin was butted up against the steep creek bank. More horses were tethered in a grove of willow trees.

Her gaze shifted from the squatter's quarters to the prize livestock that undoubtedly belonged to the Fox family.

"I'll be damned. They're here," Glenn remarked as he rode up beside Lori. "Those nesters stole our horses and set up housekeeping on our reservation land."

He glanced speculatively from her to the horses. Clearly, he was trying to decide whether to rescue the herd or escort her home. Lori wasn't allowing him to make a choice. The herd came first. She could take care of herself.

When the panther screamed again, Lori jerked to attention. She scanned the adjacent bluff that overlooked the stream. She spotted the oversize mountain lion lurking among the rocks and trees on the ledge. He switched his tail as he stalked closer to the string of edgy horses.

Lori presumed the hastily built shack was unoccupied since no one darted outside to protect the frightened horses from the black panther. If she could discourage the cat, Glenn could rescue the horses without gunplay. She could send Glenn home and she would be on her way in the opposite direction before Gideon showed up.

Before she could voice a suggestion, Glenn slid his rifle from its scabbard on the saddle and took aim at the panther. He took a shot and dropped the cat in its tracks, leaving it dangling half on and half off the overhanging cliff.

To her dismay, two men clambered from the lean-to, their rifles at the ready. Lori gasped when she recognized the two men Widow Burgess had sent to capture her. Sonny Hathaway and Teddy Collins glanced around wildly, looking for a target to return the unexpected gunfire. Lori bounded from the saddle and took cover the instant before two gunshots simultaneously exploded overhead.

Glenn slid from his horse to take aim at the scraggly-looking horse thieves. "Damn scoundrels," he muttered. "If the army would roust these squatters off our reservation, like they're supposed to do, we wouldn't have so many murders and thefts." He took a shot and hit Sonny Hathaway in the leg. "That's for Galen, you bastard," he snarled vindictively as Sonny dragged himself into the lean-to. Then he took Teddy Collins's measure on the sight of his rifle.

Lori made a pact with herself to sneak away as soon as Glenn had the situation in hand. The last thing Lori needed was for Glenn to interrogate the two men sent to apprehend her. No doubt, their story would be in direct contrast to hers.

And damn these men! she fumed. They must have anticipated that Maggie Burgess would shut down the stage station and ranch after she'd lost her husband and then her foreman. They had turned to thievery for their new career.

"Fetch my ammunition from the saddlebag," Glenn ordered after he fired off another shot that sent Teddy diving behind a boulder for cover.

Lori scrunched down to waddle toward Glenn's Appaloosa gelding. She didn't relish the idea of getting her head blown off…not before she cleared her name. Using a tree as her shield, she bounded up quickly to fish into the leather bag. She retrieved extra cartridges then she grabbed the spare pistol she found in the saddlebag.

"If you use that on my little brother, I'll make you damn sorry, hellion. Put your hands over your head. *Now!*"

Lori nearly leaped out of her skin when Gideon's menacing snarl erupted behind her. "Who'd have thought my luck could turn so sour so quickly?" she grumbled.

She lifted her arms then slowly turned to meet piercing blue eyes that glittered dangerously.

His vicious scowl condemned her to the farthest reaches of hell and she understood why outlaws feared him. He looked as formidable as the devil himself. Worse, maybe.

He aimed his Peacemaker at her heart and said, "No one outruns the long arm of the law. Not even you, hellion."

Lori swore he'd pull the trigger if she made the slightest move. So she stood as still as stone and wondered if he'd shoot her anyway.

Furious, Gideon held Lori at gunpoint. He predicted she'd planned to put the pistol to Glenn's head while he focused on his shoot-out with the man huddled beside the lean-to.

Gideon had been in a royal bitch of a mood all morning. He was infuriated with his kid brother for obstructing justice and he was outraged with Lori for seducing Glenn into helping her escape. He was certain she'd used her feminine wiles on Glenn, the same way she'd tried—and nearly succeeded—in using them on Gideon.

Had she offered her lush body in exchange for her freedom and to gain escort through unforgiving terrain? Had Glenn yielded completely to temptation, while Gideon had scraped together enough willpower to pull away before he buried himself in her silky warmth?

The thought of his brother taking the woman Gideon lusted after left him battling an unfamiliar emotion. It shouldn't matter that Lori had been intimate with Glenn, he told himself sensibly. She was a clever courtesan who used her ample charms to lead a man into trouble. To her, bedding one Fox to influence his opinion and bend him to her will was as good as another. No doubt, she would have tried to seduce Galen, too, if he could serve her devious purposes.

"Gideon, glad you're here," Glenn shouted as they approached him.

"I'll bet," Gideon scoffed at his brother.

"The other thief crawled into the lean-to after I shot him in the leg," Glenn reported. "If you'll keep this man pinned down, I'll circle around to attack his blind side."

Glenn tossed him the rifle and Gideon caught it with his free hand.

"I'll go with Glenn," Lori volunteered eagerly as she inched away from the horse.

A wild shot zinged over Gideon's head. He ducked then launched himself at Lori before she could turn the confiscated pistol on him. She yelped in pain when he wrenched the weapon from her hand and cast it aside.

"You don't have to hurt her," Glenn protested.

Damn the kid, thought Gideon. Obviously, he'd slept with this devious siren once or twice. Now he considered himself her valiant protector. The tormenting image of Glenn touching Lori as intimately as Gideon had, shot across his mind like a lightning bolt. The last shred of his good disposition went up in smoke.

"By all means, forgive my rough handling, hellion," Gideon said, his voice dripping with sarcasm.

Lori sneered at him. Not to be outdone, he sneered back.

When Glenn darted sideways, without giving Gideon the chance to reject the plan to attack the thieves' blind side, he was forced to provide a distraction and keep the gunman pinned down. While he fired rapidly, he caught movement from the corner of his eye.

Hell and damn! That cunning little vixen had dived beneath Pirate, using him as a shield, before she bounded to her feet. She knew Gideon wouldn't shoot his well-trained horse.

His one and only trusted friend in this world, he mused. He sure as hell couldn't count on his family. They had turned traitor after Lori drew them under her evil spell.

To his fury, Lori clung to Pirate's side so he couldn't get a clear shot at her. He refused to ask himself if he *would have* taken the shot, if his horse hadn't been in the way. That would signify that she mattered to him.

He'd shoot *himself* in the foot before admitting that!

Gideon swore colorfully when Lori nudged Pirate forward, mounting up while the horse was at a trot. He hated that she'd left him between the proverbial rock and hard spot. If he chased that murdering spitfire, he couldn't provide cover for Glenn who would become a moving target and likely get himself shot.

"Damn it to hell!" Gideon growled as he turned his attention to the horse thief pinned down behind a boulder. His gaze leaped back and forth between the thief and Glenn. Gideon noticed his little brother excelled in sneaking up on people. The frizzy, red-haired thief fired at Gideon, unaware that Glenn was twenty feet behind him and closing in fast.

With brotherly pride, Gideon watched Glenn launch himself through the air to knock the unsuspecting thief off balance. The man yelped loudly then lapsed into unconsciousness after Glenn hammered him on the back of the head with the butt of his pistol. Then Glenn wheeled toward the lean-to. He jerked away from the doorway the instant before the other thief took a shot at him—missing him by only a few inches.

Glenn dived in low and fast. When the second shot went over Glenn's head, Gideon smiled. The kid had learned to come in low, since most gunmen aimed for the heart.

Who would have thought his kid brother had paid so much attention when Gideon and Galen taught him to survive a gun battle.

His smile faded, wondering when Glenn would announce that he planned to put his life on the line to protect the Osage people from white invasion. Or Glenn might decide to become a Deputy U.S. Marshal. Gideon would've preferred that one Fox brother take up ranching exclusively and marry a sweet, unassuming woman.

Someone completely unlike Lorelei Russell.

He jerked to attention when Glenn reappeared from the dark interior of the makeshift shack. He dragged the second unconscious thief outside and dumped him beside his sprawled cohort. Since Glenn had the situation in hand, Gideon bounded to his feet. He vaulted onto Lori's horse to chase her.

When he reached the edge of the cliff, he realized she'd circled the hill and was crossing the meadow. His first instinct was to take her measure with the rifle. He hesitated, unable to bring himself to fire at her.

If it were any other fugitive, riding any other horse, Gideon wouldn't think twice about shooting at horse and rider. But the conniving minx knew he wouldn't shoot down his own horse!

Growling in exasperation, refusing to let Lori escape on his prize stallion, Gideon stared speculatively at the rugged slope that separated him from Lori. Then he studied the strawberry roan he had confiscated. Drifter wasn't as muscular, sturdy or sure-footed as Pirate, but he was an exceptionally fine animal nonetheless.

Gideon gouged Drifter in the flanks, forcing him to take the shortcut down the rock-strewn embankment. The horse whinnied in protest, but Gideon refused to let the animal retreat. Once they were headed downhill, momentum kept them going. Gideon practically lay back on Drifter's rump as the horse skidded through the grass and pockets of loose dirt near the boulders. The horse stumbled once but Gideon jerked the reins, keeping Drifter's head up. Then he sprawled back once again to help the horse maintain balance.

One false step, and he and Drifter would tumble head over heels down the slope to land in a broken heap. Gideon did everything humanly possible to ensure that didn't happen. Besides, he thought self-righteously, he had the law on his side.

That should count for something.

Lori unintentionally pulled Pirate to a halt and stared incredulously at Gideon. That fearless warrior of a man had forced Drifter down a treacherous slope that no horse and rider should have negotiated. It was too dangerous, with pitfalls scattered everywhere along the path he blazed downhill.

How dare he risk her horse when she had purposely circled the rugged slope to ensure Pirate suffered no injuries! Damn that daredevil marshal! He and her horse might end up with broken necks. She'd have to shoot *both* of them.

It would upset her to shoot her own horse.

Although her preservation instincts shouted at her to race across the meadow to seek shelter in the wooded hill on the far side of the creek, she sat there apprehensively, making sure Gideon didn't injure himself or her horse. She caught her breath twice when Drifter stumbled and nearly lost his footing. If Gideon hadn't been an exceptional rider with years of experience, he'd have met with disaster.

Only when Gideon reached the spot where the hillside leveled out to provide solid footing did she nudge Pirate. The powerful stallion gathered himself then shot off like a cannon, assuring Lori that he was faster of foot than Drifter, who was carrying heavier weight.

"Stop, damn you!" Gideon bellowed behind her. "Don't make me shoot you!"

Lori paid him no mind. She knew Gideon wouldn't shoot Pirate out from under her so she plastered herself against the horse's muscular neck.

She shouldn't have been surprised or disappointed when Gideon fired his pistol at her. The bullet whizzed past her head. That telling shot proved Gideon had no feelings whatsoever for her. The passion they'd shared in the moonlit darkness of the barn meant nothing to him. She could have been any female in a skirt and he would've toyed with her for his lusty amusement.

"One last chance to stop!" he bellowed at her.

Lori headed straight for the creek, hoping to scrabble up the tree-covered slope to take cover. She was halfway across the stream when Gideon let out a loud whistle. She yelped in surprise when Pirate came to a screeching halt in midstream. Lori flew over his head and kerplopped in the water before she had time to snatch a quick breath of air. She swore she'd swallowed ten gallons of water.

Gasping for breath, she climbed upon hands and knees, desperate to crawl ashore to hide in the trees. Behind her, Drifter splattered into the creek. Panicked, Lori shot to her feet, hoping to dash to safety but Gideon dived off the horse and landed directly on top of her.

Water shot up her nose and slapped her in the face as she submerged. She couldn't catch a breath since Gideon was sprawled on top of her.

When she came up for air, Gideon grabbed her by the hair on her head and forced her down. She struggled frantically, trying to land a roundhouse blow with her fists, but she couldn't see where to strike him when he held her head underwater.

He allowed her to come up for a breath then shoved her down again, without using excessive force. He simply outmuscled her to prove that he held the upper hand. She doubted he'd drown her, but it made her furious that she was no match for his strength. He delighted in driving home that point, damn him.

She should drown, just to spite this ornery devil. He might even feel guilty—for a couple of minutes.

When he pulled her up by the mop of her wet hair, she gasped and sputtered to draw breath. "I…hate…you…Gideon…Fox," she wheezed in outrage.

"That's a mean thing to say," he taunted. "I'll let you up when you say you *love* me, hellion."

"I'd rather die!" she spat, and coughed.

"Your choice, honey."

Lori barely had time to grab a breath before he forced her head underwater again. Unfortunately, her fierce preservation instincts provoked her to fight back instead of sticking with her claim that she'd rather die first. Just as she swore she'd run out of breath, Gideon lifted her head from the water and stuck his grinning face into hers.

"Still hate me?"

"Yes," she snarled furiously. "You are the devil!"

"Stop hurting my feelings with your snide insults."

"You don't have feelings. Your heart is solid rock—"

He forced her head down again then pulled her up a few moments later. "Say you love me."

"You love me," she repeated.

"No, say…*I love you.*"

When she stuck out her chin defiantly, he pushed her underwater then waited another few moments before pulling her to the surface. Lori was through with his taunting games of pushing her to the very limit of her temper. Let him think she'd drowned. Let him think she was a murderess, a horse thief and a high-priced courtesan. What did she care? She couldn't convince him she was innocent, even if she devoted a month to the task.

Furthermore, she wasn't going to say she loved this cantankerous daredevil of a lawman who amused himself at her expense. He'd done that two nights earlier and she refused to let him humiliate her again.

When she went perfectly still in the water, he yanked her up by the shoulders and stared worriedly at her. "Lori, are you all right?"

She reared back and punched him squarely in the jaw. The surprise attack stunned him and gave her a chance to shove both hands against his chest. He squawked as he tumbled off balance and went underwater. She bounded up and stepped on his chest with both feet, using him as a springboard.

To her dismay, he rolled sideways in the shallow water and grabbed her ankle. She belly flopped with a splat and a shriek. She managed to catch a quick breath before his powerful body covered her completely, weighing her down.

She was glad she didn't have to face him, knowing he'd flash that devilish grin, provoking her to try to claw the triumphant expression off his face.

She muttered when he lifted himself then grabbed her shoulder to press her onto her back in the shallows. When he sprawled on top of her, sensations that had no business whatsoever assailing her trickled through her betraying body. He'd captured her and tormented her for escaping on his own horse, but he was *not* going to see her melt beneath him like she had two nights past.

"All right. You win, Fox," she snapped as his hips settled

suggestively against hers and he braced his upper body on his forearms. "I love you. Madly. Now let me up!"

He smiled and his blue eyes sparkled like polished sapphires. It was the first time he'd really smiled at her. It wasn't one of those wry or cynical expressions he usually reserved for her. Rather a rare smile that settled into every ruggedly handsome feature and transformed him into strikingly handsome.

"Now was that so hard, hellion?" he teased. "Say it again. It's sweet music to my ears."

"I'd like to *box* your ears instead," she sniped.

He clucked his tongue and shook his wet head. "You'll have to do better than that if I'm going to let you up."

Fine. She'd say the words he demanded a dozen times— and never mean it once. Words meant nothing and she'd never forgive him for the infuriating way he made her cry uncle.

"I love you, Gideon Fox," she said, without an ounce of emotion vibrating in her voice. "Happy now?"

His dark brows furrowed and his smile faded. "Not as happy as I'd hoped."

To her surprise—or dismay, she couldn't decide which— he lowered his shaggy raven head until his sensuous lips were hovering a hairbreadth from her mouth. She turned her head, afraid that he'd kiss her and she'd be unable to stifle a response.

The feel of his muscular body gliding intimately against hers crumbled her defenses in less than a heartbeat. She wasn't sure how much more wicked temptation she could take before her traitorous body gave in. When he cupped her chin and turned her face to his, she made the critical mistake of staring into those spellbinding blue eyes. Her resolve floated downstream as he pressed his lips ever so gently to hers.

She could defy his forceful commands day and night. But his rare tenderness defeated her as nothing else could.

A moment later, his kiss deepened, savoring and devouring her at once. She wasn't aware she'd raised her head and arched eagerly into him until her arms wound tightly around his neck and she pressed her body into his. His hands prowled over her hips then his thumb grazed her nipple.

Despite the cool water in the creek, sensual fire shot through her, searing her inside and out. When his hand shifted to her buttocks to pull her against the rigid length of his arousal, another blast of heat bombarded her and unappeased desire sizzled through her. Teasing her. Tormenting her. Tempting her beyond bearing.

Brazenly, she reached between them to trace his hard length. She wanted to explore his body as completely as he'd explored hers one dark and steamy night in the barn. When he growled deep in his throat and surged toward her, she shifted against him. Then he eased her thighs apart with his knees and settled between her legs.

She wondered what it would be like to feel him moving provocatively against her without a barrier of wet clothing separating them. She wondered how his sinewy flesh and his hard arousal would feel beneath her hands…between her lips….

The deliciously wicked thought prompted her to clamp her hands on his buttocks and squirm to settle him exactly above her. When she took the initiative, he suddenly jerked away and glared at her. The mood shattered like broken glass.

"Is that how you convinced Glenn to unlock your cuffs and accompany you during your escape?" he muttered as he clamped his hand around her wrist and pulled her upright in the shallows.

"Certainly not!" she huffed indignantly.

He hauled her none too gently to her feet and kept a vise grip on her forearm, in case she tried to make a break for it. "Why don't I believe you?"

"Because you're a stubborn billy goat of a man."

"And you are the most infuriating woman I've ever met!"

"At least I'm *something* to you," she snapped then ignored him the best she could—which wasn't easy because the big galoot refused to let her go.

Chapter Eight

$\sim\!\!\sim\!\!\sim\!\!\sim\!\!\sim\!\!\sim$

Gideon cursed himself a dozen times over for surrendering—again, damn it—to his irrational desire for this spirited firebrand. Didn't he have any shame, any pride or common sense? What flaws of character left him lusting after a fugitive that *his own brother* had likely bedded when he stumbled into her conniving scheme to gain his assistance?

"Why didn't you whistle at your horse right off, instead of firing that shot at me?" she demanded as she squirmed for freedom. "And what is wrong with you! You could have killed your own horse when you barely missed me with that bullet!"

"If I'd have wanted to hit you, believe me, I would have," Gideon assured her tartly. "That was just a warning shot. The reason I didn't whistle at Pirate right away was that I gave you a chance to surrender when I ordered you to. You failed another test."

Gideon towed her with him as he strode over to Pirate, who grazed on the tender spring grasses beside the creek bed. He grabbed a coil of rope from his saddlebag to bind her hands. She glowered at him but he was too distracted by the wet clothing that clung to her curvaceous body like paint. Lusty desire tried to overwhelm him again but he resisted as best he could.

He usually had more self-control than to drool over a woman, especially one who had so many condemning strikes against her.

"And another thing," she fumed. "How dare you force *my* horse down that steep slope! I'm surprised you and Drifter didn't wind up with broken necks."

"How dare you *steal* my horse," he countered as he led her over to Drifter then secured her in the saddle. "Now you're wanted for murder, horse thieving, escape, resisting arrest, assaulting a law enforcement officer—"

"Assault!" she crowed. "You nearly drowned me!"

He wouldn't have gone that far, no matter how irritated he'd been with her. But he'd never tell her that. He was trying to break her defiancé, but he wasn't sure that was possible. The woman was bursting with more sass and spirit than any female he'd ever met.

"You clobbered me a couple of times while attempting escape, remember? And then again today," he reminded her as he mounted Pirate. "Every time I test you I realize you can be provoked to violence. *That* is assault on an officer."

"And what do you call holding my head underwater?"

"Subduing a defiant fugitive."

"You were trying to drown me so don't deny it," she shot back angrily. "There were a few moments when I wondered if dying wasn't preferable to dealing with the likes of you." She glared at him good and hard. "And do not *ever* demand that I say I love you again, as your twisted version of crying uncle. Hell will be frozen over for a century before you hear that sentiment from me!"

She was so annoyed that her face pulsed with color. She continued to glare murderously at him—which did nothing to convince him of her innocence.

"Give me your gun," she demanded abruptly.

He arched a brow. "Why? So you can shoot me?"

"No. I've decided to shoot myself. Dealing with you is more than I can bear."

"It wasn't a few minutes ago while we were lying in the shallows—"

"Don't you dare mention that ever again!" she shouted at him as her face went up in flames.

"Fine."

The thought of what they had been doing with each other in the shallows reminded him that she'd tried to use him the same arousing way she'd used Glenn to coerce him into aiding and abetting her escape. The thought made Gideon scowl. He had never shared a woman with one of his brothers and he wasn't starting now.

Gideon lapsed into silence as he led the way along the creek, heading upstream to the lean-to where Glenn had captured the horse thieves. He didn't have to look back to know his spirited fugitive was silently seething. He could practically feel her burning gaze boring into him. However, he still believed *he* had more right to be angry than *she* did.

"Ah, finally. A friendly face," she remarked. "Here is someone who treats me with kindness and respect."

Gideon gnashed his teeth when Glenn glanced up and frowned in concern—probably trying to discern what shape his ladylove was in. When his gaze roamed over her soggy clothing, Gideon battled down the ridiculous feeling of possessiveness that sizzled through him.

"What did you do to her?" Glenn demanded.

Not as much as you probably did, Gideon mused grudgingly. He hated harboring jealousy against his little brother and he blamed Lori for the tormenting feelings hounding him.

"For starters he tried to drown me," she tattled.

Glenn jerked upright and shot Gideon a disparaging glance. "Why'd you do that?"

"Because she was escaping on my horse." Gideon dismounted but he was careful not to loosen his grasp on Drifter's reins—in case Lori tried to thunder off, forcing him to give chase again.

He glanced at Glenn who was staring with masculine appreciation at Lori's wet, clinging clothes. "Show some manners and stop gaping at her," he quietly scolded Glenn.

"I'm not looking at her any differently than you are."

The comment made Gideon grumble under his breath. He was going to have to try harder to remain immune and impassive in Lori's presence. But it was nearly impossible when she triggered so many conflicting emotions.

Gideon pulled Lori from her horse, then frowned curiously when she stared intently at the two men Glenn had tied to a tree. Although their backs were to her, he could practically feel the tension coming off her in waves.

"You know them, don't you?" he guessed accurately.

She glanced at him for a moment then nodded hesitantly. "Sonny Hathaway and Teddy Collins are the two men Widow Burgess sent to apprehend me. Since I eluded them, they must have decided to take up a new line of work. Now that the widow's husband and foreman are dead, I expect she'll sell the stage station and ranch. These lazy hired hands will be out of work."

Lori glanced the other way and muttered in frustration.

Nothing Sonny and Teddy could say would convince Gideon that she was telling the truth. The men hadn't actually witnessed the bushwhacking, but Gideon preferred to believe the absolute worst about her at every turn. Honestly, she didn't know why he tried so hard to dislike her and why his opinion mattered to her. It shouldn't…but it did, damn it.

She held her breath when Gideon strode deliberately toward the stringy-haired captives. "Are you acquainted with Lorelei Russell?" he asked without preamble.

Both men nodded.

Sonny, who had taken a shot in the leg, massaged his thigh, grimacing at the pain caused by the slightest movement. "Widow Burgess said Lorelei shot Tony. She sent us to track Lorelei down, but she hid so well we couldn't find her."

"So the widow saw Lorelei shoot your foreman?" Gideon questioned intently.

Teddy lifted his shoulder in a shrug. "I suppose."

"She saw nothing," Lori insisted. "Maggie came running from the opposite side of the barn, near the stage station, *after* the sniper's bullet struck Tony. The only shot I fired was into the underbrush, hoping to hit the bushwhacker."

She doubted Gideon believed her, but this was the first time he had listened to her explanation. She wasn't shutting up until she conveyed her version of the story. "Maggie was upset when she realized Tony died and she assumed I was to blame. She grabbed Tony's second pistol from his holster and tried to shoot me, so I ran."

Gideon glanced at Sonny and Teddy for corroboration. Both men shrugged noncommittally.

"Sonny and Teddy didn't see what happened. Maggie shouted at them to fetch their horses," Lori reported.

"That's true," Teddy confirmed. "I don't know if Maggie

shot at Lori or vice versa. We heard gunfire before Maggie told us to mount up. We lit out but we lost Lori's trail."

"So you decided to pass along your misfortune of losing your fugitive by stealing horses and shooting one of the owners," Gideon growled harshly.

Teddy and Sonny clammed up. Not that Lori blamed them. Gideon's glowers could melt rock. He could be extremely intimidating when the mood suited him. Now he reminded her of the scarecrow of doom pecking away at the newly damned.

"The man you shot was my brother," Gideon snarled.

"It was self-defense," Sonny insisted hurriedly.

"No, it wasn't." Glenn strode up in front of the prisoners. "The other man you shot at was *me,* and our brother only fired a warning shot over your heads."

Leaving the captives to themselves, Gideon and Glenn strode off, bookending Lori as they went. "What are you going to do with her?" Glenn asked.

Gideon stared at her pensively, noting the red-gold hair that lay in curlicues around her lovely face. Although her clothing had begun to dry, it still accentuated her alluring figure. She kept glancing back and forth between him and Glenn and he wondered which one she'd choose as her companion, if given a choice.

As if he didn't know, Gideon thought with a smirk. Glenn was the one who catered to her, fussed over her…and no telling what else happened during their cross-country trek. Gideon didn't want to start speculating again. The prospects never failed to rile him.

"There's something you should know," Glenn blurted out hurriedly. "I told Lori last night that I was going to hunt for our missing horses. Naturally she offered to come along and help me overtake the thieves."

Gideon barked a laugh. "You are a pathetic liar, little brother. Try again. With the *truth* this time."

"All right," Glenn grumbled, dropping his head to stare at his booted feet. "Lori was in tears because you treated her so abominably. I volunteered to take her back to the scene of the crime so she could look for evidence to prove there was a bushwhacker hiding in the bushes."

"So now it's *my* fault you broke the law to help her?" Gideon asked incredulously.

"You're the one who taught me that a man was obligated to right a wrong," Glenn reminded him. "I think you've been unnecessarily hard on Lori and so do Sarah and Galen. We think she might be innocent and just ended up at the wrong place at the wrong time. She deserves the chance to clear her name and I'm taking her home to do just that."

Lori smiled gratefully. "Thank you for your vote of confidence, Glenn. At least someone around here believes me."

Gideon was quick to note that Lori had never smiled at him with such grateful appreciation.

"You're welcome, honey," Glenn said then he turned to Gideon. "I suggest you take the horse thieves who wounded Galen and return them to marshal headquarters. I'll accompany Lori."

Gideon snorted his disapproval at the suggestion.

"If I were a Deputy U.S. Marshal, I'd get all my facts straight before I convicted an innocent woman of a brutal crime," Glenn added pointedly.

"No way in hell am I going to allow you to escort Lori," Gideon said in a no-nonsense tone. "You've been too lenient already. You have less sympathy for the men who shot Galen, so *you* and your prisoners are going to swing by our ranch to check on Sarah and Galen and catch up on the chores. Then you can haul these horse thieves to marshal headquarters."

Glenn stared warily at Gideon then glanced at Lori. "I'll agree, only if you promise to be kind and considerate to her."

Gideon snorted. "I'm not mollycoddling a prisoner." In truth, he was afraid to let his guard down with this flame-haired beauty, for fear he'd become as sappy and gullible as his kid brother.

"Perhaps you could start with civility and common courtesy," Lori suggested flippantly. "For instance, if you had the slightest concern about my well-being you'd allow me to change into my skirt and peasant blouse that Sarah was so kind to loan to me. Then I wouldn't be standing here with goose bumps because you saw to it that Pirate dumped me in the creek and you held me down until I...*cried uncle*."

Gideon and Lori exchanged significant glances while Glenn's gaze bounced back and forth between them.

"Will you be nice to Gideon if he's nice to you?" he negotiated.

She tilted her chin. "If I *must*."

"Do *you* promise, Gid?" Glenn persisted. "Word of honor. *Osage* word of honor. Not the white men's version of promising something then taking it back when they decide they want it for themselves. And they call it Indian giving," he added with a disgusted snort. Then he smiled apologetically at Lori. "No offense, honey."

"None taken from *you*, Glenn."

Then she stared deliberately at Gideon.

Gideon frowned in annoyance when Glenn patted Lori on the shoulder. "You let me know if Gid doesn't treat you right, hon. I'll come running as soon as I can."

Gideon observed his brother's familiar touch on Lori. Then he glanced into those jewel-like eyes, embedded in a bewitching face. He knew he couldn't be too kind and considerate while he was trying so damn hard to resist the woman he was afraid to believe, afraid to trust because she tugged so fiercely on his emotions.

He wanted to know if she had slept with Glenn after Gideon had walked away unappeased two nights earlier. The speculations were killing him, bit by frustrating bit. However, he refused to pose the question to Lori. He didn't trust her to tell him the truth. He felt too awkward putting the question to his brother, so he held his tongue and suffered in silence.

"Well, Gideon?" Glenn pressed, demanding a promise.

"I'm still thinking it over," Gideon said as he shifted his gaze to Lori once again. "How nice do I have to be?"

Honestly, thought Lori as she watched Glenn wave goodbye then lead away the string of horses and the two prisoners. Getting Gideon Fox to agree to be polite to her was worse than pulling teeth. She stared contemplatively at the brawny lawman whose raven hair gleamed in the afternoon sunlight. She was torn between her unreasonable desire to be with him and her sensible need to have Glenn at her side instead during the trek to the trading post and stage station. As if she'd had a choice!

While Gideon monitored his brother's retreat over the hill, Lori shifted restlessly. "Are you going to allow me to change clothes or not?" she asked irritably.

"Whatever you wish," he said without glancing at her.

"Whatever *I* wish?" she smirked. "Since when did you give a damn about that?"

He clucked his tongue at her. "I'm trying to be nice to you to pacify my little brother—who's obviously infatuated with you and has visions of adding his name to your list of would-be fiancés. Unfortunately, your would-be fiancés have an unfortunate habit of dying on you."

"That only happened once."

"So it's one hundred per cent of the time," he didn't fail to point out. "Now then, I'll be on my best behavior if you'll curb your sharp tongue."

"Your best behavior?" she said, and scoffed. "On your best days, your behavior compares to everyone else's bad day."

He glared at her then remembered his promise. He flashed her one of his best smiles. "Deal or not, hellion?"

Lori blew out her breath. "Deal. Now kindly untie me so I can fetch my borrowed clothes. *Please.* And *please* forgive this slight delay," she added in a syrupy tone. "I'll make this as fast as possible."

"How very considerate," he said most politely, then dropped into an exaggerated bow.

Lori didn't know which was worse—his teasing taunts or his exaggerated manners. God help her, she preferred fencing words with this sharp-witted, sharp-edged marshal. Who would have thought it? She must be a glutton for punishment.

She expected Gideon to fasten the humiliating leash to her wrists or ankles. He surprised her by directing her attention to the chin-high bushes that might serve as an improvised dressing screen.

"Thank you for that at least," she murmured, begrudging his rare display of consideration.

"My pleasure, hell—"

When she arched a challenging brow, Gideon cleared his throat and said, "My pleasure, Miz Russell."

"I'll hurry, Marshal Fox."

Although he didn't turn his back, he accommodated

her by never allowing his gaze to drop below her neck while she peeled off her soggy clothes. Her face flushed, nonetheless, while she stood naked behind the bushes. A few minutes later, she stepped from the underbrush.

"You look very stunning," he complimented. He grabbed a fresh set of dry clothes and a pair of moccasins from his saddlebags then headed for the bushes to change.

"Thank you, kind sir. I dressed especially for you."

"I'm honored." He reappeared in a clean set of clothing. "Now haul your shapely a—" His voice dried up when she arched her brow in challenge again. "I meant to say, let me help you onto your horse."

Lori held out her hand, waiting for Gideon to boost her onto the saddle so her skirt wouldn't swirl around her and expose body parts—ones Gideon had seen and touched all too intimately. *Don't think about that,* she chided herself as he settled her effortlessly on her horse. She was never going to allow Gideon intimate privileges again. She was too susceptible, too vulnerable when he displayed his amazing brand of tenderness.

When Gideon trussed her feet to the stirrups and her hands to the pommel, she reminded herself not to expect the kind of consideration Glenn had offered. This was Gideon Rock-Hearted Fox, after all. He could only be nice to her for a little while and then he reached his limit.

Maggie Burgess seethed like the thunderstorm that loomed overhead. The flicker of lightning and grumble of thunder had nothing on her. Tapping her foot impatiently, she crossed her arms over her ample bosom and stared disapprovingly at the half-breed bounty hunter who had a habit of disappearing during the daylight hours then returning at night to roost like a pigeon. He never failed to show up for the evening meal she served at the stage station.

Reece McCree had been here a few days and had nothing to show for his nonchalant efforts. She was beginning to wonder if he were a shyster who took money from his clients without completing his cases. He was probably the one who spread the word that he was a reliable gun for hire.

She continued to glare at the approaching bounty hunter riding the bay horse she had loaned him. She thought it strange the man didn't have a mount of his own. But she had been so desperate to find that witch and have her put away forever that Maggie hadn't questioned why Reece was afoot.

"I don't see how you can track down that vicious murderess when you don't travel far from the stagecoach station and you're back here to partake of my evening meals," she grumbled as he dismounted.

Reece tapped a lean finger on the announcement Maggie had posted this morning beside the For Sale sign. "So now you're *publicly* advertising a reward to capture the woman who killed your foreman? *After* you gave me a down payment?"

Lightning flashed and reflected in his unnerving silver-gray eyes. She involuntarily stepped back a pace. The man looked as dangerous as they came. Cool, calm and deadly.

"We had a deal," he reminded her then lit his cigar. Smoke swirled around his face, making him appear even more devilish than usual. The thunderous sound effects didn't help.

Maggie gathered her nerve and said, "We do have a deal, but I haven't seen any results so I decided to offer a reward to whoever finds that murderess first. Is there some reason why you keep circling this area without heading east? After all, that's the direction she rode off, with my two hired hands hot on her heels."

He puffed on his cheroot, as if he had all the time in the world and was contemplating whether to answer her. That annoyed her to the extreme. She'd worked her fingers to the bone—cooking, cleaning and tending horses while her two missing hired hands did only God knew what! *She* was paying Reece McCree to track Lorelei and his lackadaisical approach infuriated her.

"How many killers have you tracked?" he asked with enough sarcasm to ruffle her feathers all over again.

"None," she snapped. "But I'm not a gun for hire, am I?"

"Then let me offer you some advice, in case you decide to take up my profession. Always assume the fugitive will circle back to where he or she feels safe and secure. With family, for example. Lorelei Russell's father runs the trading post and ferry located ten miles from here. She'll return to him eventually. I'd stake my reputation on it."

"Fine. And when she does, then you can bring her to me, dead or alive. I prefer *dead*. After she worked her wicked wiles on my foreman for three months, she killed him. She's made my life next to impossible because I've assumed responsibilities for my departed husband, my murdered foreman and the two hired hands who chased after Lorelei over a week ago. Now I have only one hired hand to help me with all my chores."

Reece blew a smoke ring in the air and studied her so intently that she looked the other way. The man was unnerving, as if he could read her private thoughts.

"Not to worry," he murmured. "I don't plan to leave here until I find Tony's killer."

The casual use of Tony's name took Maggie by surprise. "You knew him?"

He shrugged evasively. "A long time ago. In another place…and another way of life."

The news startled Maggie. But then, she reminded herself that Tony rarely mentioned his past.

"I'm still investigating Lorelei Russell's claim there was a bushwhacker hiding in the trees."

Maggie scoffed at him. "I'm beginning to wonder if *you* shot Tony and showed up shortly thereafter. You've been hanging around here, taking advantage of my money, my cooking and my willingness to loan you a horse."

The caustic remark didn't set well with him. His silver-gray eyes narrowed on her and he loomed over her while lightning streaked across the sky and thunder rolled.

Finally, he said, "Speaking of horses, the one you loaned me isn't swift of foot and spooks easily. Be a daisy and fetch me a reliable mount. I want the skewbald Pinto that belonged to your husband. The gelding looks like he has the stamina and endurance I require in a horse."

"What happened to your horse?" she demanded.

"An outlaw shot it out from under me. It was the last thing he ever did…. So now I'll take the skewbald as partial payment for solving this case."

Maggie stood there, fuming at the half-breed bounty hunter's audacity. The clatter of hooves and jangle of harnesses announced the arrival of the northbound stage, drawing her attention. When her lone employee, Sylvester Jenkins, limped from the barn with fresh horses, Reece released her from his piercing gaze, then glanced back at the attendant.

A moment later, he refocused his intense scrutiny on Maggie. "Now that the coach is here, what are we having for supper?"

As thunder boomed overhead, she gnashed her teeth and followed the exasperating bounty hunter into the station.

Damn the man, he was costing her money. She wanted this business concluded quickly so she could sell out, leave this godforsaken territory and move to a place where sophisticated culture prevailed.

Chapter Nine

The grumble of thunder prompted Lori to glance skyward. A bank of dark clouds piled up on the western horizon, ruining the view of a colorful sunset. Spring storms were prevalent in Indian Territory and Lori had grudging respect for them. She had suffered through dozens of them in her time. Usually she and her father were tucked safely in their living quarters on the second story of the trading post.

Now, however, she was traveling the rugged wilderness with Deputy U.S. Marshal *Thundercloud* himself. Yet, he'd become the personification of gentlemanly behavior and politeness—which didn't suit him one bit. Abrupt and plainspoken was more his style. Lori tried to picture the rugged survivalist trussed up in the fancy trappings of a gentleman. The thought made her snicker. There was too much wild nobility stamped on Gideon's features and too much brawn and muscle on his body to suit elegant attire.

"What's so funny?" Gideon asked as he looked from

her to the dark clouds boiling and burgeoning to the southwest.

"Nothing." She swallowed her amusement. "If it isn't too much trouble, I wonder if I could prevail upon you to stop here for the night. I would appreciate a cleansing bath after wallowing in the muddy shallows with you earlier this afternoon." She gestured her head toward the approaching storm. "It might be wise to eat supper before we're drenched."

"Then what's the purpose of a bath?" he asked, eyeing her warily. "Planning to sneak off and use the rainstorm to cover your tracks?"

True, she'd considered it, but she suspected Gideon would delight in the challenge of recapturing her, then hold her head underwater until she cried uncle—or rather, his annoying version of it.

"Why no, dear Gideon," she said with sticky sweet sarcasm. "You'd only hunt me down again. I know I'm no match for your scouting and tracking skills."

"Damn right." His brows flattened over his stunning blue eyes. "I may have to be nice to you, because I'll have to deal with my little brother, your lovesick admirer, if I don't. But I am not releasing you from custody."

"Even when I prove that I'm innocent?"

"*If* you prove you're innocent and I see the evidence."

He dismounted then fondly patted Pirate. Lori was ashamed to admit she was envious of that eye-catching horse because Gideon showed more consideration and respect to him than he did to her. Except when lust got the better of him and he used her as a convenient outlet, she thought resentfully.

She wondered if he would turn his attention to Maggie Burgess when he interviewed her about Tony's death. Maggie was attractive and male travelers always hovered around her, vying for her attention. Gideon might even prefer the buxom brunette with her thick-lashed brown eyes. Well, he was welcome to her, thought Lori. She didn't care one whit.

Her thoughts scattered when Gideon slid his hands around her waist and pulled her from the saddle. She hadn't realized that he'd untied her ankles until he was pulling her down. He held on to her a moment longer than necessary, prompting her to stare quizzically at him.

Fierce, undeniable attraction slammed into her when she peered into his hypnotic blue eyes. The way the wind ruffled his raven hair tempted her to comb her fingers through those thick, wavy, collar-length strands. The brush of his masculine body against hers was an unnecessary reminder of how it felt to have him lying beside her, on top of her....

Lori stifled the betraying thoughts. She would not humiliate herself again. He didn't like her. He didn't trust her. He didn't believe her story of innocence. Even the briefest of affairs would be a disastrous mistake because Gideon Fox was a lawman who traveled extensively to capture criminals. His home and his loyalty lay with his two brothers and Sarah. Lori would never have a place in his life.

She was nothing more than one of the many fugitives he transported cross-country.

Besides, she was all the family her father had. At least *he* needed and cared about her.

"About my bath," she prompted, staring at the air over his head. "Perhaps if you had more rope you could tie my leash to a nearby tree while I'm in the river."

He frowned when he noticed the raw skin left by the iron cuffs and rope leash. Muttering, he reached into his saddlebag to retrieve a tin of poultice. To her surprise, he smoothed the soothing ointment on her wrists.

Uncomfortable with his sudden display of consideration— not the excessively polite variety he'd shown all day—Lori shifted restlessly beneath his tender ministrations.

"Old Osage remedy?" she guessed.

He nodded his dark head but remained focused on applying the salve. "Made from healing herbs that were combined and perfected so the recipe could be handed down through generations. My grandfather was known as a healer during the time when our people lived in Missouri and Kansas."

He snorted disgustedly. "Of course, when whites invaded our land, the government offered a paltry sum for it then herded our people to this territory. We were confined like the other tribes that once possessed property the whites wanted. Then Osages were ordered to buy part of the land once delegated to the Cherokees, but we were forced to pay a much higher price than the government paid for our lost property."

He scowled and added, "I'm not so naive to think that vocal protests from greedy whites won't convince the government to open tribal land in Indian Territory for settlement. It's only a matter of time."

"You spurn the whites, but Glenn told me that you're half French," she remarked as she watched him rub the poultice on her left wrist.

"Don't remind me. It's our curse to bear," he grumbled. "I will always be Osage at heart. The only reason I shortened our family name of White Fox was to avoid more ridicule from racist criminals. They call me a *breed,* a *redskin* and make derogatory comments, in hopes of annoying me into becoming reckless. But their ridicule lost its cutting edge years ago."

"Gideon White Fox," she murmured, trying out his name. "I like it. You should use it since it denotes your full heritage."

His reply was a mumbled sound that could have meant anything. Of course, she didn't expect Gideon to take any suggestion from her. She, after all, counted for nothing in his book.

When he removed the rope from her wrist, Lori gaped at him in surprise.

He stared her squarely in the eye. "If you take advantage of my consideration, you will pay severely. Remember that."

"Don't I know it. That tussle in the creek was bad enough. If you ever hold me down like that again—"

"You don't like having a man on top of you?"

She glanced at him then frowned at the odd, searching expression in his eyes. He was throwing out something besides his usual taunt. This wasn't about the dunking he'd used to break her resistance after he recaptured her.

"What do you want to know, Gideon?" she asked flat out.

"What method did you use to entice my little brother?"

She gasped, affronted. She was tempted to slap him for the insult, but he'd manacle her again she predicted. She knew Gideon believed she had slept with Tony. Now he suspected she had slept with Glenn to gain his cooperation. It was glaringly apparent what Gideon thought of her morals and character.

Without a word—for fear she'd rain down every curse and profanity she'd ever heard on his head once she got started—Lori wheeled around. She grabbed the breeches and shirt to wash then stormed toward the river. She hoped she could cool off before she confronted that cynical, mistrusting, suspicious lawman again. Otherwise, she was going to wrestle him for possession of his firearm and let the bullets fly where they may.

While Lori bathed nearby Gideon glanced over to see her flaming red-gold hair and knew she hadn't made a run for it—yet. He built a campfire so he could prepare their evening meal. What he really wanted to do was wander along the riverbank and look his fill at Lori's naked body.

He wondered how much of her naked body Glenn had seen.

The thought put a scowl on his face. Wondering if Glenn had become more intimate with Lori than Gideon had been was driving him crazy. He'd worked up enough nerve to ask her earlier but the question had infuriated her and she'd refused to answer.

While the fire crackled and popped, Gideon glanced in Lori's direction again. She was still in the water so he risked tramping off to scare up a rabbit for supper. He didn't have far to go to find game. When he returned to camp, he didn't see Lori and a moment of frustration hounded him. He relaxed when he saw her wet laundry draped over tree limbs. An amused smile pursed his lips when he noticed she'd confiscated one of his spare sets of clothing. The dark shirt and breeches swallowed her so she had rolled up the cuffs on the garments.

"I didn't steal them. I only borrowed them," she said as she approached. She had piled her wet hair atop her head, revealing the slender curve of her neck, and he longed to spread a row of kisses along her soft skin. "I'll take care of skinning the rabbit while you're bathing, Gideon. It's one of my father's favorite meals. He likes it better than frog legs and fried chicken."

Gideon did something he swore he'd never do. He

retrieved one of his pearl-handled pistols and handed it to her instead of replacing the handcuffs. Stunned, she stared bug-eyed at him then looked at the weapon he'd placed in her hand.

"Just in case," he said. "There are outlaws and four-legged predators lurking around Osage Hills."

"Not everyone is an outlaw," she said absently as she tested the weight and balance of his Peacemaker.

"If they're white, there's a strong possibility of it," he replied cynically. "There are about twenty thousand of them roaming the territory and only a small percent are here legally. Most of them are wary of lawmen because they have something to hide."

The grumbling thunder caught her attention and she gestured toward the boiling clouds. "If you plan to bathe you better do it quickly. We'll be lucky to cook our meal before it starts raining. Oh, and gather my clothes off the tree branches on your way back, will you?"

He doubled at the waist in an exaggerated bow. "Anything else I can do for you, princess?"

She stuck her nose up in the air then flicked her wrist dismissively. "That will do. You can leave now."

"What happened to you being nice to me?" he tossed over his shoulder as he headed for the river.

"If this is as nice as *you* get then this is as nice as *I* get."

"Figured as much," he mumbled as he walked away.

Lori monitored the storm, speculating that it had stalled somewhere near Russell Trading Post. It seemed to build on itself, gathering more strength.

That wasn't a good sign. Once the storm began to move again it would cause downpours and fierce winds.

She stared eagerly at the meat roasting over the fire.

She had cut it into six portions, hoping it would cook faster on the makeshift skewers. With luck—and hers had been nothing to boast about lately, so she didn't hold much hope—the food would be ready when Gideon returned from bathing.

She rose from a crouch to check on him. She gasped in shock when she saw him wade ashore, naked as the day he was born. He was facing the opposite direction but she still saw more of him than she needed to see. Her face blossomed with color but she couldn't make herself look away from his sleek, bronzed, muscular body. She was fairly certain the image had burned into her eyeballs. Sweet mercy! What would it be like to see him walking naked *toward* her?

Flustered by the tempting thought, she focused her attention on the roasting meat. "No more speculations for you," she scolded herself. "You've seen too much already."

When she glanced southwest again, she noticed a curtain of rain sweeping across the rolling hills. Damnation, they were running out of time.

"Hurry up, Gideon!" she called loudly. "I'm starving and the storm is rapidly approaching."

He reappeared from the shelter of the trees to gather her scattered garments then jogged toward her. She was sitting cross-legged in her baggy clothes when he reached camp. She glanced up at him, but she kept visualizing him naked, walking away from the water. She squeezed her eyes shut, hoping to douse the inflammatory image that had a profound effect on her body.

It didn't help.

"Are you all right?" he asked, staring at her intently.

"Sure. I'm fine. Couldn't be better," she said with false enthusiasm. "Let's eat, Marshal. We're running short of time."

He sat down across from her to remove the meat from the fire. They ate their meal, serenaded by grumbling thunder and the breeze that rustled through the surrounding trees.

"Have you decided where we will hole up during the storm?" she asked.

"No. I'm not as familiar with this section of the reservation. My people are from the Heart-Stays Clan. Not the Big Hills People who populate this area."

Lori munched her food, swallowed then gestured uphill. "There is a cave on the ridge above us, but that doesn't mean it's unoccupied. We can fight whatever claims ownership, if the weather turns nasty."

"It will," he prophesied. "I can feel it in the muggy air."

She nodded in agreement, realizing it was the first time they'd agreed on anything. "I can feel it, too."

Lightning blazed across the sky and lit up the gathering darkness like the Fourth of July. The wind picked up and thunder rumbled overhead. Gideon bounded up to kick dirt on the fire and Lori lent assistance. While he dashed off to retrieve the grazing horses, Lori crammed her dry clothing in the knapsack Sarah and Glenn had provided.

With a stiff wind at their backs and a curtain of rain looming behind them, they scrambled up the rocky slope to determine who—or what—inhabited the cave.

"I suppose you've heard the tale about the creature that stalks Osage Hills, the one supposedly responsible for the mysterious disappearances of several people in the area," Gideon commented.

Lori nodded grimly. "I've heard reports of people spotting the half-animal, half-human creature. Do you believe the story?"

"I've come upon human remains a few times while

on patrol," he remarked. "But who's to say if the victims were attacked by man or beast. Sometimes it's difficult to tell—"

An ear-piercing boom exploded overhead. Lori instinctively ducked. She looked back to note that lightning had struck a tree near their abandoned campsite. The smell of burned wood swept up the hillside with the wind. Lori was anxious to take cover from the threatening storm, but she was reluctant to dart into the dark cavern.

"I'll go in first." Gideon handed off Drifter's and Pirate's reins.

"Then you'll need this back…just in case." She returned his spare pistol.

She admired and envied Gideon's fearlessness as he walked into the darkness. But she reminded herself that a man who faced down armed outlaws had learned to be prepared for anything. Still, there was no telling what lurked inside the cavern and she refused to stand here like a cowering female who sent a man to do battle for her.

On the wings of that thought, Lori pulled Gideon's rifle from the scabbard on Pirate's saddle and tethered both horses. She was going to bolster her courage and back up Gideon.

She went on high alert when she heard a low growl. Unfortunately, it was so dark inside the cavern that she bumped into Gideon and involuntarily leaped backward. He clutched her arm to steady her.

"I told you to stay outside," he murmured.

"Did you? I must've forgotten… Where did that growl come from?"

Her voice fizzled out when a ferocious snarl echoed in the darkness. Gideon tucked her behind him, much the same way Tony had that fateful night.

The unnerving thought of history repeating itself

provoked Lori to squirm free so she could place herself in front of Gideon. "No," she muttered fiercely. "No other man is going to die for me, if it comes to that in here. I already have Tony's death on my conscience and I refuse to have yours, too—awk!"

She shrieked when the furry animal slammed into her shins, tipping her off balance and knocking her against Gideon's broad chest. She felt something slash her leg and she yelped in pain.

Another snarl erupted from the darkness then Gideon's gunshot exploded. The animal—she was pretty sure it was a bear—slumped against her legs.

"You okay?" Gideon murmured against the pounding pulse beat on the side of her neck.

She swallowed with a gulp. "More or less."

"Are you injured? Yes or no?"

"Yes, but not seriously," she insisted.

"Good. Run outside and gather up some fallen branches for firewood before the rain drenches everything in sight."

Despite the burning pain in her shin, she scurried outside. She noticed bloodstains on the shredded fabric of the borrowed breeches. She forgot her discomfort when she heard Gideon fire off two rapid shots.

Carrying an armload of dry branches, she ducked into the cave then halted as Gideon dragged something toward her. She backed out of his way as he pulled the half-grown black bear past her. Then he spun around to fetch the second one.

While he disposed of the two animals that had attacked them, Lori set up a campfire by the mouth of the cave so smoke wouldn't fill the chamber. She made sure she left room for the horses to stand under the overhanging ledge without tramping on the campfire. Once she had the fire going, she retrieved the bedroll from Pirate's back. Using the light of the campfire, she inspected her leg wound.

She glanced up to see Gideon standing over her, appraising her closely. "I'm sorry about your breeches I borrowed," she said. "I have needle and thread at home to repair them."

"I was more concerned about *you* than my breeches."

She blinked in surprise. When he knelt to roll up her pant leg, she watched him inspect her wound. "You don't have to be extra nice to me," she insisted. "Glenn is long gone. He'll never know."

A smile twitched his lips as he pivoted to retrieve the tin of poultice from his saddlebag. She studied him discreetly while he concentrated on applying the soothing salve to the scrapes.

Outside, the first raindrops pattered against the leaves. A moment later, lightning flared in the darkness and thunder echoed around them. Lori felt cut off from the world as rain poured down the overhanging ledge and drafts of wind played with the dancing flames of the campfire. It was as if she and Gideon were the only two people in the world.

That wasn't good because she was battling exceptionally hard to control her irrational longings. When he ventured too close, the memories of heated passion they'd shared that night in the barn came back to torment her.

"There," he murmured. "That should prevent infection." His gaze riveted on her, making it difficult for her to breathe. "Is there anywhere else I can kiss and make it feel better?"

Gideon chided himself for voicing that suggestive comment. But when he was this close to Lori he kept remembering the addictive taste of her kisses, the feel of her silky flesh beneath his hands. He'd been craving her to such extremes that he couldn't even remember how it felt *not* to want her, despite all the sensible reasons he could list for keeping her at a safe distance.

Why this woman? he asked himself as his body moved instinctively toward her like a magnet seeking true north. It no longer mattered if she had been with Anthony Rogers or Glenn or nameless others. It only mattered that she was with him for this moment in time.

Her wide amber eyes, surrounded by thick sooty lashes, swept up. She stared at his lips then met his gaze. "I don't think this is a good idea, Gideon," she said unevenly.

"I agree completely." He angled his head toward hers to brush his mouth over her dewy-soft lips. The craving magnified tenfold and his body turned hard and aching in two seconds flat. "Problem is, I crave a taste of you and I'm not sure the miracle cures my people concoct can counter this hunger."

Then he kissed her with all the restless need prowling through him. He knew in an instant that he tasted inevitable defeat. Tomorrow he'd regain his sanity and regret his impulsiveness.

But not tonight.

He wanted this beguiling siren and he wasn't sure that holding a gun to his head would discourage him. All that might stop him was *her* protests. If she turned him down then he'd accept her refusal. Of course, sexual deprivation would probably kill him, but he refused to force this spirited beauty to succumb to his aching needs.

There would be no pleasure or satisfaction in that.

"If you want me to stop then I will," he rasped when he came up for air.

She stared at him while he crouched in front of her. Her expression suggested she hovered on a threshold, too. He held his breath while sensual anticipation buzzed around him like a hornet. When she glided her hands over his chest and settled them on his shoulders, fire seared his blood. Desire hit him like a doubled fist.

"Only for tonight," she whispered. "Not because I expect favors from you. I know you distrust me, but I am not using you, Gideon. I suspect I'm the time *you're* killing during this storm."

If it were only that simple, he mused as he eased her to her back on the pallet then stretched out beside her. Scratching an itch, he could understand. The overwhelming need to be with this golden-eyed temptress—and no one else—worried the hell out of him. She mattered when she shouldn't.

It was that simple. And that complicated.

Yet, despite the questions concerning her involvement in her would-be fiancé's death, and Glenn's obvious infatuation with her, Lori was the woman Gideon wanted. Perhaps one night with her would cure his irrational desire and he could get her out of his system for good. Then he would become the sensible, self-disciplined lawman he prided himself on being.

That noble thought flitted off as his hands—which had suddenly acquired a will of their own—worked the buttons of her shirt—*his* shirt, to be more specific. He glanced down at her breasts. They glowed like gold in the flickering firelight, matching the unique color of her eyes. Gideon was hopelessly lost. Bewitched. Captivated.

He cupped her breasts in his hands, then suckled her until she gasped and writhed restlessly beneath his kisses and caresses. So much bottled passion waiting to be unleashed, he mused, as he flicked at the beaded crests with his tongue.

When he rolled the pebbled peaks between his thumb and forefinger, a wobbly moan tumbled from her parted lips. Fascinated by her response, he flicked at her again then tugged gently on her nipples with his teeth.

Her breath quickened as she reached for him, practically tearing the buttons off his shirt in her haste to get her hands on his bare chest. The instant her fingers splayed over him, desire coiled like a spring and his aroused flesh throbbed heavily in rhythm with his pounding heartbeat. He refused to become distracted by her touch because he wanted to make a feast of her. He helped her discard her shirt—*his* shirt—then he went to work removing her baggy breeches.

When she lay naked beside him, his admiring gaze flooded unhindered over her shapely curves and swells. "You're beautiful," he murmured as he bent to spread a row of kisses along the pulsating column of her neck. "But I'm sure you know that already."

Her reply was a wispy moan of pleasure.

Gideon began his journey of discovery over the lush terrain of her body. He took his sweet time caressing her silky flesh from breast to kneecap—careful to avoid the claw marks on her shin. He swore he could spend the evening marveling at her perfection.

He'd never made a thorough study of the women who came and went so casually from his bed. But his previous encounters didn't seem as magical as learning what aroused this lovely siren. She fascinated him to the extreme. He wanted to savor the feel of her full breasts and map the trim indentation of her waist. He wanted to caress the gentle flare of her hips, the satiny flesh of her thighs. He wanted to know her body by taste, by scent and by touch and discover what made her come apart in his arms.

When his gentle suckling prompted her breathless groan, he smiled against the peak of her breast. He adored hearing the sounds of pleasure he called from her. He wanted to hear more. He wanted her completely at his mercy. It only seemed fair that this woman—who made him break every hard-and-fast rule he'd established about remaining emotionally detached from his assignments—should be overwhelmed by sensations and feelings beyond *her* control.

For certain, *he* was out of control when he touched her. The hungry want of her had become a living, breathing part of him and he couldn't remember when he hadn't wanted her to the point of aching desperation.

He heard her quick intake of breath when his hands glided from her hip to her thigh then trailed over the moist flesh between her legs. He remembered all too well how it felt to bathe his fingertips in her silken heat. He yearned to bury himself deep inside her. But she was going to have to invite him in, he vowed as he kissed his way down her rib cage to her abdomen.

"Gideon?" she gasped, and trembled beneath his kisses.

"I'm right here, love," he murmured against her fragrant skin. "Now don't distract me. I'm making a feast of you. You're delicious, by the way. I can't get enough of you…."

Chapter Ten

Each gentle, intimate stroke of his fingertip left Lori burning with exquisite pleasure. The erotic feel of his lips brushing against her heated flesh sent tidal waves of need crashing through her body. He created desires she hadn't realized existed, then he satisfied them one by one, setting off the most incredible sensations imaginable. When he flicked at her with his tongue and suckled her with the most intimate of kisses, her composure shattered. Her body quivered with phenomenal passion.

Lori was certain she was going to die. Her pulse hammered like the hailstones that pounded outside the cavern. She couldn't imagine how she could survive the intensity of his maddening seduction. Yet, one ineffable sensation built upon another until she lay helpless beneath his intimate kisses and caresses.

To her dazed amazement, he withdrew with no more of an explanation than, "Don't go away. I'll be right back."

Sprawled shamelessly naked on the pallet, she watched him walk to the mouth of the cave, then stare out into the windblown night. "If it's your intent to torture me by walking away like you did that night in the barn, it's working," she said raggedly.

"I'm torturing *myself*." His raspy voice drifted back to her. "I need a moment to gather my self-control."

"You should have plenty of it since you stole every ounce of mine."

She watched him turn toward her, a devilish grin playing on his lips. "Did I?"

When he came deliberately toward her, the anticipation of having his hands and lips working their sensual magic on her again left her throbbing with need. He did not disappoint. He knelt between her legs, guiding them apart with his shoulder. Then he reached up to brush the palm of his hand over her breast. She arched helplessly toward his caress then gasped when he kissed her intimately again.

"Come here, damn you," she demanded urgently, unsure what she needed. But whatever it was, he wasn't providing it. He was tormenting her with unappeased desire.

"Are you sure it's me you want?" he asked as he came to his hands and knees to stare at her.

Was she sure? Of course, she was sure. What kind of fool question was that? He was the only man she had ever wanted to this intense degree. He was the only man who had tempted her to discover the heights and depths of hot, overwhelming passion.

"You're making me crazy," she grumbled as she reached for the placket of his breeches. "Why all these questions? What do you want from me? An engraved invitation?"

She brushed her hand over the noticeable bulge in his breeches. At least that got a response from him. He groaned, so she stroked his hard length repeatedly.

"Hell and damn, woman," he whispered roughly when

she opened the placket to wrap her hands around his throbbing flesh.

Gideon swore his eyes were going to roll back in his
head when she curled upward to shove his breeches past
his hips with one hand while stroking him from base to tip
with the other. He tried to draw breath, though he couldn't
remember why it was necessary. He could survive quite
satisfactorily on the caressing stroke of her hand….

"Aw, damn—" he choked out when she twisted sideways
to take him into her mouth and torment him with the teasing flick of her tongue.

His brain nearly shut down when throbbing pleasure
riveted his overly sensitized body. He didn't realize she had
urged him to his back until she was bending over him. Her
long curly hair glided over his chest and belly while she
suckled him intimately and caressed him with the sweeping
stroke of her hand.

Need pounded heavily inside him, building like the
crashing crescendo of the storm raging outside the cavern.
She took command of his mind and body, enslaved him
with indescribable pleasure and made him glory in his own
defeat. The erotic touch of her fingertips and lips sent him
plunging into the blazing depths of reckless passion. He
didn't care if he ever found his way out again, either.

If she wanted the moon and a few stars, he'd find a
way to fetch them down from the sky. If she wanted her
freedom he'd give her that, too, so long as she satisfied this
maddening ache that scorched him inside and out.

"Say you want me, Gideon Fox," she demanded as she
stroked him with her thumb and held his throbbing length
in the palm of her hand.

"I want you," he admitted on a panted breath.

"Say you *love* me," she commanded, smiling mischievously at him.

"You ornery minx, I should've known you'd find a way to turn that taunt back on me—"

His breath evaporated when she took him deeply into her mouth and suckled him until every nerve and muscle in his body quivered with barely restrained need. Then she backed away momentarily, leaving him arching helplessly toward her mouth. She took him again, tugging erotically at him, flicking at him, killing him with one erotic stroke of her tongue after another.

"Cry uncle," she whispered as she traced her lips up and down the length of his pulsing flesh.

He swore he couldn't hold out much longer. Sweet, aching torment had him stumbling along the edge of hopeless abandon.

"Uncle," he choked out on a ragged gasp.

"Not good enough." She flicked at him with her tongue. Once, twice, three times.

His head spun in a dizzying circle when she nibbled at his ultrasensitive flesh and stroked him from inner thigh to ankle. "I love you, damn it," he growled finally, defeatedly. "Now say it back to me."

"No." She defied him, her golden eyes dancing with mischief.

He hooked his arm around her waist and rolled above her, pinning her down in the time it took to blink. He glided his fingertip inside her and heard her breath catch, felt her hot and moist and welcoming. He surged toward her, through with their teasing games.

He braced his arms beside her shoulders and pressed intimately against her. He nearly lost control when she reached between them to guide him exactly to her. When he arched toward her, aching to bury himself inside her, her lashes fluttered shut. He would have none of that. He didn't want to be the substitute for Anthony Rogers or his own brother or anyone else.

"Look at me, hellion," he demanded huskily. "Who is it you see?"

"A tormenting devil…with horns," she whispered. "You're driving me mad, Gideon. What more do you want from me?"

"Nothing less than everything you have to give," he insisted as he lost his battle for self-control and thrust against her.

He drove into her, then went perfectly still when she tensed. He felt the unexpected barrier give way, proving her innocence. For a moment, he couldn't believe he was her first experiment with passion. He had presumed… Well, he'd presumed all sorts of things. Obviously, he'd been wrong about her. At least wrong about *this*.

Her golden eyes, enhanced by the glow of the campfire, focused intently on him. "You wanted all I have to give, Gideon," she whispered as she moved restlessly beneath him. "It's yours. Just tell me there's more because I—"

He carefully withdrew, causing her voice to fizzle out. Then she moaned when he moved gently toward her, setting a slow cadence that was pure torture on him. His body screamed for quick release. But he'd be damned if her first time—and his first time with a woman's first time—caused unpleasant memories and disappointment. He wanted her to remember him fondly. Wanted her to know that jaded and hardened though he'd become to function and survive in his dangerous profession, he could be caring and tender when it was important.

Now it was exceptionally important.

When he felt her body melt against him, he guided his hands beneath her hips. He lifted her to him, opening her lush body so he could caress her with each rhythmic stroke.

He gritted his teeth, fighting the need to move faster. He wanted to pleasure her until she was as breathless and desperate as he felt.

As they moved together, their bodies locked in heated passion, scorching sensations welled up inside him like lava. But he swore he'd burn to a crisp in unappeased need unless Lori discovered the pinnacle of her own sexual pleasure.

A moment later, her nails dug into his shoulders and her amber eyes widened. Her body shimmered around him and he smiled in satisfaction as he followed her over the edge into rapturous oblivion.

Shudder after uncontrollable shudder rocked his body as he clutched Lori possessively to his laboring chest. It seemed hours before he could gather the energy to raise his head from the curve of her neck.

"You should have told me," he whispered as he kissed the rapid pulse in her throat.

"You wouldn't have believed me," she said, and he knew she was right.

He was a cynic through and through. A very satisfied, exhausted cynic, but a cynic all the same.

The next morning, surprised Gideon hadn't taken the precaution of tethering her, Lori dressed in Gideon's oversize shirt. She stared out the opening of the cave. Ordinarily, the sight of sunrise glistening on the raindrops that clung to leaves and blades of grass lifted her spirits. Today, however, the impact of her wild, reckless tryst with Gideon weighed heavily on her mind. To make matters worse, she had awakened Gideon at the dark hour before dawn to explore his powerful body more thoroughly and invited him to share the phenomenal pleasure she had discovered in his arms.

Lori swallowed hard and asked herself how she could have broken her determined vow to keep her distance from him. Like a fool, she'd crossed the point of no return. She'd become one of the many nameless women who came and went from his life, leaving no more than a footnote of a half-forgotten memory.

If you sleep with the devil you wake up in hell. The tormenting thought blazed across her mind, making her wince. She was shameless, that's what she was. She hadn't kept her promise to herself and her willpower had become nonexistent. The temptation to flee before Gideon awakened was so fierce she shifted restlessly from one bare foot to the other. She wasn't sure she could face him after she'd been so brazen and uninhibited the previous night.

It was one thing to surrender to forbidden desire in the flickering campfire light inside a cave and quite another to face Gideon during the light of day and remember how intimate they had been with each other. If he dared to tease her on the sensitive subject or flash a gloating grin, she might be tempted to pound him over the head.

Lori strode downhill, headed for the shallows of the river to bathe—or more specifically, to cleanse herself of the memories of the one, bittersweet night when she had succumbed to whimsical desires with the only man who had set her passions aflame.

The cold chill and fast-moving current, compliments of last night's downpour, made her gasp for breath. Nevertheless, she waded into deeper water—and wasn't that symbolic of what she'd done with Gideon last night? she mused. Grabbing a quick breath, she submerged, wishing she could resurface and find that time had rewound itself and last night hadn't happened.

When she came up for air and raked her hair from her eyes, she gasped in alarm and sank down to conceal herself.

Gideon was standing on the riverbank, bare-chested and barefoot. A long-past-five-o'clock-shadow lined his jaw and his raven hair was disheveled. Still, he had a fierce impact on her senses, testifying to her hopeless attraction to him.

"I thought you might've decided to run off while you had the chance." His words dropped like stones in the silence.

Even now, even after she'd given him a gift she'd offered no other man, he still distrusted her. He would always distrust her, she reminded herself.

"I considered it," she said honestly then flashed an impudent smile so he wouldn't know how much his lack of faith hurt her. "But the thought of how much I'd miss you kept me here."

He regarded her for a long, contemplative moment. "I think it's time I heard your complete version of the incident. From start to finish. And don't leave out any details," he surprised her by saying.

"Does that mean you think I might actually be innocent?"

He shrugged a broad shoulder. "You were…right."

She wondered how much it cost the cynical marshal to make that comment. "Really? How thoughtful of you to say so."

"I've been wrong about cases before. Rarely. But it's happened. In your case, I didn't ask enough questions about the shooting. I just presumed you were guilty because I deal with so many criminals who spout excuses and explanations that twist the truth."

"I can understand that…. Would you turn your back while I come ashore," she requested.

Wry amusement pursed his sensuous lips. "It's a little late for modesty, isn't it, hellion?"

"You might be accustomed to traipsing around in front of women, but I'm not used to being naked in front of men. The very thought makes me self-conscious." She shooed him on his way but he didn't budge from the spot.

"We also need to discuss what happened between us last night."

Heat suffused her face. Not all the cold water in the river could cool her down. "There is nothing to discuss," she decreed firmly. "In fact, I prefer to pretend it didn't happen."

"Like you pretend not to have shot poor Tony Rogers, who made the critical mistake of proposing to you? Or was it because he turned *you* down? I forget."

Damn the infuriating man! He had the maddening knack of inflaming her temper in the space of a heartbeat. "Curse you, Gideon Fox," she erupted angrily. "Now turn your back."

Chuckling, he pivoted to stare downstream. "There. My back is turned. Happy now?"

"Not particularly," she grumbled.

"You aren't going to club me over the head and run, are you?"

"I'd like to, but you'd be on my trail in nothing flat, nipping at my heels like a hound from hell."

After she donned her riding breeches and blouse, she halted beside him. "I'll have the horses saddled and ready to leave when you're finished bathing."

"Then we'll talk," he insisted as he reached for the placket of his breeches. His hands stalled when she crossed her arms over her chest and arched her brow. He unbuttoned the top button. "Do you plan to watch?"

"I'm furthering my education," she replied smartly. "I've decided to build up my resistance so I don't blush at the sight of a naked man."

He arched a thick brow. "You're planning on seeing a lot of naked men, are you?"

"The more the better," she insisted flippantly.

To her disbelief he proceeded to unfasten his breeches, then let them pool around his bare feet. Helplessly she stared at his powerful male body. Her breath clogged in her chest, as she noted that he was aroused. She averted her attention to his washboard belly, his hard, muscled thighs and athletic legs. She noticed the scar on his left shoulder, the bullet hole on his thigh and the knife wound on his ribs—souvenirs of hard-fought battles with outlaws, no doubt.

Her face exploded with color again, when he caught her making a thorough study of his incredible body.

"Never let it be said that I didn't do all I could to help expand your limited horizons, hellion."

When he sauntered into the water, smiling rakishly, she was still staring admiringly at every corded tendon and rippling muscle on his magnificent body.

Galen Fox leaned his good arm against the supporting beam on the front porch and watched his younger brother lead the string of prize horses up the path to the house. Galen frowned pensively when he noticed the two stringy-haired men tied to their saddles. The prisoners, who looked to be in their late twenties, brought up the rear of the procession.

"Glenn and Gideon must have captured the thieves," Sarah remarked as she came to stand beside him. "I wonder if this means Gideon decided to take Lorelei back to see her father and pursue an investigation. He certainly had his mind made up *not* to do it, didn't he? Stubborn man, your big brother."

"Hazard of the job, sweetheart," Galen murmured as

he slid his good arm around Sarah's waist and kissed her. "Luckily, I have you to smooth off my rough edges and keep my life in perspective. Gid doesn't have that luxury."

"That's why I decided that it would take some gentle nudging on our part to push him in the right direction."

Galen chuckled as he stared into Sarah's obsidian eyes that twinkled with mischief. "Thanks to your efforts, I hope Gideon learns a great deal on his road of discovery."

When Glenn halted in front of the house, Galen shifted his attention to his younger brother. "Everyone all right?" he asked as he strode down the steps to open the corral gate.

Glenn nodded his dark head. "Gid and Lori are fine, but Sonny caught one of my bullets during the showdown." He gestured to the dark-haired, dark-eyed man who sported a bandage on his thigh. "I patched him up as best I could but he could use some medical attention."

Sarah lurched around to enter the house. "I'll fetch my herbs and poultices."

Galen stared grimly at the captives who had shot him. "You boys should try raising your own horses instead of stealing them from other folks. Is this your first offense?"

Teddy nodded his red head and said, "We're sorry about that, mister. We got scared when you came charging from the house to fire off a shot. So we fired back."

Galen stared grimly at the thieves. "*Mine* was a warning shot and you know it. Yours wasn't and you *stole* our horses."

"We were desperate," Sonny put in as he grimaced and shifted to find a more comfortable position on the saddle. "We were sent out to capture Lorelei Russell, but she hid out too well. The Widow Burgess told us not to come back without her. Plus, the widow will sell the stage station and ranch now that her husband and foreman are dead. We're out of work. We thought we'd start up our own herd."

Galen frowned pensively as he and Glenn strode back to the porch. "These men were sent to capture Lorelei?"

"Apparently. But they claim they didn't see who shot the victim. They came from the bunkhouse and were ordered to give chase. Lori still maintains the shots came from the underbrush and the widow just presumed Lori fired the fatal shot because she grabbed one of the victim's pistols to return fire."

Galen stared off into the distance for a long moment. Then he said, "Gideon will sort it all out. All we needed to do was get him going in the right direction." He patted his young brother's shoulder. "You did your part to ensure Gid's hot pursuit, and Sarah did her part by doctoring Gid's food so he'd sleep later than usual the next morning."

Glenn grinned. "It wasn't a hardship to ride out with Lori as my companion. There is a lot about that spirited female to like and I did my best to make Gid jealous."

Galen and Glenn chuckled conspiratorially and Galen said, "It's obvious he's interested in her, but he's fighting the attraction tooth and nail."

"How is it that a man who's brutally honest most of the time can't be honest with himself? He has to know that Lori intrigues him. Why is he fighting it so fiercely?"

"I think he's afraid he'll make a mistake, like our mother did when she married our stepfather," Galen remarked. "She let herself be fooled into thinking he was kind and considerate. Then he got what he wanted."

"Yeah, our home, control of our finances and our mother," Glenn added on a bitter note.

"Gideon was the oldest and he was left to deal with Mama's mistake. We all suffered because of it, but Gideon vowed never to be deceived again. He doesn't want to believe Lori's claim of innocence because she intrigues him so much. He's afraid he'll be wrong about her and come away looking like a fool."

"Well, I believe she's innocent," Glenn maintained.

"I sincerely hope we aren't wrong since all three of us conspired to throw Gid and Lori together. If things turn out badly we are going to make a pact never to tell Gid that we set him up. Agreed?"

"Agreed," Glenn said, "Gid would probably shoot us both if he knew we tampered with his fate."

Galen nodded and grinned. "At least he'd go easy on Sarah, even if he found out the matchmaking scheme was her idea. Gid likes her better than us or so he says. That's all that will save her."

Chapter Eleven

Gideon and Lori were a quarter of an hour into their westward trek to the trading post when he glanced sideways to study her captivating profile. It would be so easy to believe Lori's version of the story because—despite his better judgment—he'd become physically and emotionally involved with her. But he'd been deceived once before and the repercussions to his entire family had been disastrous. He did not intend to live through an ordeal like that again.

Nevertheless, Lori was burrowing her way into his well-guarded heart as no other female ever had. Yet, Gideon vowed to proceed with great caution and he absolutely refused to let her make a fool of him. No matter how much he desired this flame-haired firebrand, he vowed to maintain a mental distance. Even if he'd been unable to keep his hands off her. Because one touch demanded another. Until they'd become as intimate as a man and woman could get.

Before he became sidetracked again, he said, "Start

at the beginning of your...er...friendship with Anthony Rogers and don't leave out anything, no matter how awkward or embarrassing," he insisted.

"Tony had been in the area for two years," Lori informed him as they circled a boulder-strewn hillside to follow the tree-lined creek. "He never mentioned his past, just said he'd lived here and there and worked in the Creek Indian reservation by Tulsey Town. I always wondered if he'd become crossways with the law since he avoided the subject so noticeably. He might have started a new life with a new name."

"So that's why you wondered if a bounty hunter had taken a shot at him that fateful night?"

"It was the only thing that made sense," she replied. "If his past was about to catch up with him that might explain why he proposed suddenly and insisted that we elope to anywhere I wanted to go, as long as we left the territory immediately."

"He courted you for how long?" Gideon asked.

"About three months. He usually came by the trading post to gather supplies so I knew who he was. Occasionally, I delivered supplies to the ranch and stage station. Before Hubert Burgess died accidentally, Tony began stopping by in the evening and we spent more time together. He was pleasant company and very respectful." The look she shot him indicated she couldn't say the same about Gideon.

"What kind of accident killed Hubert?" Gideon asked.

"What does that have to do with anything?"

"Nothing. But as I said, I want to get a general idea of what was going on during the time leading up to the murder."

"Hub Burgess was chasing off cattle thieves when he

took a fatal fall from his horse," she reported. "No one has any details because he was alone when it happened."

"Who found him?" Gideon asked.

"Maggie Burgess and Tony, I think. When Hub didn't come home for supper they went looking for him."

"And Tony was pursuing you *before* the accident? Correct?"

"Yes. About three weeks." She stared quizzically at him. "Do you think Hub knew about Tony's past and threatened to expose him? Maybe the accident wasn't an accident."

Gideon waved her off. "I'm just trying to put the events in chronological order. Go on, please."

"Tony showed up to gather supplies one evening and asked if I wanted to go riding. So I did. He came by to see me once a week, even though he said he had more chores to tend after Hub died. I wondered at the time if Hub's sudden death inspired him to live in the moment instead of working constantly."

Gideon had certainly adopted that live-in-the-moment philosophy the previous night. He'd turned a deaf ear and blind eye to caution. He'd surrendered to his forbidden desires for this amber-eyed beauty whose questionable involvement in Tony's death tormented him to no end.

Absently, Lori patted Drifter's muscled neck then shifted to a more comfortable position in the saddle. "It seemed Tony became more serious in our friendship the following month. His kisses…" Her voice trailed off and she squirmed awkwardly on her horse.

"I need *all* the details and facts," he insisted. "Go on."

"They became like yours," she described without glancing in his direction. "But my responses were lukewarm."

"Unlike your responses to me?" He couldn't help but tease her. He loved to tease her, just to watch her feisty spirit burst to life.

Sure enough, she glared at him. "Do you want to hear the details or not?"

He bowed nonchalantly from atop Pirate. "Please proceed and I'll try my best not to interrupt."

Her response was a smirk that implied he couldn't keep his mouth shut if he tried.

He thought they had that in common.

"Tony was more like a brother, sort of like my relationship with Glenn," she explained. "Enjoyable company and interesting to visit with, but not—"

"Got it," he inserted, feeling extraordinarily pleased that she didn't lump him in the lukewarm category with Glenn and Tony. Even if Gideon couldn't explain or control his compelling attraction to Lori, he didn't want the feelings and sensations to be one-sided. He did have his pride, after all.

Too much, if the truth be told.

"The day before the disastrous incident, Tony sent me a message. I stopped by the stage station after I delivered supplies to one of our elderly customers," she elaborated. "When I met with him, he made the odd comment that he hadn't meant to fall in love with me, but he'd come to care deeply about me. Then he proposed and suggested we elope that very night."

"Hadn't meant for it to happen?" Gideon repeated curiously.

She lifted her shoulder in a shrug. "I wasn't sure what that meant, either." She shot him a quick glance. "I doubted my irresistible charm got to him. It doesn't seem to have any effect on *you*."

A lot she knew. He'd found her impossible to ignore. She'd haunted his dreams since the day she'd walked from the fog like every man's fantasy come true. Apparently, Tony had fallen into the same trap that lured Gideon.

Unfortunately, Tony's desire for Lori turned fatal.

"Let's not deny the truth, honey," he suggested. "You're tempting and alluring. A man would have to be dead a week not to notice you."

She scoffed. "Thank you so much for that flattering compliment."

"You're welcome. Now get on with your story."

"I didn't know how to respond when Tony said he loved me. Then he dropped down on one knee and proposed. He insisted he would take care of me and that we'd go wherever I wished so we could make a clean break and a new start."

"Clean break and new start. That's what made you wonder if his past was about to catch up with him," Gideon presumed.

She nodded her flame-gold head. "He didn't sound desperate exactly, but he was *most* insistent. I told him that I cared for him, but I wasn't in love with him." She stared somberly at Gideon. "It was difficult to say that to him because I considered him a dear friend. I didn't want to hurt his feelings."

"It doesn't bother you to hurt my feelings with your snippy remarks?" he asked teasingly.

"Again," she said, tossing him a dour glance, "do you want to hear this or don't you?"

"I'm all ears, hellion, and I'm sitting on the edge of my horse," he claimed, tossing her a wry grin.

She shot him another dirty look, but she went on. "I urged Tony back to his feet and that's when we heard the rustling in the underbrush on the west side of the barn. The first shot zinged over our heads and struck a tree. That's when Tony stepped protectively in front of me and caught the bullet."

She clenched her hands on the pommel of the saddle

and it was a moment before she cleared her throat and continued, "He collapsed against me and I grabbed one of his pistols to return fire when the sniper fired the third shot."

Gideon had checked the pistol to note one shot had been fired, but he only had *her* word that she had fired into the underbrush and not at Tony.

"He said he was sorry he'd gotten me into this. Then he told me to run. But I refused to leave him when he wilted to the ground. When the gunfire caught Maggie Burgess's attention, she dashed toward us."

"Where was she?" Gideon asked.

"I'm not sure. In the station on the far side of the barn, perhaps. She might've come down from the house. I'm not sure because the barn and trees blocked my view. But I'll admit my focus was entirely on Tony's injury."

She swallowed hard and tears glistened in her eyes. Clearly, the incident had affected her. Gideon gave her a moment to compose herself. Yet, distrust flared in his mind. He wondered if this story was a hoax and *she* was the one who secretly desired Tony, despite what she said about feeling nothing but friendship.

Gideon had heard criminals weave many an elaborate and twisted tale in his time in law enforcement. The fact that he was vulnerable to this alluring woman made him fight like the very devil to keep an unbiased perspective.

"When Maggie came running, she commenced screaming and blaming me for shooting Tony. But she didn't arrive in time to see what really happened. She looked at the gun in my hand and assumed I'd shot Tony. Then she grabbed Tony's spare pistol and tried to shoot me."

"So you ran," he finished for her.

She nodded bleakly. "Maggie went a little crazy and she was intent on shooting first and asking questions later.

She'd lost her husband and her foreman and I suppose she was so overcome with grief and anger that she directed it at me."

Gideon could understand that. Grief and anger were powerful emotions. He'd dealt with them during those abusive years with his stepfather where he'd taken the brunt of the man's violence to protect his brothers and mother as often as he could. Emotions had exploded inside him when he rode off to find the man who'd caused his mother's death. The situation had come to a head—and ended badly. But Gideon didn't regret sending the devious bastard to hell where he belonged.

"I mounted Drifter and rode in the opposite direction of the trading post so I wouldn't drag my father into this," she told Gideon. "I heard Maggie shouting for Sonny and Teddy to give chase because I'd murdered Tony. As Sonny and Teddy said yesterday, they didn't see what happened and only followed Maggie's orders. They trailed after me and I hid out in caves for several days before I saw you taking Pecos Clem into custody. Then I came to you for help."

She stared at him stonily. "My mistake was believing that I'd be considered innocent until proven guilty by the Deputy U.S. Marshal I willingly contacted for assistance."

"If you're trying to make me feel bad it won't work," Gideon replied. "I had received the message about a female murderer on the loose, same as the other marshals had. I rarely encounter a fugitive who isn't a prime suspect in a crime. There's a price on your head and someone passed the word throughout the territory."

"Maggie," she guessed. "She kept screaming and crying and claiming I would pay dearly for what I'd done."

"This presents another problem," Gideon mused aloud.

"With a price on your head, someone might decide to shoot you. Dead or Alive. That's the standard procedure for suspected murderers on the loose."

"Even if I haven't been formally charged?"

"Even if," he maintained. "Judge Parker is a no-nonsense kind of man. His main concern is protecting his law enforcement officers from harm and incarcerating criminals."

Lori glanced uneasily around the wooded area. "If something happens to me, please promise to get to the bottom of Tony's death. Someone was hiding in the bushes, taking shots at him."

"Are you sure it wasn't you?" The cynical question popped from his mouth before he could bite it back.

Lori glowered at him. "No, it wasn't me. I still maintain that Tony's death has something to do with his secretive past and his eagerness to leave the area as soon as possible. With or without me, I expect."

When she lapsed into silence, Gideon did the same. He would have to do some checking with the other marshals and with Judge Parker about a possible fugitive who might have taken an alias to escape captivity. Somewhere there might be an outstanding warrant with Tony's physical description. That might answer the puzzling questions that pertained to this case.

"How long before we reach your trading post?" Gideon asked in a lull in their conversation.

"We should arrive this evening," she predicted.

Gideon surveyed the unfamiliar terrain, wondering if bushwhackers lay in wait, hoping to make a profit from the price on Lori's head. *His* head might get in the way, he mused, taking another careful survey of the area.

"We'll stop here for a meal," he decided, then swung from the saddle. "I prefer to arrive after dark. No sense making ourselves sitting ducks, in case your high-profile case draws greedy bounty hunters."

He could almost guarantee it had. Gideon would bet his reputation someone was out there waiting to collect. Someone might shoot at him, and that never failed to ruin his good disposition—whatever he had left of it.

Lori felt she'd taken gigantic strides with Gideon. For the first time since she approached him, he had listened intently and posed questions. He might not believe her side of the story, but he had admitted to her that he shouldn't have judged her guilty so quickly.

Anticipation sizzled through her as she led the way through the darkness to reach the trading post. She hadn't seen her father in almost two weeks and she knew he was worried—and horrified—by the charges against her.

"Halt," Gideon murmured as he grabbed Drifter's reins.

Her senses went on full alert as she scanned the moonlit path, wondering what he had heard that she had missed.

Without warning, Gideon dismounted and pulled her down beside him. "We're going to get off this path," he whispered in her ear. "Something or someone is out here. I'm not familiar enough with this area to take a shortcut through the trees. Lead the way, Lori."

She veered south, weaving in and out of the trees to follow the bend of Winding River. It required an extra quarter of an hour to reach the place where her father docked their ferry each evening.

Home again, Lori mused as she stared uphill at the trading post. She saw the flickering lantern light in her father's upstairs bedroom, shining like a beacon. Bubbling with emotion, she pivoted to fling her arms around Gideon's neck. Impulsively, she planted a loud, smacking kiss on his lips.

"Shhh!" he hissed when she allowed him to come up for air. "What the hell was that for?"

"For allowing me to come home to reassure my father that I'm all right." She kissed him again. "And that's for opening your mind to the possibility that I might be telling the truth and for coming to investigate."

"You're welcome, hellion." He bent her over his arm to deliver a lip-sizzling wallop of a kiss that left her hungry for more. When his caresses moved possessively over her, she arched into him, aching to rediscover the amazing pleasure she had experienced with him the previous night.

"What are the chances of your father allowing us to share the same bedroom?" he mumbled against the pulsating vein of her throat.

"None whatsoever."

"Figured as much."

He stepped away long before she wanted to let him go. Inhaling a steadying breath, she grabbed Drifter's dangling reins and headed toward the stone-and-timber trading post she'd called home for a dozen years.

A moment after she stepped into the clearing between the ferry and post, a gunshot shattered the peaceful darkness.

"Ooofff!" Lori grunted uncomfortably when Gideon launched himself at her, knocking her to the ground and covering her body protectively with his.

His pistol cleared leather before she could blink and he fired off a shot.

"Don't ever do that again," Lori erupted as she tried to buck him off.

He came onto his knees, his gaze still focused on

the clump of weeds and trees near the river. "Don't do what?"

"Don't try to protect me from gunfire," she grumbled as she came up on her hands and knees. "That's what got Tony killed, and I refuse for that to happen to you. I told you already, one death on my conscience is plenty. I don't want yours, too."

"Can we argue about this later," he said absently as he scanned the area. He moved in a low crouch to approach the sniper's hiding place. "And stay put, damn it."

Huffing out a breath, Lori came to her feet to duck behind the nearest tree. In the moonlight, she watched Gideon move stealthily toward the place where she had seen the flare of gunpowder and puff of smoke.

A moment later, her father flung open the door. "Who's there?" he called anxiously.

"A weary traveler," Gideon called back to ensure Lori didn't commit the critical mistake of answering her father and inviting more gunfire. Who knew how many bounty hunters were waiting in the darkness to pick her off. "I need food and supplies for my journey south."

A minute passed before Gideon returned to Lori then grabbed Pirate's reins. "Whoever took that shot is hell and gone already, but that doesn't mean he's alone or he hasn't shifted position. I'll check for discharged cartridges and tracks in the morning. The bad news is that whoever took the shot knows you've returned home," he told her grimly. "This is where *I*'d lie in wait if I knew where you lived."

The comment assured Lori that she'd be dodging bullets in the near future. Gideon had prophesied bounty hunters and fortune hunters would lurk about, waiting to collect the reward on her head.

She wondered how much she was worth.

Well, I'll worry about that tomorrow, she decided as she approached her father anxiously.

"Stay behind me," Gideon ordered as he took the lead. "Even better, try to become invisible."

Lori leaned heavily against Drifter's side as she made her way toward her father. Excitement roiled inside her and she involuntarily quickened her step. Gideon reached over to slow her down.

"Be careful," he cautioned. "I'll use the horses to block you from any prying eyes in the bushes. I don't want you to end up dead on your doorstep. That's guaranteed to ruin your father's evening."

Gideon could feel the tension in Lori's arm as they approached the tall, lean, older man. He was a few inches shorter than Gideon, and he looked to be in his late forties. He carried himself with the proud military bearing of an officer.

Sandy blond hair capped his square face. His jaw was rimmed with whiskers that looked to have been growing for about the same length of time Lori had gone missing.

"Move aside, please, sir," Gideon commanded. "I'm Deputy U.S. Marshal Gideon Fox."

"Clive Russell," Lori's father introduced himself quickly.

His hazel eyes widened when he saw Lori sandwiched between the two horses. Thankfully, he didn't dash toward her. He backed away as Gideon requested.

The moment Gideon escorted Lori through the door and shut it behind them she flew into her father's outstretched arms.

"Thank God!" Clive gushed as he hugged the stuffing out of Lori. "I've been worried sick about you, sugar. Maggie Burgess is so convinced that you shot Tony that she's posted Wanted posters at every stage station along the route. She's offering a reward for your capture. You've become notorious in less than two weeks!"

Gideon watched as the emotional reunion continued for several minutes. While father and daughter exchanged whispered conversation, he surveyed the trading post. It was full of shelves lined with neatly organized stacks of various and sundry supplies to satisfy travelers and local residents. Obviously, the Russells were successful at business. Plus, the building was clean, spacious and tidy. Not like some he'd visited in other parts of the territory.

"What about supper?" Clive asked Gideon as he tucked Lori protectively against his side. "Have either of you eaten yet?"

"We had hard tack during the ride," Gideon reported. "But that was several hours ago."

Clive smiled broadly and Gideon noticed a family resemblance. "I'm indebted to you for returning my daughter safely to me, Marshal Fox. With your authority in the territory maybe we can find out who really shot Tony."

The man had no doubt whatsoever that Lori was completely innocent, despite not hearing any of the details. Gideon would never trust so blindly or unequivocally. And for good reason. Outlaws were liars, cheaters, thieves and often cold-blooded murderers. But he had to admit that his opinion of Lori had changed drastically over the past few days. Yet, the cynical voice inside his head kept asking if he'd allowed himself to be seduced into giving this beguiling female the benefit of every doubt.

Even as Clive tucked Lori possessively beside him, Gideon felt the insane urge to grab her hand and lead her away to treat himself to another helping of her addictive kisses and caresses. He chastised himself for not waylaying her this afternoon so he could enjoy the erotic pleasure they had shared the previous night in the cavern.

The titillating thought sent a jolt of fiery desire sizzling through him. Gideon shifted uncomfortably from one booted foot to the other.

"I'll tend the horses if you'll tell me where I can stable them for the night," he eagerly volunteered.

"I'll take care of—" Lori tried to offer but Clive interrupted with a slashing gesture of his arm.

"You are staying inside so no one else can take more potshots at you." Clive's blond brows flattened over his hazel eyes. "I'll show Gideon where to put the horses while you round up something to eat."

"Yes, sir, Lieutenant Colonel, sir," she said, giving him a snappy salute. Then she wheeled like a soldier on parade and marched to the kitchen.

"So she *can* follow orders," Gideon said to himself. "Just not mine."

Reece McCree lit his cigar and puffed on it until a wreath of smoke floated in front of him. "Well, well, Gideon Fox. Long time no see," he murmured as he stood at a distance.

He had held his position, watching the shapely flame-haired woman dash through the front door, with Fox guarding her back. When Fox closed the door on what Reece predicted to be an emotional family reunion, he puffed on his cheroot. His gaze shifted to the lantern light glowing in the second story window. He debated with himself about scaling the rock-and-timber walls.

When the front door of the trading post opened a few minutes later, Fox and Lorelei's father exited to tend the horses. Reece smiled slyly. This was the perfect time to make Lorelei's acquaintance—without the inconvenience of having Gideon Fox breathing down his neck.

Crushing the cheroot beneath his boot heel, Reece

tethered his horse a safe distance away. Then he moved silently toward the side of the trading post, looking for the shortest route to an upstairs window.

After Lori's playful, military-style retreat to the kitchen, Clive grinned good-naturedly. "My daughter is a handful." He grabbed Drifter's reins and led the way to the oversize barn. "Feisty and independent to a fault, too."

"I've noticed," Gideon said. "We've clashed a time…or three."

"I won't apologize for raising Lorelei to be self-reliant and spirited," Clive declared. "I've met too many timid females in my time. They were never allowed to develop minds of their own or interesting personalities." He smiled ruefully. "Lorelei is like her mother in appearance and disposition. To tell the truth, there are times when I notice that Lorelei's expression or gesture is so similar to her mother's that it nearly breaks my heart."

No doubt, Clive had never recovered from the grief of losing his beloved wife all those years ago. Gideon wondered what it would be like to care so deeply and devotedly for a woman that her absence in his life left him without a heart beating in his chest. Not that he had much of a heart left these days—at least in the eyes of fugitives that called him a heartless devil.

"Do you know of anyone around here who might have held a grudge against Anthony Rogers?" Gideon asked as they strode into the barn.

"One or two, I suppose. There are always hired hands that covet a better position on the job."

"Do you know Teddy Collins and Sonny Hathaway very well?"

"Not well enough to predict whether they would ambush their boss to take his place at the station and ranch."

"After they chased Lori and couldn't locate her within a few days, they decided to steal my family's prize livestock," Gideon remarked as he unfastened Pirate's girth strap. "By the way, your training paid off. Your daughter avoided her would-be captors with relative ease."

Clive chuckled. "But she couldn't match your skills, I take it, since she didn't return home alone."

"She came to me for assistance, but I wasn't sure I believed her story. A messenger arrived in marshals' camp, offering a very different account than she told. There's also a high price on her head."

Clive's expression sobered as he stared intently at Gideon. "But you believe her, don't you?"

Gideon pulled the saddle from Pirate's back. "I'm a cautious man whose been bombarded with countless false claims of innocence from the guilty-as-sin outlaws I've tracked down."

"But she's a woman," Clive reminded him—as if Gideon didn't know that all too well.

"So is Belle Starr. She has a long list of crimes to her credit. Only now are she and her husband, Sam, serving a nine-month sentence for horse thieving. But in the past, she's gotten off on technicalities by hiring expensive lawyers and paying them with stolen money. I transported her to Fort Smith to face Judge Parker once myself. She offered me all sorts of incentives to look the other way while she escaped."

Gideon clamped his lips together and mentally kicked himself for not shutting up one sentence sooner.

Clive glanced speculatively at him and frowned. "And do you *demand* or *invite* favors to give leniency to your prisoners, especially those of the female persuasion, Marshal?"

He'd known that was coming before Clive spewed out

the question. Gideon didn't want to answer, for fear he'd incriminate himself.

"Well?" Clive prodded, staring at him in consternation. "We are discussing my daughter. If you resorted to asking for favors in exchange for bringing her home and investigating the charges against her, I want to know and I want to know now!"

Chapter Twelve

Lori sighed contentedly as she fried steak and potatoes in the skillet. She'd never been so glad to be home. She still faced an uphill battle, but at least her father knew she was safe and Gideon had opened that steel trap he called a mind to the possibility that she might be telling the truth about that awful incident that took Tony's life.

Humming a soft tune, Lori hurried to the cellar to fetch a jar of beans that she had canned the previous summer. When she returned to the kitchen, she heard an unidentified creak from the second floor. Warily, she stared up the staircase leading to their private quarters.

Then she glanced expectantly toward the front door. She had been perfectly serious when she'd told Gideon that she didn't want anyone to take a bullet for her. Tony would be alive today if he hadn't tried to be so blasted noble. No one was going to fight her battles for her, she vowed as she set aside the steaks and potatoes.

Lori grabbed the pistol her father kept stashed beneath the counter, then headed quietly toward the staircase. She knew which steps didn't creak and which ones did. She was careful to avoid them during her ascent. Her heart pounded fiercely against her ribs, but she reminded herself that Gideon faced this sort of danger on a regular basis.

So had her father during his stint in the army.

Her father hadn't raised her to be a simpering female who stood aside and waited for a man to protect her. She intended to protect the two most important men in her life because she loved them both—

Dear God! she thought with a start that nearly caused her to miss a step. Was she really in love with that hard-edged, cynical marshal? When had that happened? Why had she allowed it to happen? She knew Gideon was simply using her as a pleasurable diversion. She was convenient. No more. No less.

And *still* she'd allowed her foolish heart to enter into that steamy, wildly erotic tryst one dark and stormy night. Gideon Fox, it turned out, was the only man who set fire to her desires and compelled her to live in the moment, for as long as it lasted. Defying all consequences.

Lori willfully cast aside the unsettling epiphany that took the worst of all possible moments to reveal itself. She had the sneaking suspicion that someone was upstairs and she needed to concentrate on nothing but the potential threat awaiting her.

When she reached the landing, her courage faltered. Maybe she should have waited for Gideon and her father. But no, *she'd* decided to be the protector. She wanted to prove she was brave enough to face unseen danger the way Gideon and her father did.

Cautiously, she glanced down the shadowed hall, but she'd taken only one step forward when someone pounced from the darkness. Fear blazed through her when a man's powerful body slammed her broadside, knocking her off balance. He wrenched the pistol from her hand before she could turn it on him.

She tried to scream bloody murder, but he clamped his gloved hand over her nose and mouth, making it difficult to breathe. She bit into his fingers as he dragged her into the nearest bedroom—the one that belonged to her father. The man growled in pain when she bit a chunk from his finger but he refused to remove his hand.

Instead, a long-bladed knife appeared in his free hand. He laid it against her throat and said, "Do that again, wildcat, and you'll be bleeding all over the carpet. If you keep quiet, I'll spare the marshal and your father. If not…"

His hushed voice trailed off, leaving her to speculate on the grim possibilities in store for Gideon and her father. The vivid memory of watching Tony collapse and die was too fresh in her mind. She stilled instantly in the circle of her captor's unyielding arms.

"You're worth a lot of money, but I still want to hear the boiled-down version of *your* side of the story," her brawny captor demanded in a hushed tone. When he settled his arm diagonally across her breasts she struggled against him—and felt the sharp prick of his dagger.

"Easy now," he murmured. "Tell me what happened."

That he was willing to listen to what she had to say surprised and confused her. But when he moved his hand so she could speak, she responded hurriedly. "I was talking with Tony when someone tried to shoot us from the bushes."

"Did you see who it was? Could you identity this supposed bushwhacker?" he questioned intently.

Lori frowned. Something about the man's tone puzzled her. She couldn't put her finger on why the questions sounded odd. However, she was too overwhelmed with fear to question him, especially since he held a knife to her throat.

"No, I didn't see who took the three shots at us. Whoever it was hid in the thick underbrush, and darkness was closing in quickly. Tony stepped in front of me to shield me. His self-sacrificing deed cost him his life. *I didn't kill Tony,*" she said adamantly. "He was my friend."

"I heard that he was your lover," her captor contradicted. "You killed him because he rejected you."

"You heard wrong," Lori insisted. "He asked me to marry him and to leave the territory. I got the impression he was in some sort of trouble or he was on the run from the law. Perhaps he suspected he was about to be captured and he felt compelled to escape immediately."

The man's grasp eased ever so slightly. "You think he *knew* someone from his past was about to catch up with him?"

She nodded—or at least as much as the knife at her throat allowed. "I believe he planned to leave, with or without me."

"Why did you refuse to go with him?"

"Because I didn't love him. I wished I did, though."

"So you just led him on, is that it?" he asked sharply.

Honestly, there was something about this mysterious intruder that reminded her of Gideon, in size and extraordinary skill. And that made him a formidable enemy. This man was cautious by nature and habit and he posed intimidating questions meant to rile her temper—just like Gideon.

"I didn't lead him on," she insisted. "I cared about him and I intend to avenge his death—"

When her captor made the crucial mistake of relaxing his grip, she exploded into action. She shoved the heel of her hand against his wrist, forcing the blade away from her throat. With lightning quickness, she used her elbow to deliver a sharp blow to his crotch. He doubled over, grunted in pain then cursed her soundly as he staggered backward.

She tried to make a run for it but he grabbed her hair and gave it a quick jerk to maintain control of her. But Lori had found herself in tussles with drunken men on numerous occasions and she knew how to defend herself. She'd even gotten in a few good blows on Gideon because he hadn't given her full credit for her training in self-defense—thanks to her father's relentless instructions.

Lori yelled at the top of her lungs and spun out of her captor's reach. When he tried to recapture her, she groped in the dark for any object that might become an improvised weapon. She latched onto the coatrack beside the door and swung it sideways to catch the man upside the head. While he stumbled backward, stunned and disoriented, Lori screamed a few more times for good measure, hoping he would dart away.

Scowling, he wheeled toward the window. In the moonlight, she noticed his collar-length hair and muscular build. Of course, she'd been vividly aware of his strength since he had clamped hold of her.

"We'll meet again, wildcat," he assured her gruffly. "And next time I'll be better prepared to deal with you. Your father and the marshal won't be nearby. Count on it."

He slung his leg over the windowsill and disappeared from sight. Lori turned and ran to safety, then cursed herself for not slamming down the window sash on the man's hands while he hung on the outer wall.

Well, it was too late for that now, she mused as she took the steps two at a time to return to the kitchen. Her survival instincts had kicked in and put her to flight. Even as she huddled in the kitchen with knives in both hands, she could still hear the mysterious man's vow wringing in her ears.

He'd return if she made the careless mistake of venturing away from Gideon and her father's protection.

In other words, he'd be watching and waiting.

The realization that the darkness had eyes made the hair on the back of her neck stand on end.

Clive stood in the barn, bristling with a father's indignation about the possibility of his daughter's damaged virtue. Gideon scrambled to find a tactful reply so he and Clive wouldn't come to blows.

Lori's wild scream shattered the brittle silence in nothing flat.

Gideon lurched around and dashed to the trading post. Hell and damn, one of them should've remained with her, he scolded himself.

If Lori had been abducted or injured because of Gideon's careless neglect, he'd never forgive himself. He knew better, damn it. Yet, he'd broken his own rules so many times where Lori was concerned that he was in danger of tarnishing his spotless reputation as a Deputy U.S. Marshal.

However, his pride and reputation weren't his main concern as he sprinted to the trading post. He bounded onto the porch, bypassing the steps, and barreled through the door. Both pistols drawn, he was prepared to shoot anything that moved—except Lori.

If she were still here. *If* she were still alive.

The unnerving thought hit him so hard he practically stumbled over his own feet. Relief washed over him like a tidal wave when he saw Lori scurrying from the kitchen with two knives clenched in her fists. Her face was as white as flour and a dribble of blood trickled down her neck.

She dropped the knives and flew into his arms. Gideon

held her close as he pointed his weapons in every direction, expecting attack.

"What happened?" he panted, out of breath—not from the mad dash but from fear for her life. His heart was bouncing around in his chest, nearly beating him to death! Being afraid for someone else was a new experience. He didn't like it a damn bit.

"A man came through the upstairs window to grab me."

Gideon swore mightily, uncaring if Clive—who came through the front door, breathless and wild-eyed—took offense when he saw Gideon cuddling Lori close.

"What the hell were you doing upstairs in the first place, damn it?" Gideon demanded harshly.

"I didn't want anyone shot on my account." She raised her chin to defy the two disapproving glares directed at her. "I keep telling you that Tony was one too many. I am *not* risking either of you, and I damn well mean it!"

"It's *my* job to take risks," Gideon told her sharply.

"I don't care if it's a direct order from the Lord above," she countered hotly then stared down Clive. "Same goes for you, Papa. I can take care of myself and I escaped tonight without help from either of you."

"Right. Never mind that Clive and I nearly suffered heart seizure when we heard you scream," Gideon muttered caustically as he headed for the steps. "Did you get a good look at your captor? Can you identify him?"

"He was about your size and height," she reported as she followed him up the staircase. Clive was two steps behind her. "He grabbed me in the darkness then fired questions about the night Tony died. He seemed exceptionally intent on hearing what I had to say about a possible bushwhacker. He wanted to know if I saw the supposed sniper and if I could describe him."

Gideon frowned, bemused. "You mean, as if it mattered if you could positively identify the sniper? As if *he* might be the sniper and wondered if he needed to dispose of an eyewitness?"

Lori blinked. "I believe you might be right. I wasn't thinking straight at that unsettling moment, but something bothered me about his peculiar questions. He was intent on knowing everything I knew about Tony and the shooting."

"Do you think he really might be the sniper?" Clive questioned. "The less you know, Lori, the safer you'll be."

"If that's true then he knows I can't identify him. Maybe that's why he exited the window without trying to dispose of me. I put up a fight and escaped but he could have shot me if that had been his intent."

"Lori, for God's sake," Clive howled in dismay. "You shouldn't have fought back! You might have provoked him to kill you for being so much trouble!"

Gideon wanted to rail at her, too, but Clive was doing a bang-up job for the both of them. Gideon swore colorfully to himself as he stared out the window into the darkness. The thought of a prowler scaling the outer wall and capturing Lori unnerved him.

He'd faced the prospect of his own death so many times over the years that he'd grown accustomed to danger. But the prospect of *Lori* dying during his watch rattled him to no end. If this feisty, independent hellion wasn't out there in the world somewhere… Well, it wouldn't be the same. *He* wouldn't be the same because she'd imbedded herself in his memory and she'd touched emotions that he'd buried beneath cool, callous reserve for over a decade.

"I'm going outside to look around," Gideon announced as he spun away from the window.

"No, you aren't. Supper is ready." Lori stood in his path like an immovable obstacle.

He tried to stare her down, but knew she wouldn't step aside.

"Fine. Supper sounds great," he said with false enthusiasm.

She spun on her heels to lead the way downstairs while Gideon cursed himself for giving in to her—again. He also cursed his unruly male body for focusing on the hypnotic sway of her hips while his mind transported him back in time to relive the night he'd shared indescribable passion with Lori. *Damnation,* he thought. *I'm getting in so deep with her that I'll never find my way out...* And he wondered if he cared if he ever did....

"You didn't answer the question I asked in the barn," Clive reminded Gideon the moment he returned from scouting the area after their late supper.

"Damn, back to that again," Gideon mumbled under his breath as he closed the front door behind him.

"Papa, it's been a long, tedious journey." Lori ambled over to latch onto Clive's arm and guide him toward the staircase. "The marshal and I are exhausted. Let's save further conversation for tomorrow, shall we?"

Gideon decided the golden-eyed female had her father wrapped around her finger. She flashed Clive a dimpled smile. He relaxed his defensive stance and went with her without complaint.

"I can't tell you what a relief it is to be home so I can snuggle up in my own bed, after living like a soldier on bivouac," she said.

"You're right, sweetheart. We all need our rest." The glance Clive sent Gideon assured him the subject of possible favors wasn't over—only postponed.

"I'll show you to your room, Gideon," she offered.

"I'll take care of that," Clive said a little too insistently.

"I've been heating water for an honest-to-goodness bath." She cast Gideon a smile then headed upstairs. "Good-night to both of you."

"I'll take my bath in the river after your father shows me to my room," Gideon said.

"Whatever you wish." Lori veered down the hall to her room.

Clive blocked his view, as if that would stop Gideon from figuring out where Lori would be sleeping. Wherever it was, it would be the wrong place, if he wasn't there with her. Gideon didn't know why he considered it vital that Lori slept in his arms. Maybe because someone had tried to shoot her and abduct her to collect a high bounty. Or perhaps sharing one night of amazing passion hadn't been enough to appease him.

Perhaps two nights would satisfy his craving.

He doubted it, but he could only hope.

"Your room is down here." Clive gestured forcefully in the opposite direction as Lori disappeared at the far end of the hall.

Clive halted beside a spacious room. He stared pointedly at Gideon, who wore a carefully blank stare. "I expect you to stay in here. Marshal or not. I believe we understand each other."

"I believe we do." Gideon turned on his heels. "I'll scout the area again, just to be on the safe side, after I bathe."

"Thank you, Marshal Fox. And beginning tomorrow, you will resolve these ridiculous accusations against my daughter so you can go back to what you do best. Tracking ruthless fugitives, not *innocent* women who should be home under their father's *vigilant* protection."

Gideon inclined his head ever so slightly. "Exactly what I was thinking," he said before he walked away.

It was an outright lie, of course. Clive Russell would skin him alive if he knew the thought of sharing Lori's bed was the only recurring thought on his mind.

Lori opened her window, then stared down at the dark silhouette moving gracefully across the lawn toward the river. She frowned pensively, remembering that her would-be kidnapper reminded her of the way Gideon Fox moved. She contemplated that for a moment as Gideon disappeared into the bushes near the ferry. She couldn't recall any of the locals who reminded her of Gideon's size, stature and lithe economy of movement. Whoever was stalking her wasn't from the area, she assured herself.

Impulsively, Lori wheeled toward her bedroom door. She wanted to speak with Gideon, wanted to be with him. She halted halfway across her room and grumbled under her breath. Her father had become excessively protective after her extended absence and he seemed determined to keep Gideon a respectable distance away from her.

Ordinarily, she would have appreciated his concern, but she'd made the mistake of falling in love with a man who could only be hers during the course of this investigation. Their days were numbered—hers perhaps more than his, if unidentified snipers kept shooting at her then trying to take her captive.

Which made it even more important not to waste a single moment of the limited time she had left with Gideon.

Lori reversed direction and returned to the window. If her would-be captor could scale the outer wall then so could she. If she could balance on the jutting stone momentarily, then she could reach the gutter pipe to steady herself while she climbed the rest of the way to the ground.

Determined of purpose, she slung her leg over the windowsill then twisted sideways to anchor her hands on the ledge so she could let herself down until she could place her foot on one of the rough, protruding stones. Slowly, carefully, she reached sideways to latch onto the drainpipe. From there, stepping from one stone to the next was much easier and she made it to the ground without mishap.

Concealing herself in the trees to ensure her father couldn't see her, Lori crept toward the river. An amused smile quirked her lips when she spotted Gideon backstroking across the moonlit water that rippled like a sea of shimmering diamonds. Fascinated, she peeled off her boots, breeches and shirt to join him for a swim. Lori shook her head, amazed at her own reckless abandon. She'd never considered sneaking from her room to be with any other man....

Her thoughts trailed off when Gideon swirled suddenly to stare in her direction. She walked into the river, headed directly toward him.

"What are you doing here? How did you get past your father? There might be a sniper lurking around and Clive will have my head if he catches us together...." His voice became a husky growl. "Lord, you're beautiful. I never tire of looking at you."

Lori smiled, pleased by his compliment. Praise from a man like Gideon Fox was rare and was meant to be savored.

Despite the chilly water, Lori warmed up the moment her body glided suggestively against his muscular torso. She looped her arms around his broad shoulders, then kissed him with all the pent-up emotion bubbling inside her.

Gideon moaned hungrily as he plunged his tongue into her mouth and all but devoured her. She melted beneath his ravishing kiss, delighting in the feel of his hands gliding from the peaks of her breasts to the curve of her hips then back again.

"Your father thinks I'm demanding favors from you in exchange for investigating the murder," he whispered against the curve of her neck.

"Did you tell him I was offering you favors in exchange for lessons in passion?" she teased playfully.

He raised his damp head and stared quizzically at her. "Is that what's going on here, hellion? We never got around to discussing what happened last night. Maybe we should now."

She wasn't about to tell him that she'd fallen hopelessly in love with him. That's the very last thing Gideon would want to hear.

He cupped her chin in his hand and raised her face to his intent gaze. "What *is* going on here, Lorelei?"

She moved suggestively against the whipcord muscles, hard contours and sleek planes of his masculine body, well aware that he was aroused. "I'm seducing you into helping me, of course. I'm calculating and manipulative and I want to get my hands on you every chance I get. So stop wasting precious time talking when I want everything you have to give."

Then she kissed him for all she was worth and skimmed her hand down the washboard muscles of his belly to curl her fingers around his rigid shaft.

"Honesty," he rasped. "I like that in a woman."

"What else do you like, Mister Marshal? This…?"

He groaned aloud when she stroked him from base to tip then cupped him in her hand. Hungry desire throbbed heavily through him as she caressed him gently and teased his mouth with light, feathery kisses that made him crave a deeper taste of her. Her touch made him burn with a fever that only she ignited and only she could satisfy.

That worried the living hell out of him—but not enough to prompt him to back away from her. She was the one temptation in life he couldn't resist. His Waterloo. His Achilles' heel... He could go on and on, but her arousing touch was boiling his brain down to mindless mush.

He swore softly when the erotic stroke of her hand had him arching toward her in shameless defeat. It amazed him that a previously inexperienced woman could devastate him so easily, so thoroughly. He'd almost swear she'd cast some sort of unbreakable spell over him because the self-discipline and good judgment he'd spent years cultivating seemed nonexistent when this feisty beauty was in his arms.

Need riveted him and he wrapped her legs around his hips, aching to bury himself inside her. He sighed in satisfaction when she guided him to her and he pressed intimately against her. The instant he became the burning flame inside her, all seemed right with his world.

Definitely a mystical spell, he decided as he moved ardently against her and she matched him thrust for thrust. He had her protective father to worry about and a sniper waiting to collect a reward. Yet, all that mattered was having Lori heart-to-heart and flesh-to-flesh with him, sharing her incredible passion and leaving him spiraling through time and space to revolve around her, as if she were the sun in his universe.

"Say you love me," she whispered as passion overtook him, despite his attempt to hold on to his crumbling restraint.

"You love me," he murmured breathlessly.

He felt her shimmering around him as he shuddered in helpless release...and he thought to hell with the consequences. For once in his hardscrabble life, he felt wild and reckless and fulfilled. Not wary and cautious. He wasn't looking over his shoulder, expecting the worst. He was savoring the feel of Lori's lush body joined intimately to his while he treated himself to a few dozen more intoxicating kisses.

He wondered if his brother, Galen, and Sarah experienced anything remotely close to the soul-shattering pleasure that consumed him when he was with Lori. Then he felt guilty because his other brother, Glenn, had developed a fascination for this alluring woman. Gideon hadn't stepped aside for his brother and he maybe should have. He'd always placed his family first—except with Lori. He'd made her top priority and he wasn't sure how to deal with that undeniable, but unsettling, realization. His perspective had changed drastically and he didn't know how to stop it from happening.

Chapter Thirteen

"What are you thinking?" Lori whispered as she nestled her cheek against Gideon's shoulder while they clung together in the river.

"That Glenn made it clear he was interested in you… and I betrayed him."

She leaned back to peer up at him. "I told you that I hold him in the same regard that I did Tony. You're the one I wanted, Gideon. You want honesty? There it is."

"That's good for my self-esteem, but it isn't much consolation for Glenn."

Lori pressed a kiss to his lips then eased away. "I can't help what I feel," she murmured before she dived underwater then reappeared near the riverbank.

"How *did* you get past your father?" he asked curiously.

"The same way the intruder came in. I climbed through the window and down the outer wall by holding on to the gutter pipe for support."

"What!" he yelped in disbelief, then lowered his voice

so Clive wouldn't come running to blast him out of the water. "You have snipers shooting at you. Don't do them any favors by breaking your own neck and making it easy to haul you in and collect a reward."

"Why not? It would make your life infinitely easier. You'd be rid of me and you'd end the investigation that places you in the line of fire." She pulled on her breeches—while he admired the erotic sway of her bare breasts.

"Getting shot at goes with my job," he said, distracted.

She halted in the process of grabbing her blouse. "Is that all I am to you, Gideon? Another job and a diversion while you're off duty?"

"Is that all I am to *you,* while you're waiting for me to find evidence that clears your name?" he shot back.

Disappointed, he watched her cover her full breasts with her shirt then fasten the buttons. He could make a dedicated study of her curvaceous body and never tire of admiring her. What did that mean? That he was in lust with her?

"I told you last night that I expected nothing from you." She sank down on a fallen log to pull on her boots. "I wanted you. You needn't feel obliged to me in any way because of it."

"You *had* me," he reminded her. "*Thoroughly.* And I wanted you so much that I couldn't find the willpower to back away. Even now, I wouldn't let you sleep alone if your father wasn't lurking about, trying to prevent impropriety."

"Yes, well, that's a moot point now, isn't it?" She turned away. "Good night, Gideon."

"Wait up. I'll give you a boost up the wall." He waded ashore to hurriedly pull on his breeches—backward. He cursed, then started the process all over again.

The damnedest thing happened on the way to the trading

post. Gideon slipped his hand into hers. He'd never been the romantic type, inclined to hold a woman's hand. But he couldn't make himself let go of her, couldn't set aside the magical moment they had shared in the river.

He was losing his edge and getting soft, he decided, grinning wryly. Except when he was with Lori. In those instances, her touch, her kiss, her smile left him hard and aching in the time it took to blink.

His thoughts scattered when they halted beneath her bedroom window and he stared at the obstacle course of stone-and-timber wall. "You climbed down from there?" he choked out.

She nudged him with her shoulder. "Just proves how eager I was to be with you."

"I'm flattered," he said, and he meant it.

"Good, but you should know I've been a hopeless tomboy all my life. I haven't spent much time worrying about what a lady should do and what she shouldn't."

"I prefer self-reliant tomboys to useless, whimpering females." He linked his fingers together to give her a boost.

Impressed, he watched her grasp the drainpipe for support then step from one jutting stone to another. When she reached out to grasp the windowsill, Gideon held his breath and moved directly beneath her, just in case. But she agilely shifted sideways and pulled herself through the window. Smiling triumphantly, she poked her head outside and waved good-night.

Knowing she was safe and sound, Gideon spun on his heels to circle the building one last time. He halted beside the rough wall below Clive's bedroom—the one the would-be abductor had scaled to attack Lori. The climb looked to be more difficult, but a clump of trees obscured this side of the trading post, making it vulnerable to siege.

Gideon frowned worriedly as he headed toward the front door. He wasn't dealing with a dense, fumbling bounty hunter. Whoever the man was, he was skilled and patient. First thing in the morning, Gideon vowed to scout the area and search for clues that might lead him to the man who had shot at and then captured Lori briefly this evening.

He was still unsure of the man's true purpose. The questions the intruder had posed, while holding Lori at knifepoint, sounded as if he were verifying that she *couldn't* identify Tony's killer. Was *he* the killer? Would he leave Lori alone now that he knew she couldn't identify him…?

Gideon snapped to attention and asked himself at what point in time he had convinced himself that Lorelei Russell hadn't committed murder. He wasn't sure, but he was beginning to think the amber-eyed minx really had seduced him into believing her. He swallowed a smile as he opened the front door. She could seduce him every night during this investigation, if she were so inclined, and she wouldn't hear a single complaint from him.

He pulled up short when Clive appeared from the shadows at the head of the stairs and glared down at him.

"Long bath, Marshal."

"A long bath to end a long day."

He climbed the steps and brushed shoulders with Clive, who stared speculatively at him. Then Gideon ambled into his room and closed the door. He wondered if Clive planned to stand guard in the hall between Gideon's room and Lori's. If he did, he'd waste his time and miss sleep.

Gideon flopped on the bed, tired and sated. He dreamed of the flame-haired hellion who scaled walls and brought him to his knees with the kind of incredible passion he never realized existed.

* * *

Reece McCree returned to the bunkhouse at Burgess Ranch and Stage Station sporting a hellish headache, compliments of the surprisingly feisty Miz Russell. Next time he'd know better than to take her for granted.

He inwardly groaned when he noticed Maggie Burgess awaiting him. He was in no mood to answer questions while dealing with this blinding headache. But Maggie gave him no choice because she blocked his path.

"Well? Where have you been?" she demanded tartly.

"Around."

Her back went ramrod stiff and she glowered at him. "*Around* is not a sufficient answer, considering what I'm paying you. Have you checked the trading post to see if Lorelei has sneaked home yet?"

"Despite what you think, I don't answer to anyone," he retorted sarcastically then lit his cheroot. "That's the luxury of my job—"

When she swatted at his cigar, knocking it from his hand, he glared at her. Then he bent to retrieve it from the dirt.

"You are trying my patience, Mister McCree. If you cannot produce satisfactory results in the next few days then I will dismiss you without further pay."

She stared pointedly at the horse he'd been riding. "And you can return my mount, too. That well-bred Pinto is the property of this ranch and stage station. Both of which I intend to sell to the highest bidder," she said huffily. "Far as I'm concerned, the Indians are welcome to this god-awful territory. I don't know why those silly Boomers keep invading the place and insist on having the territory opened to settlers. This uncultured, uncivilized country is not my idea of the promised land!"

Reece arched a brow. "It doesn't bother you that the government promised this territory to *all* the Indian tribes they herded here after confiscating their original properties and sacred ground?" Reece snorted sourly. "The government will inevitably give in to the Boomers and conveniently forget this territory was supposed to belong to all Indian tribes, for as long as rivers run and stars twinkle in the night sky."

"I have my own problems and I don't have time to worry about Indians," Maggie snapped petulantly. "I've lost a husband and foreman. I want to quit this place. But before I go, I want the murderess responsible for Anthony Rogers's untimely death captured and punished."

"Are you certain she is to blame?" Reece questioned as he watched her pace back and forth on the bunkhouse porch.

She wheeled around to glower at him. "I saw what I saw," she insisted stubbornly. "Lorelei is like a black widow who disposes of her mate when she is finished with him."

Reece rubbed his throbbing head. Watching Maggie pace back and forth was making him dizzy. "I'm thinking of pursuing the possibility that there was a bushwhacker in the underbrush," he announced.

"What?" She lurched around, then puffed up with irritation, making her ample breasts heave, drawing his unwanted attention. "I told you what happened that night. Do you think just because I say the killer is a *woman* that I must be mistaken?"

She shook her finger in his face. "First thing in the morning I want you to ride back to the trading post and stand guard until you see that murderess. She has to be around here somewhere. *You're* the one who prophesied she'd come to roost in a familiar place eventually."

"So I did," he murmured as he turned away.

"Good night, Mister McCree," she muttered as she started down the steps. "I have a long hard day of work, thanks to the disappearance of my two hired hands. I have another coach of travelers to greet and feed tomorrow morning. You will *not* be welcome at the table. Buy something at the trading post while you're standing guard."

Reece watched the agitated widow storm to her house. Then he entered the bunkhouse to nod a greeting to Sylvester Jenkins—the one-and-only hired hand left on the premises.

"Was that Maggie I heard yapping like a dog?" Syl asked as he limped over to pour himself a cup of coffee. When he glanced back at Reece, who passed by the lantern, casting light on the injury, he frowned curiously. "What happened to you?"

When Syl tried to inspect the knot on Reece's head, he moved away. "Nothing worth mentioning. I simply forgot to duck."

"You might have to start ducking around Maggie if you don't find Miz Russell soon," Syl said before he sipped his coffee. "Ask me, she's obsessed with seeing Miz Russell convicted of killing Tony before she sells out and moves away. It's like unfinished business hanging over her head."

Reece studied Syl carefully. "Do you believe the girl killed Tony? Or do you think there might have been an unseen sniper gunning for him?"

Syl lifted his thin-bladed shoulders in a noncommittal shrug. "All I know is what Maggie told me."

"Where were you the night Tony died?" he asked abruptly.

Syl took a slow sip of his coffee, then stared into the distance. "Riding fences."

"Do you know anything about Tony's past? Did he confide in you or anyone else?"

"Nope. Most folks in the territory don't like to discuss their past."

"You included?" Reece inquired as he stared pointedly at Syl's stiff leg and wondered how he'd come by the injury.

Syl shrugged enigmatically. "All Tony ever confided in me was that he'd lived southeast of here for a time." He took another sip of coffee then added, "I think he had a lady friend...or two...hereabouts, before he began courting Miz Russell. But he was secretive, not one to kiss and tell."

"You think he was seeing someone besides Miz Russell?" Reece questioned as he dipped a cloth in water and held it against the side of his throbbing head.

"There was always someone. Women liked Tony and he liked women," Syl replied. "But I doubt Miz Russell was the only one he was seeing. Ladies offered him all sorts of invitations, but I don't know them by name."

Reece frowned pensively as he grabbed the whiskey bottle he'd tucked in his leather pouch. "How many ranches are nearby?"

"Four or five. Three belong to Osage families. The other two are Boomer camps. The army patrols don't bother to chase squatters across the Kansas border."

"Maybe I need to check around to see who else might have wanted Tony Rogers out of the way," Reece mused aloud.

"Good idea." Syl watched Reece pop the cork on the liquor bottle. "If you scare up some interesting facts, maybe it'll get Maggie off your back. And mine. She's been nagging at me since we became shorthanded. I'll be glad when she sells out and moves away. I only hope the new owner will hire me."

"She's difficult to work for?" Reece ventured as he sipped his whiskey.

"And then some… Got enough bug juice to spare a friend?" Syl limped over to extend his cup—and Reece wondered again how Syl had come to have that noticeable limp. "It's been a long damn day and I could use a stiff drink," Syl added.

Reece poured a generous amount of liquor into Syl's coffee then said, "Tell me exactly what you thought of Tony Rogers."

Maggie Burgess muttered and scowled her way to the house. "Blast that incompetent hired hand and curse that cocky bounty hunter!" She swore the man was lollygagging about, trying to collect his wages without putting serious effort into apprehending Lorelei Russell.

"How long does he think I'm going to let him drag this out?" she asked no one in particular as she stamped upstairs to her elegantly furnished bedroom.

Her room. The one she didn't have to share with all her brothers and sisters in that shabby shack on the bayou. The room she hadn't had to share with her older husband, either. This was *her* private domain and Hub Burgess had agreed to leave her in peace, except for a few intimate visits. That was their agreement when she married him and he'd pestered her only a handful of times in the six years they were married.

She glanced at the expensive furnishings as she pulled the pins from her dark hair and shook it around her shoulders. This was a far cry from her childhood home, thank God. But it still wasn't good enough. Maggie wanted the best proper society had to offer.

And this wasn't it.

She spat a curse at the infuriating image floating in her mind. She would be gone from here, sitting in the lap of luxury, if not for the unfinished business of Lorelei Russell. She was not getting away with this! Maggie fumed as she discarded her gown. Lorelei would pay her due. Then Maggie would pack up and leave this godforsaken place.

And damn that arrogant bounty hunter for wasting time asking impertinent questions. Starting tomorrow, she would offer his job to any man on the stagecoach who agreed to accept a gunfighter's wages and promised quick results.

Competition was what Reece McCree needed, the sarcastic scoundrel. She wasn't wasting another week with his nonsense.

Maggie flounced on her feather bed and blew out an agitated breath. All that kept her going these days was visions of elegant hotels and restaurants in a thriving city. She would become the envy of her family. They had laughed at her dreams, but all of them would be wishing to exchange places with her one day soon.

The thought of lounging in luxurious accommodations put a smile on her face. There would be a wealthy suitor in her future, she promised herself. Someone with style, polished manners and enough money to shower her with jewels and fashionable clothing. After touring the world, she would have at least two grand mansions, complete with servants, to return home to when she tired of extensive traveling.

With visions of grandeur dancing in her head, Maggie snuggled into her soft bed and fell asleep.

The next morning when Lori came downstairs she noticed her father's abrupt manner toward Gideon, who took it in stride. He was used to being treated without respect—and she'd been guilty of that, too, come to think of it.

After her ordeal and Gideon's lack of trust, she knew how it felt to be looked upon with suspicion and treated like a second-class citizen. No one had questioned her integrity or morals until she'd had the notorious distinction of having her name plastered on Wanted posters. She had been labeled a criminal and that incensed her.

Gideon had been ridiculed because of his job and his mixed heritage. Watching her father cast Gideon disparaging glances and all but ignore him was too much for Lori to bear. She was sensitive to his plight, as well as her own.

"A word, please, Papa," she murmured as she strode over to pour herself a cup of coffee.

"I've had more than one word to say to that lawman and none of them were pleasant," her father huffed, then sent another sizzling glower toward the back of Gideon's raven head while he ate breakfast. "And you shouldn't be downstairs where someone might walk in and see you. At least Gideon and I agree on that count."

With her father at her heels, Lori ascended the steps, then ducked around the corner. "I appreciate your attempt to protect me from harm, but you need to have faith that you've trained me well enough to take care of myself."

"With pistols, rifles, knives and hand-to-hand combat, yes," he agreed as he glared down the steps to where Gideon sat. "Now we're discussing a hard-edged man who's accustomed to wielding authority and knows how to use—and abuse—power."

"Like you when you were a high-ranking military officer?" she supplied helpfully.

He scowled at that. "I tried not to abuse my power."

"Did you occasionally use it to your advantage?"

He scowled again. "Once or twice, but this is different.

You were alone with Gideon during the cross-country trek."

"That's true, but I also traveled alone with his younger brother, Glenn, until Gideon rejoined us."

"*How* young?" Clive demanded, brows furrowed.

"Twenty-six."

Clive muttered under his breath.

"Let me repeat," she said emphatically. "I can take care of myself around men, the respectful and disrespectful ones alike. Have you already forgotten that I thwarted an abduction attempt just last night in this very hallway?"

Clive blew out an agitated breath. "No, I haven't forgotten...but I don't like Gideon Fox."

"I'm sorry to hear that, Papa, because I'm exceptionally fond of him," she admitted. "If he manages to clear my name in this murder case then he's going to become my very favorite man on the planet." She grinned impishly at her father. "Present company excluded, of course."

Her attempt to cajole him back to good humor was marginally effective. He stared at her with intense hazel eyes that sought to bore into her private thoughts.

"How much do you like him, Lorelei?" he asked.

"At lot. More than anyone else I've met."

"Damn it, you know he leads a gypsy lifestyle, riding all over the territory to hunt down criminals. His dangerous profession makes him the worst kind of candidate for a husband," he lectured.

"Sort of like marrying a soldier who fights one battle after another and moves to one military post after another?"

Clive gnashed his teeth. "All right, so your mother moved all over creation with me. I can't see you following Gideon Fox while he's on foray. People try to shoot at him all the time, I'd imagine."

"People have been shooting at *me* lately. We seem to have a lot in common."

Her father rolled his eyes at her dry humor.

"I didn't say I planned to follow Gideon to the ends of the earth," she reminded her father.

But *if* he asked, *after* he said he loved her madly and couldn't live without her, she'd do it at the drop of a hat.

Unfortunately, that wasn't going to happen. There was no fairy-tale ending, she told herself sensibly. Even if Gideon wouldn't admit that he was merely killing time with her during this investigation, *she* knew it.

"All the same, I don't want you to get your heart broken," her father said. "He's a bad risk—"

"Am I interrupting?" This from Gideon who'd moved silently up the steps to join them.

"Yes, as a matter of fact," Clive said in a clipped tone, then grunted uncomfortably when Lori gouged him with her elbow.

"No, you aren't," she told Gideon then stared deliberately at her father. "*You* be nice."

His reply was a snort.

"Thank you for breakfast, Clive," Gideon said politely.

"Don't mention it."

"I'm going to ride over to Burgess Ranch and Stage Station to ask a few questions and have a look around," Gideon announced.

"Then you'd best pin on your badge, so no one tries to blow your head off," Clive suggested in a tone that indicated he wouldn't mind doing it himself.

"I'm coming with you," Lori volunteered.

Gideon shook his raven head. "You're staying out of sight while your father tends to business and waits on customers."

"And what am I supposed to do here?" she grumbled.

"I don't know. Knit something," Gideon suggested.

"I don't knit."

He slid a Peacemaker from his left holster. "Then make yourself useful by cleaning my pistol. I don't want it to misfire after getting wet in the downpour the other day."

Scowling, Lori accepted his Peacemaker.

"Good, you look like you'd like to use it on him, too," her father observed as Gideon descended the steps.

She cocked her head and peered up at her father. "What would you do if it came to pass that Gideon began to like me as much as I like him?"

"I'll borrow that pistol and shoot myself," her father said before he lurched around to descend the steps.

"Then it's a good thing marriage isn't in my future," she murmured as she strode off to clean the pistol. "We'd end up with a wedding and a funeral."

Chapter Fourteen

Gideon took the business of scouting the wooded area near the trading post where the shot had been fired the previous night very seriously. He checked for boot prints, horse prints and shell casings. Sure enough, he found a discarded cartridge and a man's boot prints, but no sign of a horse.

Canvassing a wider area that led to and from the sniper's nest in the underbrush near the river, Gideon discovered a cigar butt, horse tracks and more boot prints. He frowned pensively as he squatted down to compare the prints to the ones by the river. Then he shifted his attention to the window of Clive Russell's upstairs bedroom.

"That's strange," he mused aloud.

"You there! Are you looking for a ferry ride across Winding River?"

Gideon rose to his feet, then ambled toward the young man who'd apparently arrived for work. He was short, stout, raven-haired, dark-eyed and looked to be in his mid-twenties. Full-blood Osage, Gideon guessed. The man's eyes widened when he noticed the badge Gideon had pinned on his leather vest.

For the most part, Gideon didn't display the badge because most white folks were leery about offering information to lawmen. But Clive had recommended it—probably because he wouldn't mind seeing Gideon shot by the nearest outlaw.

"If you're looking for whoever shot Tony Rogers I can tell you it wasn't Miz Lorelei."

Gideon inwardly smiled at the man's blind loyalty to his employer's daughter. Another secret admirer, no doubt.

"I'm inclined to believe that myself," Gideon confided then extended his hand. "Deputy U.S. Marshal Gideon Fox. I used to work for the Osage Police near Pawhuska. My family is from the Heart-Stays Clan."

"John Little Calf." He smiled cordially. "My clan is the Big Hills People. I've been working part-time for Clive Russell since Lorelei disappeared."

"You were well acquainted with Lorelei before the shooting?" Gideon prompted.

John nodded his head. "I am one of her many friends and admirers."

"Figures." Gideon mumbled, drawing John's quizzical stare. "How well did you know Tony Rogers?"

John shrugged a thick-bladed shoulder, making his long black braids ripple over his chest. "Well enough. I saw him here on occasion, while gathering supplies. I recall a few women vying for his attention at the trading post. But I don't know them by name. I've also filled in occasionally at the stage station the past year when Hub Burgess and his wife were traveling. Tony was a hardworking man and a fair-minded boss, even to the two white men who went chasing after Lorelei. They were short on ambition."

"What about the other hired hand?"

"Sylvester Jenkins?" He shrugged nonchalantly. "I suppose he got along all right with Tony. But I was only there for a week at a time. Then I returned to our family farm to catch up on my work."

"Do you have any reason to want Tony dead?" Gideon asked for shock value.

John's surprised expression was answer enough. "No. Except that he courted Lorelei and I never worked up the nerve to do it myself."

"How many other men around here envied Tony's close association with Lori?"

John smiled wryly. "You'll need a notepad if you want me to list all the names. She's a favorite in the area. She's kind, considerate and she delivers supplies to families who cannot always come themselves. She treats our people as equals. Not like some whites who intrude on our reservation lands and look at us with disdain," he added in a bitter tone.

When Gideon nodded in agreement and turned away, John called after him. "Find the man who shot Tony Rogers. I know it wasn't Lorelei. I can feel it in my heart, Gideon Fox."

Gideon ambled over to fetch Pirate, then headed northeast toward Burgess Stage Station. The ten-mile jaunt on the stagecoach route gave him too much time to reflect on his obsession with Lori. And it didn't sound as if he was the only one around here who was fascinated with that golden-eyed, flame-haired beauty.

Gideon couldn't pinpoint the time and day when the emotions he'd kept in cold storage for a decade began to give him fits. Naturally, he was physically attracted to her. Most men seemed to be, his brother included. Plus, John Little Calf insisted she was kind, generous, caring and willing to help her neighbors and customers.

He wondered why he was the one who got on the wrong side of her feisty nature and her sharp tongue. He freely admitted that Lori wasn't your garden-variety female. Not with an ex-army officer for a father, who had trained her to hold her own against the unwanted advances of men. She was competent, bright, beautiful, witty and—

When Pirate pricked up his ears, Gideon reflexively plastered himself against his horse's neck. A gunshot ripped through the trees and whistled past his head. Reining sideways, Gideon made a beeline toward the spot where the shot was fired. Puzzled, he glanced at the river bend that was clogged with trees, making it difficult to see in either direction. He frowned when he noticed stepping-stones on the riverbank. The only telltale clue Gideon noticed was one heel print from a boot in front of the nearest stone.

"Come on, Pirate," he murmured to his valuable horse, whose keen senses had saved Gideon's life more times than he could count. "Unless you want to take a swim, we can't find out who took that shot then floated away."

An hour later, Gideon drew Pirate to a halt on the rise of ground overlooking the stagecoach station. A two-story clapboard home, bunkhouse, oversize barn and several corrals filled with horses sat in the distance. Cattle and sheep grazed in adjoining pastures. The place looked a mite run-down, what with untrimmed grass and weeds waving in the breeze. He supposed that was to be expected since the owner and foreman had died recently.

Gideon rode downhill, noting the spacious house abutting a grove of trees and creek that provided a convenient water supply for the owners and their livestock. There were two groves of trees on either side of the gargantuan barn. Gideon veered toward the one Lori claimed a sniper had used for cover while he fired a fatal shot at Tony Rogers.

From his position in the shadows, he saw a

woman—Widow Burgess, he presumed—exit the house and head toward the stage station that sat beside the corrals. Maggie Burgess was well dressed and extremely attractive with her shapely figure and chestnut-brown hair.

Unfortunately, she didn't draw Gideon's masculine interest. For some reason, he'd developed a single-minded fascination for a flame-haired, golden-eyed temptress, who had quickly learned how and where to touch him and make him forget everything he ever knew.

Giving himself a mental kick in the seat of the breeches, Gideon focused on the widow, who veered toward the simply constructed cabin. He predicted she was on her way to check on the meal she planned to serve incoming passengers.

A tall, lanky man with thin-bladed shoulders and a slight limp exited the barn. In the distance, Gideon heard the clatter of a stagecoach and the pounding of hooves. Good. He wanted the inhabitants of the station occupied while he scouted for clues without someone looking over his shoulder.

This was critical, Gideon reminded himself as he dismounted to survey the area where the fatal shot was fired. Gideon squatted down to take a close look then cursed when he realized the area had been wiped clean by recent rains. There were no footprints or shell casings to indicate anyone had fired three shots from this location. Which made it impossible to prove Lori's claim that someone else had shot Tony while he and Lori were together.

"I wondered when you'd show up."

Gideon wheeled on his haunches, reflexively drawing his pistol in one swift motion that testified to years of practice. When the man who'd called out to him emerged from the underbrush with his hands in the air, grinning wryly, Gideon reholstered his Peacemaker.

"Reece McCree, it's been a long damn time." Gideon shook his hand and added, "I heard you were dead."

The bounty hunter, who matched Gideon in size, stature and mixed breeding, smiled in greeting. "Never believe rumors, Fox. You know better than that."

Reaching into his vest pocket, Gideon retrieved the cigar butt that he'd recovered this morning near the trading post then handed it to Reece. "Yours, I presume. I found this in the trees near the place where you waited to scale the wall and pounce on Lori. I've never known you to miss very often with a rifle or pistol." He glared disdainfully at his former friend. "You might as well know that I take serious offense to you taking potshots and trying to kidnap a woman under my protection."

Without changing expression, Reece tucked the evidence in his pocket. "Careless of me." He lit a fresh cheroot.

"What the hell were you trying to do last night?" Gideon growled irritably. "*Scare* Lori into confessing to murder?"

Reece puffed leisurely on his cigar, sending a cloud of smoke drifting into the air. "I didn't take the shot," he said very simply. "Like you, I rarely miss with a pistol or rifle. I was standing off to the west, as I've been doing every night for the past few days. I anticipated the woman would sneak home. I wasn't expecting you to be with her, however. How did that come to pass?"

"I'm still a marshal, working an investigation," Gideon reminded him. "Unlike you, I didn't put my gun up for hire."

Reece frowned darkly. "I discovered there are times when a marshal is restricted by laws and killers walk free."

"I can't argue with that." Gideon arched a curious

brow. "So why did you take this particular case for bounty money?"

Reece grinned around the cigar he had clamped between his teeth. "Why not? A beautiful woman wanted for murder? It's an intriguing case. And she *is* beautiful and well rounded in all the right places. I should know. I had the good fortune of holding her close for a few minutes last night during our question-and-answer session. It was all very enjoyable until she put a knot on my head. The woman is a wildcat…. I like that about her."

Gideon tried extremely hard not to react to the teasing taunt, for Reece was studying him all too closely with silver-gray eyes trained to observe every detail. Hell, watching Reece look for telling reactions was like looking at himself in the mirror because he used the same tactics.

Reece McCree had been an exceptional Deputy U.S. Marshal until he became personally involved in a case. Like Gideon was now. The incident had ended badly and bitterness had consumed Reece. He'd turned in his badge and disappeared from sight for over a year. There had been rumors of his death and other rumors indicating he'd turned to bounty hunting and took only the most dangerous cases that left him traveling hither and yon.

"I thought it was odd that Lori's abductor asked several questions about whether she could positively identify the supposed sniper. Where were you when Anthony Rogers died? And what did you have against him? Or were *you* hunting him for reward money?" he asked with rapid-fire precision.

Reece's bronzed face became an unreadable mask. Gideon swore he was looking at his reflection in a mirror again. Like Reece, Gideon had shut down emotionally on dozens of occasions.

The exception being Lori's case. He'd tried to remain uninvolved. And look where that got him. In too deep.

"Was he the elusive killer you've been tracking since you turned in your badge?" Gideon persisted.

"No."

"Did you kill him and let Lori take the blame?"

"Hell, no!"

"Then what's your connection to Tony Rogers, if he wasn't the man who killed Angela—"

"Don't!" Reece interrupted sharply. "I've spent over a year trying to forget. The last thing I need is you bringing it up."

Gideon surveyed Reece's angular features. He wondered how it felt to be haunted by memories that a year's time still couldn't cure. If something tragic happened to Lori, he wondered if a decade would be enough time to ease the pain.

Gideon didn't want to find out. He wanted to solve this case and spread the word that Lorelei Russell had nothing to do with Tony's death so no one else would hunt her for bounty.

And from now on, he promised himself resolutely, he'd compensate for mistrusting her and taunting her unmercifully. He'd be kind, understanding of her crusade to clear her name and exceptionally considerate of her needs.

She deserved that after the cynical way he'd treated her.

"Tell me something, Fox."

"If I can."

"Do *you* think she did it? The bewitching but feisty little wildcat I tangled with last night?"

"No, I don't think she's involved."

Reece smiled slyly as he puffed on his cheroot. "And

which head would be doing your thinking in this case, Fox?"

"Are you implying I'm involved with her?" he asked with a carefully blank stare.

"I know you are," Reece said matter-of-factly. "I was there last night when the shot was fired. I saw you put yourself in harm's way to protect her."

"She's in my custody," Gideon defended self-righteously.

Reece snickered. "Is that what you call that midnight swim the two of you enjoyed yesterday evening?"

Gideon felt heat rise instantly in his face to stain his cheeks. He gnashed his teeth when Reece waggled his thick brows suggestively. "You need to shut up, McCree," Gideon muttered. "That's between her and me."

"I'll say it was," Reece teased unmercifully. "In the past, I've seen you *cover* a prisoner under your protection with *gunfire,* but not with your *body.* That was never your style." His expression sobered. "But a man can change. I did."

Apparently so. Gideon didn't feel like the same man he'd been before the beguiling female walked from the fog. She'd turned his life upside down and resurrected emotions he'd kept dead and buried for a decade.

Hands on hips, Gideon blew out his breath. "Are you going to help me solve this case or pester the hell out of me?"

Reece bit down on his cheroot and grinned wickedly. "I plan to do both because I find your dealings with this accused murderess beyond fascinating." He cocked his head and studied Gideon astutely. "Just so we're clear, are you using each other for sex or is something else going on with you two?"

Gideon purposely ignored the personal question and

fired one of his own. "Tell me why you captured Lori and demanded to know if she could identify the supposed sniper."

"Because I wanted to know if she *could* identify the sniper," Reece said reasonably.

"So you don't think she's guilty, either," Gideon speculated.

"No." Reece's smile faded. "I'm here to deal with Tony's killer. The Widow Burgess is paying me to do it. She's complained regularly about my methods because she's anxious to wrap up this case."

"Is she as attractive up close as she is at a distance?" Gideon questioned, scrutinizing Reece carefully.

"Attractive enough, but she plans to sell out and quit this place after losing her husband and foreman. She's thoroughly convinced Lorelei Russell fired the fatal shot then dashed off. I've questioned her, but she's adamant about what she thought she saw. She doesn't want Lorelei going free, just because she's a woman."

Gideon stared into the distance. "Someone took a shot at me at the bend of the river about an hour before I arrived here. That wasn't you, was it?"

"Nope. I was here."

"What about Sylvester Jenkins?"

"He was gone for a while but he returned to feed the horses he's hitching up to take the coach to the trading post and ferry, and then to the next station in the Pawnee Nation. But I'm not ready to rule him out completely."

"And the widow?" Gideon inquired.

"She was in the station making stew this morning. Then she returned to the house for a while. I saw her walking out to check on the meal a few minutes ago."

Gideon frowned pensively. "Whoever took that shot last night and again today has to be lurking around somewhere.

My guess is that he's trying to discourage me from searching for clues and protecting Lori."

"Could be another bounty hunter who wants to collect the reward," Reece suggested. "I've encountered several unscrupulous scoundrels in the business over the past year."

"I'm wondering if whoever killed Tony is trying to prevent Lori from presenting her side of the story in court."

"I agree," Reece said.

Gideon's eyes narrowed on his former cohort. "So tell me again why you've decided to give this case your undivided attention. Was Tony a fugitive using an alias? Does he have a criminal past that interests you?"

Reece blew a smoke ring in the air, then stared solemnly at Gideon. "No. He's my stepbrother and I want his killer to face the consequences. Not like the case that left the woman I loved dead and her killer still running loose."

While Reece made another thorough sweep of the bushes, hoping to find overlooked clues, Gideon waited for the stagecoach passengers to take their meal then pile into the conveyance that traveled to the trading post. He noticed Widow Burgess cast him several curious glances after she saw his badge, but she went about her duties. No doubt, the shapely chestnut-haired widow was itching to get him alone so she could fire questions about her foreman's murder at him.

Sure enough, once the stagecoach rolled off, the widow, who looked to be about five or six years older than Lori, marched up to him. She stared deliberately at his badge then narrowed her dark eyes on him.

"I hope you're here to inform me that Lorelei Russell is under arrest and awaiting trial."

"No, ma'am, I'm not."

"The name is Maggie, not ma'am," she corrected as she rearranged the pile of hair atop her head. "I am not that old yet, Marshal…?" She arched her brow, waiting for him to offer his name.

"Deputy U.S. Marshal Gideon Fox."

"Then what *are* you here to tell me?" she questioned as she motioned for him to follow her into the house.

His gaze dropped to the feminine sway of her hips, but it didn't remain there long. When compared to a certain shapely Lori, the widow couldn't measure up.

Gideon forced himself to focus on business. "There are too many unanswered questions about this case," he said on his way up the front steps.

"Oh? Such as what? It looked cut-and-dried to me when I found Lorelei standing over Tony's body, holding a smoking gun."

"But you didn't actually *see* her fire the weapon at him, did you?" Gideon probed intently.

Maggie blew out a frustrated breath. She strode over to the stove to pour herself a cup of tea, then offered one to Gideon, which he politely declined. "No, but I heard the shots and witnessed the end result," she maintained.

"How many shots?" he questioned.

"Two or three, I think." Maggie sank down in a chair at the dining table. "Everything happened so fast. I became upset when I dashed over to see Tony dead on the ground."

Gideon frowned. According to Lori, the sniper fired three shots and she fired one. "Two shots or three?" he persisted.

"I don't recall for sure," she admitted. "I was on my way from the house to the station to make sure everything was in order to serve passengers on the early-morning stage from Greenleaf Store in the Creek Nation."

Gideon was familiar with the place since he'd passed through it several times during forays to track outlaws.

"I heard the shots and dashed around the barn to see Lorelei holding Tony's spare pistol." Her intent gaze zeroed in on him. "What would you presume if *you* arrived on that unpleasant scene, Marshal Fox?"

"Probably the same thing." Yet, he'd reached the point that he wanted the woman who intrigued him to be innocent of wrongdoing. "Reece McCree thinks perhaps there was a sniper hiding in the underbrush."

She sniffed in annoyance. "That arrogant bounty hunter is wasting my time and money with his nonchalant approach to finding Lorelei. I don't know who else would want to kill Tony, except the woman he'd been seeing for the past three months. I suspect he'd grown tired of her and tried to break off their affair. She must have gone a little mad and decided that if she couldn't have him then no one could."

Gideon was sorry to say he'd worked cases exactly like that.

"How do you know Tony was courting Lorelei?"

She shrugged casually. "He told me so, for one. I've seen them together on occasion. So have other folks around here."

Gideon glanced around the expensively furnished home. "John Little Calf mentioned there were at least two other women who showed an interest in Tony."

"Oh? Who?" Maggie questioned interestedly.

"I'm not sure yet. But a jealous husband or forsaken lover might be involved in this case. Someone could have fired shots from the underbrush and let Lorelei Russell take the blame. Since you can't *swear* you saw exactly what happened, we have only circumstantial evidence. I doubt it will hold up in court. Jumping to conclusions doesn't solve cases."

He'd done it with Lori and he sorely regretted it.

Maggie slumped back in her chair and stared at him for a long, pensive moment, as if wrestling with some sort of decision. "I suppose you're right," she said eventually. "I didn't know there were other women in the area that might be resentful or jealous of Lori's connection to Tony. Maybe I assumed too much and let my grief and anger over losing my husband and foreman consume me. I was striking out for revenge and justice to ease my sorrow."

"Understandable," Gideon commented. "Nonetheless, I'm taking down the signs you've posted and I intend to notify other stage stations to remove the Wanted posters."

"Do what you must, Marshal Fox." She sat upright in her chair and leaned her forearms on the table. "I suppose I should pay Clive Russell a visit to pick up supplies and apologize for believing the worst about his daughter. I demanded vigilante justice without gathering all the facts.

"But in my defense," she added, tilting her chin to a proud angle, "law and order doesn't always reach across this wide-open territory. My husband served as lawman and judge on several occasions. I suppose I tried to take up where he left off in order to track down Tony's killer."

"This case is better left to proper authorities who have legal jurisdiction," Gideon stated firmly.

He didn't need a hotheaded, grieving widow resuming her crusade after he rode off today. He wanted her promise that she would give Lori the benefit of the doubt and let him handle the case.

"I agree that you should speak to Clive Russell and make amends," Gideon said. "You lost a foreman and Clive is dealing with concern over the charges against his daughter, as well as the damage done to her reputation."

Maggie nodded her head as she stared into her teacup. "I'll contact Clive when I have the chance, Marshal Fox." She glanced up to stare intently at him. "But in my mind, Lorelei is still a prime suspect and should not be discounted."

Gideon pivoted toward the door. "I hope to wrap up this case soon. Reece informed me that you plan to sell out."

"Indeed I do," she said as she followed him outside.

"Have you decided where you're headed?"

"Anywhere but this uncivilized country and the Louisiana bayous where I grew up," she remarked. "There has to be a better way of life in big cities like Saint Louis or Kansas City."

"Thank you for your time," Gideon said then strode off.

He doubted he could convince the attractive widow to change her story or her thinking, but at least she had admitted there were other possible explanations.

Gideon tore down the Reward posters on his way to retrieve Pirate. He didn't know how many stage stations Maggie had contacted and asked to circulate the posters, but he suspected there were too damn many.

He wadded up the posters offering a hefty reward for Lori's capture. Then he tucked them in his saddlebag. It would take time to call off bounty hunters looking to collect the reward on Lori's head. He made a mental note to post a few notices of his own during his return trip to marshal headquarters and the Fox family ranch.

Chapter Fifteen

Lori paced the confines of her upstairs bedroom until she swore she'd worn a rut in the carpet. Gideon had been gone for hours. All day, in fact, and she was worried about him. Plus, inactivity made her crazy. She couldn't wait until dark so she could prowl outside and pounce on whoever had tried to blast holes in her last night….

Her frustrated thoughts trailed off when she heard voices and footfalls on the staircase. She ducked behind the partially opened door. When Gideon came into view at the far end of the hall, she veered around the door, eager to greet him. But she froze in her tracks when she saw the shadowed silhouette of the man trailing behind Gideon.

Instant recognition and alarm assailed her. Hurriedly, she tucked herself behind the door. Didn't Gideon realize the man he'd brought upstairs was the very same one who had attacked her? Her captor certainly wasn't wearing the metal bracelets Gideon had clamped on *her*.

Lori swallowed apprehensively. Dear God, was Gideon

here to arrest her because he'd discovered planted evidence that supposedly proved her guilt?

While her heart pounded like a galloping stallion, Lori darted to the window. Before Gideon reached her room she climbed out, taking the same route she'd used the previous night when she joined him in the river.

Now she was running *away* from him as fast as she could.

"Lori?" Gideon called out softly.

So deceptively soft, unlike his usual tone, she noted as she grabbed hold of the gutter pipe to scramble hurriedly downward. Something had changed, she realized. He was probably trying to deceive her so she wouldn't realize he was no longer her ally but rather her antagonist once again.

Feelings of anger and betrayal swamped her as she bounded to the ground then dashed toward the concealment of the trees. She was on her own again. It was up to her to figure out who had lurked in the underbrush to kill Tony that fateful night.

Gideon had never been eager to take her side. Now he was back to being his cynical self and she was hugely disappointed in him.

When Gideon poked his raven head out the window and scowled, a jolt of betrayal shot through her like a lightning bolt—straight to the heart. Then the other man appeared at the window beside Gideon. Lori studied his bronzed face, his shaggy black hair and high cheekbones that indicated Gideon's new sidekick shared his mixed heritage.

No wonder the stranger reminded her so much of Gideon. Both were ruggedly handsome, handy with weapons and exceptionally skilled as scouts and trackers.

They would test her mettle, but she vowed to remain one step ahead of them.

Lurching around, Lori zigzagged through the copse of cottonwood trees to retrieve her horse before the two men charged after her. She ducked into the back door of the barn then hurriedly stuffed a bit in Drifter's mouth. She slung the saddle on his back and quickly fastened the girth strap. As an afterthought, she exited the front of the barn to fetch Pirate and the stranger's skewbald Pinto from the hitching post.

No doubt, Maggie had convinced Gideon and his new friend that Lori was guilty as sin. They'd come to drag her away.

If Gideon—the traitor—and his new cohort planned to chase her down then they'd do it riding horses pinned in the corrals. None of them compared to Pirate and the powerful-looking skewbald pinto she recognized as the one that had belonged to Hub Burgess—another sign Gideon and his sidekick believed Maggie's version of the deadly incident.

Drawing the two horses into the barn, Lori bounded onto Drifter's back then ducked out the back door. She led Pirate out of shouting distance of the barn because she knew the stallion responded to Gideon's piercing whistle. Gouging Drifter in the flanks, she raced off, leading the two horses behind her and cursing Gideon's betrayal with every breath she took.

"Hell and damn," Gideon grumbled as he stared out the window.

"This doesn't say much for your ability to keep a prisoner in custody," Reece mocked wryly.

"The woman has a mind of her own and an independent streak a mile wide. She must've decided to do her own investigating while I wasn't around to discourage her."

Gideon pivoted on his heels and strode from the room.

"Damn, if she gets herself shot, I'm going to strangle her!"

Reece chuckled in amusement. "Good idea, Fox. Maybe you can stab and poison her while you're at it. That'll show her."

On his way down the hall, Gideon hurled a glare over his shoulder. "You are no help whatsoever, McCree."

"Really? I thought I was the very picture of helpfulness. Watching you bungle an investigation and misplace your lovely prisoner is the most fun I've had all year."

"Glad I'm providing entertainment," Gideon muttered, his voice oozing with sarcasm.

He halted abruptly at the foot of the steps and waited until Clive's customer exited the trading post. Despite Clive's glance—one that testified to his dislike—Gideon stalked toward him.

"Did you bother to check on your daughter at all today?" Gideon demanded accusingly.

The former military officer puffed up with so much indignation he nearly burst the seams of his cream-colored shirt. "Of course I checked on her. I took her lunch and supper tray upstairs. Why are you giving me the third degree?" He shot Reece a quick glance, then zeroed in on Gideon. "Did you uncover any evidence whatsoever while you were gone the whole blessed day?"

"I know she didn't commit the crime," Gideon declared.

Clive rolled his eyes. "Any idiot knows that."

Behind Gideon, Reece snickered. Damn the man. "When was the last time you saw her?"

"An hour ago. Why all these questions?"

"Because she's gone!" Gideon huffed in frustration.

Clive's hazel eyes nearly popped from their sockets. *"Gone?"* he tweeted. "How can that be?"

"If she didn't sneak downstairs and out the door while your back was turned then she must have sprouted wings and flown out the damn window."

Clive scowled. "Why the devil would she leave?"

"I don't know. I gave her specific orders to stay here and clean my spare pistol…. Oh hell. She's armed *and* missing."

On that unsettling thought, Gideon lurched toward the door. Reece was a step behind him. Clive muttered sourly when another customer arrived, forcing him to remain behind.

Good, thought Gideon. He didn't need Lori's overprotective father breathing down his neck and criticizing him while he tracked her down, then gave her the good shaking she deserved for defying his orders.

When I catch up with her, I won't stop with giving her a good shaking—Gideon didn't have the chance to finish the spiteful thought. He was halfway to the barn when he realized his horse was gone. So was Reece's.

Reece chuckled beside him. "That answers the question of *when* she took flight. Clever of her to take the two fastest horses on the place when she left."

"I told you she wasn't your average female."

"Certainly not. Otherwise I wouldn't have a knot on my head and your mind and body wouldn't be in constant turmoil."

"It's time once again for you to clam up because you *aren't* helping," Gideon muttered resentfully.

He charged to the corral to commandeer the first horse he could get his hands on. Within a few minutes, he and Reece had saddled two brown geldings and raced off, following the three sets of fresh tracks he picked up behind the barn. If he didn't overtake Lori soon, darkness would descend and she would be impossible to find. Especially since she was skilled at going to ground and exceptionally familiar with the area.

"I'll follow the tracks as far as I can," Gideon said to Reece. "You travel perpendicular. Maybe she'll circle back here, in hopes of keeping watch for our mysterious sniper tonight."

With an agreeable nod, Reece reined east.

Gideon cursed Lori up one side and down the other. Why in hell had he allowed himself to become mixed up with that independent-minded, high-spirited female who defied his orders every chance she got? Just when he'd decided to put his faith in her, and planned to compensate for his lack of trust and mistreatment, she ran off, making him chase her all over creation.

The next time he became involved with a woman she was going to be meek, mild and domesticated. She was going to be able to knit, too, he decided spitefully. She wasn't going to thumb her nose at his direct orders, either.

Lori muttered irritably when the two horses trailing behind her kept lurching sideways and tugging on her arm. Pirate was the worst because Gideon's loud whistle erupted in the distance. Curse it, she didn't want to release the two horses. Unfortunately, Pirate would yank her arm from its socket if he kept resisting her.

Finally, she stopped to tether the two horses to a tree. That done, she raced off again, hoping to circle the trading post then cover her tracks beside the river. Soon, John Little Calf would dock the ferry for the night. Then she'd lie in wait to see if Gideon and her would-be abductor arrived to capture her. Or shoot her. Whichever came first.

"Damn him," she muttered when Gideon's tormenting image floated across her mind. He'd betrayed her in the worst possible way. He'd turned on her now that she'd fallen in love with him. He'd become the curse of her life—

"Awk!" Lori's breath gushed out in a pained grunt when a man's body soared through the air and slammed into her.

She cartwheeled from the saddle, then bolted to her feet. He grabbed her ankle and jerked her sideways, tossing her off balance. Frantic to escape the powerfully built man who'd teamed up with Gideon, she kicked his shoulder with her boot heel.

"Hey, wildcat. I already have a knot on my head, thanks to you. Stop fighting me. I'm on your side!"

"Like hell you are!" she growled, then gouged him again.

"I'm Gideon's friend," he said with a pained grunt.

"Then you're no friend of mine." She reached for a fallen limb and tried to whack him on the head.

He dodged the oncoming blow then wrenched the makeshift club from her hand. She grabbed another one.

"Will you calm down, wildcat!" he barked at her.

"This is as calm as I'm ever going to get if you don't let me go!" she snarled in her most intimidating tone.

They were like two swordsmen locked in heated battle. She thrust her club at the man who held her ankle. He parried adeptly. She tried to smack his head again, but he deflected every brain-scrambling strike. When she tried to slam her club against his wrist, he blocked the attack. Then she aimed for his shoulder but he countered that strike, too.

To her surprise and dismay someone sneaked up behind her to yank the tree limb from her hand, just as she reared back to deliver another powerful blow. That someone, no doubt, was the traitor she'd made the disastrous mistake of falling in love with. Left without a makeshift weapon, she reached for Gideon's spare Peacemaker she'd tucked in the back band of her breeches.

"Oh, no you don't, hellion," Gideon scowled as he clamped his fist in the back of her shirt and yanked her against him to retrieve the pistol before she grabbed hold of it.

He swore foully when she gave him a mule kick in the shins and twisted sideways, attempting to wrest free. But Gideon Fox was no novice at hand-to-hand combat. He swung his leg to take her feet out from under her. Unfortunately, she was ready and waiting. She leaped over his outstretched leg as if she were jumping rope.

"Hell and damn," Gideon muttered when he nearly spun himself into the ground with his unsuccessful maneuver. "Stop fighting me. What is wrong with you?"

"*You're* what's wrong with me," she railed, as she took full advantage of the fact that Gideon had stumbled off balance.

She jerked her arm from his grasp, but he grabbed hold again—until she bit his fingers.

"Ouch! Damn it, hellion!" he yelled at her.

"Careful, Gid," Reece said, battling a chuckle, now that he wasn't engaged in heated battle with Lori. Gideon had heard Reece singing a different tune while she'd tried to knock him silly. "She might have rabies, what with all that growling and frothing at the mouth in fury."

Lori shrieked when Reece pounced, knocking her face-down in the dirt. She squirmed furiously and struck out in every manner possible when Reece plunked down on top of her. Before she could take another swing at him, he grabbed her wrists and pinned them to the ground.

"Gee, and it only took two of us to subdue her." He smirked. "Hand me the cuffs, Gid."

"I don't have them with me. They're in the saddlebags on Pirate. And where the hell is my horse, hellion?"

"I'm not speaking to you for the rest of my life," she snapped angrily. "Or *your* life. I hope you go first."

Still holding her down, Reece snickered at her fiery remark then glanced over at Gideon.

Reece was enjoying this too damn much.

"This is not funny, Reece, and you can get off her right now!" Gideon demanded sharply.

"And risk suffering another painful blow? Not a chance," Reece refused. "Get some rope. Anything to tie her down."

Gideon stalked around to stare down at her. If he made her say uncle in his unique way, he suspected she'd buck off Reece and go for his throat. So he said, "If you promise to behave I'll have Reece release you."

"I'll behave," she said all too quickly.

"I don't believe her," Reece said. "She's bristling with bad temper. I'll lay odds she'll come up swinging."

Gideon squatted down in front of her. Her golden eyes flared like flaming arrows and her lips curled in disdain.

"You lied to me, damn you," she said with an infuriated hiss. "You deceived me."

He frowned, confused. "What the devil are you talking about? I haven't talked to you since this morning."

"Him." She jerked her tousled red-gold head toward Reece, who was still sitting on her rump and smiling in amusement. "You joined up with the very man who put a knife to my throat and tried to drag me away last night. And *he* calls *you* friend!"

Finally, Gideon understood what had put Lori to flight and left her thinking he'd betrayed her. She must've recognized Reece and assumed he'd joined forces with Gideon so they could arrest her for murder.

"He is a former Deputy U.S. Marshal," Gideon explained as he reached out to comb his fingers through the curly strands that dangled over her flushed face. "He and I worked together for three years."

"So naturally he tried to shoot me last night," she said caustically. "When that didn't work he tried to kidnap me."

"I didn't shoot at you," Reece protested, still holding her in place. "If I had, you'd be wounded or dead. I happen to be an exceptionally good shot. Same as Gideon. Judge Parker doesn't hire law enforcement officers who can't hit the side of a barn, you know."

Her reply was another skeptical scoff.

"This is Reece McCree," Gideon introduced. "He left Judge Parker's force to hunt high-profile killers for bounty. He is also Tony Rogers's stepbrother."

"Tony wasn't pleased when his mother married my father, but he lived and worked with us in the Creek Nation until he was old enough to venture out on his own," Reece elaborated. "Tony and I got along fine. I'm here to find his murderer."

"So you have a personal vendetta against me?" she muttered cynically. "Gee, that makes me feel so much better."

She felt the brawny bounty hunter go still above her. "Are you admitting that *you* killed Tony?"

"Certainly not! I already told you he took a bullet for me when the sniper shot at us," she told Reece. "If you were worth your salt, you and your friend, Fox, would be trying to figure out what Tony was running *from* that earned him a bushwhacking."

"Lori," Gideon said too softly, putting her sense of self-preservation on alert again. "We are on your side, no matter what you think right now. In addition, our mysterious sniper took a shot at me while I was on my way to the stage station this morning."

She jerked up her head sharply and stared warily at him.

Gideon nodded somberly. "I followed the shooter to the river, but I couldn't find any tracks. When I reached the stage station, I discovered it was Reece who had been on hand last night when the shot was fired. He sneaked upstairs for only one purpose. To get answers from you, not abduct you… Let her up, Reece."

"Only if she cries uncle," Reece stipulated.

Gideon and Lori exchanged glances. She glared at him, wondering if he had shared the intimate details of *cry uncle* with his former associate.

"I didn't," he insisted, as if he'd read her mind.

"You didn't what?" Reece asked as he eased off her back and came agilely to his feet.

"Nothing," Gideon said, casting her a discreet glance.

Reece gallantly helped Lori to her feet then doubled over in a bow. "I'm hoping this will be our last tussle, Lorelei." He smiled wryly, his silver-gray eyes glittering with amusement. "I'm still nursing a hellish headache after we tangled last night. I'd rather not battle you again, if you don't mind. You play rough for a girl."

Lori rubbed her stinging wrists then stared accusingly at him. "So do you, Reece." She studied him long and hard. "You really didn't try to kill me last night?"

"Nope." He reached into his vest pocket for a cheroot and lit up. "I wanted to know if you could identify the elusive sniper, but I don't know who shot at you or why. I wanted to question you before I spoke privately with Gideon this morning. After we exchanged information, we joined forces, in hopes of finding the sniper."

Lori expelled a self-deprecating sigh. "I've become so

suspicious of everyone's intentions that I've turned into Gideon Fox."

Gideon scowled and Reece snickered at that.

The anger and frustration drained out of her and she offered Reece a peace-treaty smile. "I'm sorry I assumed the worst about you. When I saw you and Gideon in the hallway together, I thought you'd convinced him that I was responsible for Tony's death and you'd come to take me prisoner."

"You should have trusted me," Gideon grumbled, then gnashed his teeth. "Oh, right. What was I thinking? You've become as much of a cynic as I am."

That was true. Now she understood why Gideon reacted so cautiously when working cases. Blind trust could get you killed, and she'd operated on that philosophy today.

"When you're wanted for murder and have a reward on your head, you don't hang around to find out why a bounty hunter and Deputy U.S. Marshal have come to call," she retorted. "Your tone of voice made me wary, as well, Gideon. You sounded a little too nice, which is completely out of character. So I figured it must be a ploy to trap me."

Reece choked when he tried to inhale smoke and laugh at the same time. "Not accustomed to niceties from Fox?" he wheezed. "Smart woman to question his agenda."

"Go away, Reece," Gideon demanded sourly. "*Again,* you aren't helping."

"No, I told you this is more fun than I've had in ages."

"Make yourself useful and go fetch our horses," Gideon requested in a sticky-sweet voice. *"Please?"*

Reece winked conspiratorially at Lori. "I see why that syrupy tone makes you suspicious. It's not his usual gruff, authoritative style."

When Reece left—*finally*—Gideon reached out to

pull Lori into his arms. Then he kissed her thoroughly, repeatedly. "I'm sorry about the misunderstanding and the tussle."

She reared back in his encircling embrace and studied him with somber, amber eyes. "Why *are* you acting differently all of a sudden?" she asked suspiciously.

"Because I'm convinced you had no part in Tony's death."

Apparently, she was having none of that because she gave an unladylike snort. "When did you come to that conclusion? *After* you spoke to Reece? You certainly weren't willing to believe *me* when *I* told you. Which proves how little faith and respect you have for me."

He inwardly winced because he knew she was right. He owed her a dozen apologies for his bad behavior. "I'm sorry about that, too. But I told you that I have to assume the worst about people to get the job done. Now I know you aren't capable of murdering anyone…except me for doubting you."

He flashed a charming grin, hoping to return to her good graces, but she continued to study him skeptically. "Reece and I compared notes. Now we're both on your side." He tried out his very best smile and said, "Actually, I'm a reasonably nice person once you get past my tough exterior."

She smirked, assuring him that it would take time to convince her of his redeeming qualities. But he vowed to make up for the past week, no matter how long it took.

"And you call me cynical and suspicious?" he murmured when she continued to stare doubtfully at him. He reached out to wipe a smudge of dirt from her creamy cheek. "You turned and ran the instant you thought I'd betrayed you. You didn't ask questions first. That is a shining example of the pot calling the kettle black."

"Fine, Mr. *Kettle,* we're too much alike," she agreed. "But I'm fed up with hiding and being labeled a criminal. Tonight I intend to set a trap and catch whoever is responsible for shooting at me. I don't know if it's the same person who shot Tony or if an unscrupulous bounty hunter is trying to beat Reece to the reward on my head. But I damn well plan to find out."

Gideon nodded pensively as he retrieved the pistol he'd confiscated from Lori. Then he handed it back to her. "You're right in thinking there might be two snipers running loose. But I suspect whoever shot at *me* this morning is the same person who shot at *you* last night.

"When I canvassed the areas where both shots were fired, at the trading post and near the river, I found boot prints and empty shell casings. Unfortunately, the tracks led nowhere. Whoever took the shots cleverly retreated, as if he hadn't been there at all."

He led Lori toward her strawberry roan gelding then boosted her into the saddle. "As for Tony's killer, he might have gone into hiding. Or he could be lurking around, waiting to see if you're convicted of the crime before he skulks off."

"Did you find any useful evidence near the stage station?" she asked while she waited for him to mount the borrowed horse.

"Nothing on the scene. It's rained since the incident. Plus, the sniper carefully removed any evidence that he was there."

Her shoulders slumped defeatedly. "So there is no way I can prove my innocence or the existence of a sniper since I'm the only one who claims to know where the shots originated."

"There is no one to prove you *didn't* see a sniper," Gideon clarified. "According to what Sylvester Jenkins told me when I interviewed him this afternoon, Tony had been courting someone else in the months leading up to his interest in you. John Little Calf mentioned the same thing this morning."

Lori glanced up quickly then frowned. "Are you suggesting a spurned girlfriend? But we know the shooter is a man."

"The one who shot at you and me," he corrected. "We didn't see any boot prints from the night someone shot Tony so we can't say for certain. Did Tony mention another woman or did you hear any rumors that he was seeing any local women?"

Lori frowned pensively. "He mentioned a few families in the area on occasion. But I can understand why a man wouldn't want to drop another woman's name while courting me."

"Reece and I are going to make the rounds in the morning to find out if there is a 'woman scorned' in the area. Either that or a cuckolded husband might have retaliated to spite his cheating wife and eliminate the temptation. I've handled similar cases before."

"Did you speak with Maggie?" she questioned attentively.

He nodded. "She didn't seem to be aware there were other women besides you in Tony's life. I made an effort to drive home the point that we only have circumstantial evidence against you. She finally admitted she didn't actually see what happened, just jumped to conclusions. I ordered her to remove the Reward posters until I close the investigation."

When Reece arrived with both horses in tow, his silver-gray gaze bounced back and forth between them. "Have we kissed and made up yet? We're all done hitting one another, I hope."

Lori nodded and graced Reece with a dimpled grin. Gideon watched his hard-edged friend melt into a puddle of mush. Reece's all-consuming gaze swept over her curvaceous body in masculine appreciation, testifying that she had a potent effect on *all* males of the species. Proof positive that no man was immune to this unique female's dazzling smiles and irrepressible spirit.

Gideon knew his friend had suffered a tragic emotional loss when his fiancée died. Reece lived with the constant torment that her killer remained on the loose. Even so, Reece was captivated with Lori and it showed, just as it had with Gideon's younger brother, Glenn.

"Now that we're all grand friends again," Gideon said as he led the way through the trees, "can we go to the trading post and eat? I'm starving. I plan to grab a quick bite before standing lookout tonight and finding out who's taking potshots at us."

While they rode toward the trading post, Lori questioned Reece about his formative years as Tony's older stepbrother and about Reece's service as a Deputy U.S. Marshal. Although Reece carried a torch, and a burden of guilt because of Angela's death, Lori's attention was good for him and she won him over in nothing flat.

Before long, they were talking and laughing like old friends. Which left Gideon riding in silence and feeling like an extra person in the world. He tried to convince himself he wasn't a tad bit jealous because it gave him time to mull over what Syl Jenkins, Maggie, John Little Calf and Reece had told him earlier.

Someone was definitely lurking about, waiting for the opportunity to collect the reward on Lori's head. Gideon didn't intend to locate the culprit *after* he shot Lori. He didn't want to endure the hellish torment Reece suffered.

Although…Gideon mused as he cast his troubled friend

a pensive glance, Reece didn't look quite so miserable now that he was basking in the glow of Lori's radiant smile. Again, Gideon told himself he wasn't envious or jealous of the undivided attention Lori showed Reece....

But he couldn't quite make himself believe it.

Chapter Sixteen

"Well, it's about damn time," Clive grumbled when Lori slipped in the back door of the trading post after dark.

Her father smothered her in a bear hug and held her protectively while Gideon and Reece filed in behind her. "What is going on around here? Or is a father not supposed to know?"

"I didn't realize Reece was Gideon's former acquaintance and it spooked me," she told her father. "He's the man who—"

She shut her mouth so fast she nearly snipped off the tip of her tongue. Her father's hazel eyes narrowed on Reece, who tried to flash an innocent smile, but her father didn't appear convinced.

"*You* are the man who sneaked in here last night and held my girl at knifepoint?" he growled accusingly.

"I was trying to restrain her but I hadn't planned to draw blood. She turned out to be a handful," Reece explained. "If it makes you feel better, she drew *my* blood when she hammered me on the head with the coatrack."

Her father glanced down at her. "No wonder you ran scared." He focused his disdainful gaze on Gideon and Reece. "You are peas in a pod. If this is any indication of how you bungling lawmen protect my girl then you are dismissed," he said with the authoritative tone of a military officer.

"We are not soldiers under your command," Gideon protested.

"Damn good thing, too. You'd be in the stockade for failure to perform your duties satisfactorily."

"Everything is fine now, Papa," Lori reassured him. "We cleared up all the misunderstandings. Gideon and Reece have learned that Tony was seeing someone else before he turned his attention to me. Do you have any idea whom he was seeing? Did you hear any rumors that might provide promising leads?"

Her questions diverted his attention from Gideon and Reece. He frowned thoughtfully. "I recall a couple of women who fawned over Tony when they were at the post at the same time he was picking up supplies for the ranch and stage station."

Gideon nodded pensively. "John Little Calf thought there were one or two, as well, but he couldn't name names."

"Syl Jenkins thought the same thing. He said Tony didn't mention names but he slipped off at night on a regular basis."

"One of them is Beatrice Ogden," her father informed them. "The other is Theresa Knott. Their families live in the Boomer camp a few miles east of the stage station near the river."

Gideon and Reece muttered sourly. It was evident they had no use whatsoever for the invading whites who squatted on tribal lands and petitioned the government to open the Indian reservations for settlement.

"One of them wouldn't happen to be married, would she?" Gideon asked.

Her father nodded. "Theresa is married, but that didn't stop her from flirting openly with Tony while she was here. However, both women seemed eager for his attention. Bea was buzzing around him, batting her eyes so furiously that she was causing a draft."

Lori strode off to throw together a quick meal for Gideon and Reece while Gideon offered her father an account of the ambush he endured this morning. It bothered her that someone was trying to dispose of Gideon—probably to scare him off and collect the reward without competition. She wondered if Reece would be next on the list since he'd united with Gideon.

Even her father might be in danger, she mused uneasily. The sniper knew she'd returned and he could be waiting to pick off the men protecting her.

The thought unsettled Lori. The haunting torment of watching Tony die trying to protect her made her squirm restlessly while eating her meal.

"Are you all right?" Gideon asked, watching her astutely.

She favored him with a smile. "Thinking the worst about you and Reece tonight upset me. But I'm better now."

The answer seemed to pacify him. But later, when he followed her upstairs, he tugged her into his arms. "I'm sorry you got the wrong impression when I brought Reece here with me. You scared ten years off my life when I realized you were gone. I thought the sniper might have captured you when you dashed off. Do *not* scare me like that again, hellion."

He angled his head to kiss her and Lori fell in love with him all over again. This evening she'd been so angry and disappointed in him that she'd felt utterly betrayed. Now he was being so attentive and nice to her that she lost her whole heart to him.

The gentler side of Gideon Fox was impossible to resist so she didn't bother trying. She yielded to his breathtaking kiss and arched into his masculine contours, wishing they could spend one uninterrupted night together in the privacy of her room on her feather bed instead of the hard floor of a cave or the chilly water in the river.

"Ahem." Reece cleared his throat and grinned devilishly. "Clive sent me up here to chaperon, in case something *untoward*—his word, not mine—might be going on."

"Don't you have somewhere else you could be for a few minutes?" Gideon asked irritably.

"No. I told you, I'm the designated chaperon."

Gideon dropped one last kiss to Lori's lips, and she savored the addictive taste of him until he backed up to stare imploringly at her. "Please don't climb out the window while Reece and I are standing watch. *Promise me.*"

She expelled an agitated breath. "I don't know why I can't stand guard, too. I'm handy with a pistol and rifle."

"You're the target," he reminded her darkly. "Now promise me." He cupped her chin in his hand and forced her to look him squarely in the eye. "If you're in here, I won't be distracted, wondering if someone sneaked up to knock you out and drag you into the trees. *Promise me,* hellion."

She sighed heavily. "Oh, all right, if you insist, but I'm doing this under protest."

"Duly noted." He gave her a loud, smacking kiss.

"How much longer are these negotiations going to take?" Reece checked his timepiece. "Our sniper might be setting up camp already, and we aren't in position to do anything except get shot."

"Neither of you will do anything to put yourself in harm's way," she said adamantly. "Is that understood?

No grand heroics on my behalf. I'll have none of that. *Promise me.*"

"Fine. We promise all the way around," Reece said with an impatient flick of his wrist. "Now go to your room and stay there, wildcat. We have scouting to do."

Reluctantly, Lori pivoted toward her room. If she didn't know her gallant protectors would be checking up on her, she'd take her own position as posted lookout.

"Keep a pistol handy," Gideon told Clive as he descended the steps. "You are Lori's last line of defense."

"You don't have to worry about me," Clive said loftily. "I know how to defend a position on a battlefield and how to protect my only child. You two, I'm not so sure about."

When Gideon and Reece closed the door behind them, Reece said, "We let one pint-size female pull one over on us and our reputation is ruined for life. Clive will never let us live this down."

"Probably not. Never mind that Clive had no idea she'd gone missing," he said with a snort. "But Clive dislikes me because he's convinced himself that I demanded favors from Lori to make her captivity more tolerable during our trek cross-country."

"Ah…" Reece grinned slyly. "Shame on you, Fox, for taking unfair advantage of that helpless little daisy of a female. Overpowered her, did you?"

"Right. You know how easy it is to subdue that firebrand."

Reece massaged the knot on his head. "Indeed I do."

Gideon's smile faded as he walked off the front porch He'd be ready and waiting if the sniper struck again tonight. If not, he'd ride to the Boomer camp, first thing in the morning, and interrogate the two women Clive mentioned by name. The sooner he found a likely suspect the sooner he could prove Lori's innocence and remove the rest of those Reward posters that were plastered around the stage stations and trading posts in the area.

On that determined thought, Gideon gestured for Reece to prowl the perimeters on the east side of the trading post while he scouted the west side.

Lori paced the room for an hour, pausing at irregular intervals to crane her neck out the window. Careful not to make herself an open target, she didn't burn the lantern or stand directly in front of the window.

One hour became two then two became three. Still, she didn't hear shots fired or shouts of alarm in the darkness.

Finally, she bedded down for the night, dismayed that Gideon and Reece felt the need to stand guard until dawn. She was still tossing and turning when she heard a faint tap on her door.

"Lorelei? Are you still in there?" her father called softly.

"Yes, Papa, I'm still here."

He took it as his cue to open the door. He walked over to the end of the bed. "I'll stand guard outside your room."

"That isn't nec—"

He flung up his hand, halting her protest. "Yes it is. No one is getting past me. Those young bucks might stumble but I'm your father. You're all I have left in this world. I refuse to lose you, sweetheart."

His fierce comment put tears in her eyes. She knew it haunted her father that he could protect his family from most threats but he'd been helpless when disease stole his beloved wife and young son. He was an ex-army officer and he would defend her with his life, even if she objected to anyone making the supreme sacrifice.

As Tony had done.

"I love you, Papa," she murmured softly.

"I love you, too, Lorelei. I probably haven't told you often enough, but I'm telling you now."

He walked over to drop a kiss on her cheek. She looped her arms around his neck and held him close for a moment.

"Try to get some sleep." He patted her shoulder comfortingly. "One of us around here needs to be mentally sharp tomorrow."

When he exited, she really did try to rest, but she swore she only nodded off once or twice the whole livelong night.

The next morning the three men serving as Lori's bodyguards showed up bleary-eyed at the breakfast table. All they had received for their efforts were cramped muscles from trying to rest on the ground—or in her father's case, in a chair with a pistol draped over his lap.

"I think this is a waste of time," Lori declared.

Gideon's ruffled raven head came up and he stared at her through bloodshot eyes. "Who's running this investigation?"

"A better question might be, who's running it *right?*" Clive put in as he massaged his aching shoulder. "This can't go on indefinitely."

"Reece and I are headed to the Boomer camp to interrogate the women you mentioned yesterday," Gideon declared. "Maybe we can wrest pertinent information from one of them."

"Then maybe we'll finally get somewhere with this case," Clive grumbled before he bit into his toast smothered with plum jelly.

After breakfast, Gideon escorted Lori upstairs and confined her to her room.

She complained, of course. "I don't care how long this takes, I am *not* going to take up knitting and I cleaned your spare pistol already. I have nothing else to do since I swept and dusted the upstairs rooms yesterday."

He chuckled as he kissed away her pout. "I'm sorry, but letting folks know you're back in the area is an invitation for trouble. Our sniper knows you're here. We don't need to see how many bounty hunters you can attract, as well."

Lori heaved an audible sigh. "If the possibility of a jealous rival for Tony's affection, or a jealous husband doesn't pan out, we'll be out of options, won't we?"

Gideon nodded somberly. "We'll have to deliver you to Fort Smith and take the case to court. With Reece and me as character witnesses, I think we can convince Judge Parker there isn't evidence to file formal charges."

"Right," she said, and smirked. "The 'hanging judge' is going to set me free."

"He's a fair and just man," Gideon defended.

"So are you, but *you* didn't believe proclamations of my innocence," she pointed out.

Gideon grinned guiltily as he traced the curve of her lips. "I have an excellent excuse for not believing you."

She arched an eyebrow. "Oh? What excuse is that?"

"I was wildly attracted to you the moment you emerged from the fog, looking like a curly-haired angel. I was fighting like the devil not to be deceived by your cherubic face and sinfully alluring body."

She chortled softly. "You can be suave and charming when you want to be, Marshal." She draped her arms around his neck and leaned suggestively against him. "And now what do you think of my version of the story and of me?"

"I believe you," he murmured before he kissed her deeply

and hungrily. "And I'm still wildly attracted to you. Now behave yourself while I'm gone and stay out of sight."

She backed up a step and eyed him warily. "You're trying to flatter me into obeying your orders, aren't you? What happened to all those gruff commands you usually hurl at me?"

"They didn't work worth a damn so now I'm changing tack," he said with a grin. "Besides, kissing you instead of arguing with you is a lot more fun."

His smile and the teasing glint in his hypnotic blue eyes nearly melted her into a gooey puddle.

He dropped another kiss to her lips then spun on his heels. "I have to go, hellion. Be safe."

"Gideon, I—"

"Yes? What is it?" Gideon pivoted to stare curiously at her when her voice trailed off.

She clamped her mouth shut before she made the colossal mistake of blurting out she was in love with him. Even if he did believe she was innocent, he might think she was professing affection to assure his loyalty when they stood before Judge Parker.

Furthermore, and most importantly, Gideon didn't love her back. From recent experience, she knew how awkward it was to deal with one-sided love. When Tony declared his love, she'd scrambled to find the right words to let him down gently.

Lori wasn't ready to deal with rejection right now. Being wanted for murder and becoming the target for a mysterious sniper was enough on her plate.

She flashed a blinding smile and blew him a kiss. "Just be careful, too. I want you back in one piece because I have a few experiments I want to try on you."

He smiled rakishly. "I'm at your service, but your father won't let me near you to experiment."

"He'll like you, given time," she insisted. "You're the kind of man who grows on a person."

To the point of hopeless infatuation and unrequited love.

"Thanks…I think." He made a stabbing gesture with his forefinger. "Now stay put. I don't want to chase you down when I'm cranky and deprived of sleep. I can guarantee I'll take it out on you, hellion."

Lori watched him walk away. She memorized the cat-like grace with which he moved, admired his horseman's thighs, his muscled shoulders and the shiny raven hair that brushed against his shirt collar.

She hadn't expected to experience the kind of love her parents had discovered. But now she knew how it felt to want someone with every beat of her heart, to need him to the very depths of her soul.

Heaving a dispirited sigh, Lori wheeled around to closet herself in her room. It tormented her to no end that her father was shorthanded today, since John Little Calf had asked for the day off to tend to pressing chores on his family's farm. She should be working the counter in the trading post or running the ferry across Winding River. Instead, she was stuck in her room with nothing to do—and all damn day to do it.

Maggie Burgess parked the supply wagon directly in front of the trading post, then climbed down. She grabbed the peace-treaty peach pie she had made for Clive Russell and ascended the steps. She met Clive and one of his customers on their way outside to the ferry.

"Maggie?" Clive halted to stare warily at her then glanced at the fresh-baked pie.

"Marshal Fox convinced me that I should make amends," she explained. "Even if we still don't know what happened to Tony, the marshal assures me that *assuming* what happened is not the same as actually *seeing* it. I came over to apologize and to gather a few supplies before the noon stage arrives."

Clive smiled in relief. "We'll talk after I transport my customer across the river. Pick up whatever you need and I'll be back as soon as I can."

Maggie set the pie on the table that was tucked around the corner from the store counter. Then she strode off to gather necessary supplies for the house and stage station. By the time Clive returned, she had three stacks of goods on the counter and two slices of pie and coffee waiting on the table.

"If you'll tally my expenses for these goods, I'll cart them out to the wagon," she insisted.

"I'm sorry for the delay. I'm shorthanded today." Clive rang up the items. "John Little Calf can only work a few days before he gets behind on farm chores."

Maggie nodded in understanding. "We have the same problem when he fills in at the stage station." She picked up several cans of peaches and beans then headed toward the door. "I've gotten used to tending chores. Especially now."

A few minutes later, she had the supplies loaded in the wagon. She seated herself at the table across from Clive. "Now, about my formal apology for jumping to conclusions and thinking the worst."

Clive took a bite of the warm pie, then chased it with a sip of coffee. "It was an unfortunate misunderstanding."

"I assumed Lorelei and Tony had a squabble that ended badly," she went on to say. "But Marshal Fox has pointed out several other possibilities that I was too distressed and grief-stricken to consider."

Clive nodded slightly. "Yes, he's checking a few leads this morning…and this pie is delicious, by the way."

"Thank you." Maggie smiled at him. "I know you must be upset, as I have been. I've lost two men suddenly and I've been overwhelmed with work. Especially since the two hired hands who chased after Lorelei never returned. I know it has been worrisome for you, not knowing where your daughter is."

"It's very upsetting and I've spent too many sleepless nights walking the floor," Clive admitted then took another bite of pie. "As for your two missing hired hands, they won't be back. They stole horses from the marshal's family. Now Sonny and Teddy are headed to Fort Smith to stand trial."

"The marshal didn't mention that yesterday…Clive?"

When he wobbled slightly in his chair, she reached for his hand. "Are you feeling all right?"

The color seeped from his face and his fork clattered against the table.

"Clive? Can you hear me?"

His mouth opened and closed. His eyes rolled back in his head. He toppled from the chair then collapsed on the floor.

"Clive? Dear God! Someone help! Clive has collapsed. I'm not sure if he's breathing. *Someone help!*"

Alarm shot through Lori while she hovered in the upstairs hall. She'd seen Maggie enter through the front door and watched her make several trips to load her supplies. Lori overheard bits and pieces of Maggie's conversation with her father. She was greatly relieved to know Maggie had decided to give her the benefit of the doubt and had come to make peace with her father.

Knowing that, Lori disobeyed Gideon's orders to remain

upstairs—no matter what. When Maggie yelled for help, Lori bounded down the steps two at a time. Her father had missed sleep and had fretted about her welfare and her whereabouts. Knowing he had collapsed sent her into a state of panic. She couldn't lose her father, too! She knew she'd lose Gideon when he rode out of her life, never to return. But she'd expected her father to be here, as he always had.

She shrieked when she saw him sprawled lifelessly on the floor beside the table. "Oh, God! Papa, can you hear me?"

He didn't respond.

"Lorelei, you're here," Maggie said unnecessarily as she stood up to allow Lori to kneel beside her father.

"Yes, I heard what you said. I swear that I had nothing to do with Tony's death," Lori insisted as she eased her father onto his back to check his breathing. "Maggie, fetch a cold cloth from the kitchen, will you?"

"No, I don't believe I will…."

Before Lori could twist around to stare quizzically at Maggie, her skull exploded with blinding pain. A dull groan tumbled from her lips as she sprawled atop her father.

That was the last thing she remembered before the world turned pitch-black and became deathly silent.

Chapter Seventeen

Gideon was frustrated to no end. His attempt to gain information from Beatrice Ogden and Theresa Knott at the Boomer camp had caused a domestic quarrel between a husband and wife and disrupted a budding new courtship between Bea and her beau. No one admitted to anything except a fleeting fascination for Tony Rogers.

"I'm going to have to tote Lori all the way to Fort Smith, and Clive will want to come along to make sure nothing *untoward* happens," Gideon grumbled.

"Cheer up, I'll come along with you," Reece volunteered. "I'll run interference while you and that lovely wildcat wander off to do something untoward."

Gideon smiled. "You're a good friend, McCree. A little too much like me at times, but a good friend all the same."

"I used to be," Reece murmured. He stared into the distance, as if it were a window through time. Smiling ruefully, he glanced at Gideon. "Seeing you again has inspired me to offer my services to the judge. Although I still contend the law doesn't protect innocent victims like it should."

"I can't argue with that. Lori is a perfect example of being condemned without a fair trial. I contributed to that injustice. Even now, the lack of evidence and Maggie Burgess's version of the incident points to Lori's guilt. But she didn't turn on Tony Rogers."

"You're saying that because you're too involved to make an unbiased judgment," Reece said before he lit his cheroot.

Gideon shot him a reproachful glance.

"I'm just saying what you already know." Reece shrugged a broad shoulder then blew smoke into the air. "I believe she's innocent, because there are too many unanswered questions about what was going on in Tony's life. Not because I'm involved with her as you are. Which is a *lot*." He shot Gideon a stern glance. "Knowing what I know about the two of you, I'd take a few shots at you, if *I* were Lori's father."

"Now I remember why I didn't like you much," Gideon teased. "I never could get you to shut up."

While Reece snickered in amusement, Gideon focused his attention on the stage station in the distance. He frowned curiously when he noticed the familiar Appaloosa gelding tied to the hitching post. He nudged Pirate into a gallop to reach Burgess Ranch.

"Glenn? What the hell are you doing here?" Gideon demanded when his younger brother came around the corner of the two-story house.

"Checking on you." Glenn said then focused his attention on Reece. "I heard you were dead, or turned outlaw. I don't remember which." He grinned broadly. "But obviously you're not dead."

"Nice of you to notice," Reece remarked. "I felt dead

for a while, but I'm doing better, after watching your big brother fumble his way through this investigation."

Gideon scowled at his mischievous friend then stared apprehensively at his brother. "Again, Glenn, what are you doing here? Is something wrong with Galen or Sarah?"

Glenn shook his ruffled head. "Nope, Galen is doing much better after being shot," he added for Reece's benefit. "Sarah is fine, too. She sends her love, though why she wants to waste it on you is beyond me."

"Hell's bells," Gideon groaned. "I'll die of old age before you get to the point!"

Glenn chuckled in amusement. "Galen sent me here to make sure you were treating Lori fairly."

The guilt of knowing he'd betrayed his little brother who was infatuated with Lori, made Gideon inwardly grimace. "You'll be glad to know I'm convinced she's innocent."

"It took you long enough," Glenn said, and snorted. "Any fool could see that." He pivoted toward the house. "I had planned to introduce myself as a bounty hunter, looking to collect a reward on Lori, so I can snoop around. But no one answered my knock at the door. I went around back, looking for Widow Burgess, but I didn't see anyone. Just a canoe tied up at the end of the path beside the creek."

"*Canoe?*" Gideon's heart dropped to his belly and a coil of fear knotted in his chest. "A canoe would easily explain how someone might slip away undetected after taking potshots at Lori and me, wouldn't it?"

"Damn sure would." Reece stared speculatively toward the bunkhouse. "I wonder if Syl Jenkins, with his limp, prefers to use a canoe rather than a horse when he sneaks around, looking to make extra money by collecting a bounty on a certain murder suspect."

"You go check on Syl while Glenn and I look around."

Gideon bounded from his horse to jog around the side of the house. The uneasy sensation rippling through him while he jogged down the overgrown path to locate the canoe magnified tenfold. He glanced speculatively from the watercraft to the back door of the house then back again.

Suddenly something Maggie Burgess had said yesterday exploded in his mind and nearly knocked him off his feet.

"I want to be anywhere except this uncivilized territory or the Louisiana bayous where I grew up."

"Gid? Are you okay," Glenn asked, staring at him in concern.

"No, damn it," Gideon snarled as he dashed toward the back door of the Burgess house.

"Damn it, *what?*" Glenn demanded as he rushed after him.

"Go fetch Reece. Tell him to leave Jenkins until later. We have a bigger problem right now."

Furious, Gideon bounded onto the back porch while Glenn dashed off to summon Reece. "Maggie Burgess! I'm coming in. Like it or not!" he bellowed as he stalked through the door.

He heard nothing in response, but he kept right on walking through the kitchen to reach the staircase. He bounded up the steps then wheeled around the corner to find a spacious bedroom decorated with frills, ruffles and lace. Swearing foully, he whipped open the closet door to survey the contents. Nothing incriminating, damn it to hell!

Reversing direction, Gideon stamped down the steps to see Reece and Glenn staring curiously at him. "Maggie told me yesterday that she grew up in bayou country. I suspect that canoe belongs to her, not Syl Jenkins."

"Oh, hell, I knew there was something about her I didn't like," Reece muttered.

Gideon lurched toward the door beneath the staircase. "We're looking for a pair of men's boots and clothing that Maggie might have used to charade as a man while she bushwhacked Lori and me. There was no incriminating evidence in her upstairs bedroom, but my guess is she used her dead husband's garments as her disguise to seek her revenge."

"This is the same widow that arrived on the scene to point an accusing finger at Lori?" Glenn asked.

"The very same," Reece confirmed. "That devious bitch! She used me to locate Lori. Like an idiot, I told her that I was keeping surveillance on the trading post, expecting Lori to come to roost."

"So *she* decided to take matters into her own hands by shooting Lori herself," Gideon snarled. "She shot at Lori then fired at me yesterday, trying to get me out of her way so I couldn't protect Lori. Then she paddled off in the canoe to return here."

Gideon descended into the cellar, then exploded in outraged fury. A pair of mud-caked boots—with socks stuffed in the toes so they'd stay on Maggie's smaller-size feet—sat on the floor. She'd tucked the set of men's clothes and hat in the back corner of a shelf lined with canned goods.

As Gideon swore the air blue, Glenn stared warily at him. "Now what, big brother?"

"That cunning shrew," he muttered as he gathered the evidence and shook it in Glenn's and Reece's faces. Wheeling around, he headed up the steps. "Maggie told me yesterday that she decided to make amends with Clive, after *I* supposedly convinced her there might be another explanation for Tony's death. I practically gave her my blessing to pay Clive a visit. She knows Lori is there, and I suspect she plans to walk in and dispose of Lori once and for all."

"Damnation," Reece growled. "She's already on her way there. Syl told me that Maggie took the wagon to purchase supplies from the trading post. She could be there right now. The next stage isn't due to arrive until noon. I'll bet she plans to return and act as if she knows nothing."

Cursing inventively, Gideon led the way out the front door then raced to his horse. He rode hell-for-leather toward the trading post, knowing that conniving widow was setting some sort of trap. She'd taken advantage of Gideon and Reece's absence and she was using the excuse of making an apology to lower Clive's guard. The older man wouldn't be suspicious of a woman coming to pick up supplies and apologize for jumping to conclusions about his daughter.

Sickening dread bombarded Gideon as he raced down the road, wishing Pirate could sprout wings and fly. What if he arrived too late? he thought in panic.

The grim prospect of losing Lori turned him wrong side out. He regretted every suspicious thought and every disparaging comment he'd made to her. She hadn't deserved his criticism. Maggie Burgess was the manipulative, deceitful schemer who'd decided to become judge, jury and executioner.

Maggie had been on a crusade to see Lori captured and punished. She'd put up reward money and circulated Wanted posters at stage stations along the route. Wanted Dead or Alive. Preferably *dead,* Gideon mused bleakly.

Most women wouldn't have managed to elude the two-man posse Maggie sent to apprehend Lori. Maggie expected Lori to be locked in jail in Fort Smith, awaiting trial, so Maggie could feel vindicated before she sold the stage station and ranch and left the territory she disliked so much.

"When I get my hands on that sneaky woman for taking the law into her own hands and using me to do it, I'm going to show her no mercy," Reece snarled viciously.

"You'll have to get in line," Gideon scowled. "You can have what's left of her after I'm through with her."

He just hoped and prayed Lori would be alive to watch Maggie Burgess pay for her vigilante justice.

Lori regained consciousness and groaned when the splitting headache made her nauseous. She dragged in a shaky breath and opened her eyes. She realized she was covered by a moldy canvas tarp. She was bound and gagged, and she presumed Maggie had managed to drag her into her supply wagon that moved along at a fast clip.

Where Maggie was taking her was a mystery. She assumed the widow planned to turn her over to Gideon. She could only hope it was Gideon and not some greedy bounty hunter Maggie paid to tote her to Fort Smith for hanging.

When the wagon skidded to a halt, Lori frowned, wondering how long she'd been unconscious. She fretted over her father's condition. No one was there to check on him. Lori hadn't had time to figure out why he'd collapsed before Maggie clubbed her on the head and dragged her away.

The instant Maggie jerked off the canvas tarp, Lori glowered at her, then cursed beneath her gag. Maggie reached over to remove the gag with one hand and kept a pistol trained on her with the other.

"Any last words, Lorelei?" she asked sarcastically.

"Yes, I want you to go check on my father."

"He'll be fine in a few hours. The doses of laudanum I put in the pie and coffee will wear off eventually."

Lori stared suspiciously at the smug-looking brunette. "You drugged him so you could take me captive?"

"You won't be a captive for long," she muttered hatefully.

Another thought struck like a sharp blow. "You *knew* I was at the trading post, didn't you? The only way you could have known is because you were the one who tried to shoot me."

"Precisely," Maggie said without the slightest hint of shame. "I used my canoe to travel downriver then hid in the bushes. Reece was kind enough to offer his trade secret of outwaiting a criminal that eventually returned to familiar surroundings. A pity I'm not a better shot. We could have concluded this business almost two weeks ago."

The comment drew Lori's suspicious frown. She watched Maggie hold her at gunpoint while grabbing the rope tied around Lori's ankles. When Maggie tried to tug her forward, Lori squirmed the other way.

"You were there the night Tony was shot," Lori muttered as she resisted Maggie's attempt to drag her off the wagon bed. "You came around the opposite side of the barn by the station…."

The pieces of the puzzle began to fall into place. Lori stared at Maggie in disbelief. "You circled around the barn to make it *look* like you were coming from another direction. But *you* were the one hiding in the bushes. That's why you arrived before Sonny Hathaway and Teddy Collins. You knew I didn't shoot Tony, but you were quick to point an accusing finger at me to protect yourself."

Maggie gave another fierce jerk to pull Lori to the edge of the wagon bed. "Congratulations," she said caustically. "You finally figured it out. It's too late to do you any good, of course. But you'll die knowing the truth, if that helps."

Lori tried to wriggle loose, but Maggie refused to release her grasp on the rope tied around her ankles. "Why would you want to shoot Tony? You ranted and raved about losing your husband and then your foreman."

"I wasn't trying to shoot Tony, you little idiot," Maggie snapped as she gave a mighty heave-ho, forcing Lori to topple off the wagon bed and land on the ground with a thud and a groan. "I was trying to shoot *you!*"

Gideon reached the trading post and bounded from Pirate's back before the laboring horse skidded to a halt. He tried to barge through the door, but it was locked. Scowling, he stepped back, raised his foot and slammed his boot heel against the latch. On the third try, the door splintered and gave way.

With Glenn and Reece a step behind him, Gideon raced through the store and headed upstairs, afraid of what he was going to find. Afraid he'd arrived too late to prevent Maggie from shooting Lori and leaving her for dead.

He hurried into her room, holding his breath. He couldn't decide if he was relieved or more alarmed when he found no sign of Lori.

After a quick check of the other upstairs rooms, he hurried down the hall then heard Reece shouting at him to come to the kitchen immediately. Icy dread flowed through his veins as worst-case scenarios exploded in his mind.

What was left of his heart was going to shrivel up and die if he found Lori sprawled in a pool of her own blood.

Grimly, he raced around the corner to see Glenn and Reece down on their knees, huddled around a body. Gideon sagged in relief when he realized Clive lay unmoving. Two coffee cups and a peach pie sat on the table.

"No gunshot wounds," Reece reported as he stared at Clive. "He's still breathing." He glanced at the food and drinks on the table. "My guess is the widow drugged Clive rather than poisoning him. She put him out of commission so he couldn't protect Lori."

Bleak, silver-gray eyes settled on Gideon. He knew Reece was reliving the awful incident that had taken his fiancée's life and left him wandering like a lost soul for a year. Gideon was beginning to understand all too well how it felt to suffer all the torments of the newly damned. Not knowing Lori's fate was like standing in hell's hottest bonfire with no relief in sight.

"She's not upstairs," Gideon said bleakly. "Glenn, check the cellar."

Nodding somberly, Glenn descended the stone steps. He returned a moment later. "She isn't there, either."

Gideon half collapsed in relief. "Maggie must have dragged Lori away in the wagon."

Glenn frowned, "How can a woman drag a body away and load it on a wagon?"

"Ramps," Gideon replied then turned to see the discarded rug lying by the front door. "She probably used the rug to pull Lori across the wooden floor and up the ramp. I noticed ramps in the wagon bed yesterday while I was snooping around the stage station searching for clues."

Reese rose to his feet to fetch a cup of water, then dribbled it on Clive's face. The man didn't move a muscle. "He might be sedated for hours. Lori doesn't have time to spare. We can't wait for Clive to regain consciousness."

"He might not know what happened to Lori," Gideon muttered. "So much for leaving the ex-lieutenant colonel on guard against a sneaky, deceptive bitch like Maggie."

Wheeling around, Gideon made a beeline toward the door. He noticed the tracks from the wagon she'd parked near the front steps. Wherever Maggie was, with Lori in tow, she was using the wagon, not the canoe…unless she had a second one tied up nearby.

The unnerving thought that Maggie might consider letting Lori sleep with the fishes had Gideon spewing one foul epithet after another. A child of the bayous probably had all sorts of experience with disposing of unwanted objects in places where they would be difficult to recover.

Gideon bounded into the saddle to follow the tracks that veered into the weeds and underbrush. He prayed to white and Indian deities alike as he raced off, hoping he'd find Lori before Maggie disposed of her.

The dreadful thought nearly shattered his composure. If he couldn't gaze into those entrancing golden eyes, embedded in that beguiling face surrounded with flaming hair, he wasn't sure he'd survive—or have a reason to.

He thought again of Reece McCree battling his private demons. Gideon knew without question that he'd be carrying around a passel of his own demons if he failed to rescue Lori.

"Kill *me?*" Lori stared blankly at Maggie as she sat upright on the ground. *"Why?"*

"Because you made Tony fall in love with you," she sneered angrily. "You lured him away from me after *I* went to the trouble of planning the pretense of an affair for him so we could cast suspicion away from *us.*"

Lori gaped at Maggie. "You were the woman Tony was seeing? Not one of the women from the Boomer camp? You were cheating on your husband?"

"Yes, and the old goat never suspected a thing. I was cautious when Tony and I sneaked off in the canoe."

Maggie gnashed her teeth as she glared disdainfully at Lori. "I wanted Tony to dispose of Hub so we could leave this place, but he refused to do the deed. I had to take care of it myself."

Lori swallowed uneasily as she discreetly surveyed her

surroundings beside the swift-flowing river. "You killed Hub?"

"Well, *someone* had to do it," she said peevishly. "Tony was my ticket out of here. If I was going to keep the money from the sale of the ranch and stage station, then Hub had to go, didn't he?"

"And Tony approved the idea?"

"No, his conscience kept getting in his way," Maggie said, and scowled.

Thank God for that, Lori mused as she studied the odd gleam flickering in Maggie's dark eyes. She swore the widow was losing touch with sanity, for she kept pacing about, tossing her head and muttering to herself at irregular intervals. Lori didn't know what else to do but keep the crazed widow talking until she figured out how to extricate herself from this potentially deadly ordeal.

"I can see what you mean," Lori said as calmly as she knew how. "You can't depend on men to do what you want."

Maggie whirled around. "You have to *manipulate* them," she insisted. "I swore years ago that I was going to escape from my family's poverty. I married Hub so I'd have money for the first time in my life."

Lori realized that Maggie had become obsessed with money.

It was the only god she worshipped religiously.

"Even if Hub was sixteen years older, he was my *escape* and I took it. Then I met Tony and decided he would suit my purpose. I seduced him and I told him to court you publicly so no one would suspect we were lovers.

"When Tony refused to help me dispose of my unwanted husband, I drugged Hub before he went to check cattle. He toppled off his horse, hit his head and that was the end of it."

She said it so matter-of-factly that Lori inwardly grimaced. Killing had become second nature to Maggie. Her twisted code of ethics refused to allow anyone to interfere with her self-serving schemes.

"So you invented the story about Hub falling to his death while chasing off cattle rustlers," Lori presumed.

Maggie jerked up her head and smirked loftily. "Who was going to contest my story? Certainly not Tony. He was suspicious of the accident but he said nothing." Her expression turned vicious and her eyes glittered dangerously. "But you lured him in and used your younger body to entice him, didn't you? After all I went through to control him, *you* foiled my plans."

Now Lori understood the baffling comments Tony had made that fateful night. *"I didn't mean for this to happen. I want you to come away with me so we can make a clean break and fresh start,"* he'd said.

Lori thought the law was after him and he needed to take a new name, a new identity and make a quick escape. But it wasn't a lawman who was breathing down his neck, making him uneasy. It was a ruthless madwoman who had murdered her husband. And when she accidentally shot Tony, Maggie had rushed in to point an accusing finger at Lori.

Maggie went back to her rapid pacing. "Everything would have been fine if Sonny and Teddy weren't such bungling morons or if I hadn't missed when I scrambled into the canoe to circle around so I could take another shot at you while you were riding east that night." She glared accusingly at Lori. "Then you came back, dragging that Deputy U.S. Marshal into this. You worked your wiles on him, just like you did on Tony."

Lori wondered if Tony had been using Maggie for convenient sex or if he had once fancied himself in love with her.

When he realized she was a scheming lunatic, he probably tried to distance himself from her but she'd murdered her husband and Tony expected to be next if he crossed her.

It was a shame Tony hadn't hightailed it off to ask for his stepbrother's assistance. Either that or he should have run for his life without waiting to ask Lori to leave with him!

"I tried to dispose of the pesky marshal, but my gunshot missed its mark," Maggie muttered irritably.

Lori was eternally grateful Maggie wasn't a crack shot. Otherwise, Gideon would've suffered the same fate as Tony.

Maggie halted and cackled fiendishly. "But I fooled him, as well as that annoying bounty hunter who refused to succumb to my charm. I fooled your father, as well. The situation worked out perfectly. I had an excuse to appear at the trading post to make peace with Clive and no one is the wiser. Now I'll make it look like you took off on your own, just as you did after Tony died."

Suddenly Maggie swooped down to grab the rope to Lori's ankles then dragged her toward the river. Lori tried to latch on to striplings with her bound hands, but Maggie cursed her violently then kicked at her wrists until the excruciating pain forced Lori to recoil.

"*I* was the woman that men looked at and coveted around here until *you* came of age," she said, huffing and puffing for breath. "But you began turning heads, damn you. Then you used your body to steal Tony. For that, you're going to die, Lorelei. I'll board a stage, toting the money I've tucked away for safekeeping the past six years. I'll quit this place for good and I'll have my revenge on you for taking Tony away while I was still using him!"

Maggie gave another tug on the ropes to drag her captive closer to the river. Fear rose inside Lori like a tidal wave when she saw the canoe tied to a tree. When Maggie propped her upright, Lori tried to hop away. She ducked when Maggie, who commenced screeching like a banshee, tried to whack her skull with the butt of a pistol. The blow grazed her head, dazing her and making her lose her balance.

Maggie rammed her broadside, launching her into the canoe. It was impossible to crawl out before the crazed woman shoved the canoe into the river's swift current.

"Fare-thee-well, once and for all," Maggie cackled triumphantly as she used both hands to steady the pistol she aimed at Lori's head.

The weapon exploded and Lori's life flashed before her eyes.

Chapter Eighteen

Gideon heard the gunshot in the distance. He prided himself in being cool under pressure and he didn't scare easily. But he was *terrified* now. His heart ceased beating for several vital seconds. He couldn't draw breath. No matter how hard he pushed Pirate he felt as if he were moving in slow motion.

The prospect of arriving too late to save Lori crushed his fighting spirit as nothing ever had. All that kept him going was his fierce determination to make sure the vindictive widow paid her dues—and *he* was a man who meted out consequences. Especially now, he vowed vengefully.

"Maggie!" he yelled at the top of his lungs, hoping to distract her from taking another shot—just in case there was the slightest hope Lori had survived.

He thundered through the underbrush toward the sound of gunfire. When Gideon spotted Maggie braced to fire off another shot at the sinking canoe being swept into the swift current, he headed directly toward her. Maggie shrieked in furious outrage when Gideon jerked his foot from the stirrup to kick her in the shoulder. She spun like a top, causing her shot to strike the bow of the canoe.

Gouging Pirate in the flanks, Gideon rode into the water, bellowing Lori's name as he tried to catch up with the fast-moving canoe. Behind him, he heard Maggie railing in demented fury. Then another shot whistled through the air, missing him by mere inches.

Gideon heard Glenn and Reece cursing loudly. He glanced back momentarily, glad to see they had run Maggie down and subdued her. He focused his full concentration on reaching the sinking vessel and the tangle of red-gold hair barely visible in the rising water.

Frantic, Gideon swam Pirate to the spot where the canoe went down. He dived into the water, groping desperately to locate Lori. When his foot struck something below him, he submerged to latch on to the motionless body. He'd have screamed in fury if he could—without swallowing a few gallons of water.

Fearing the worst, Gideon yanked Lori upward and struggled to grab a breath as he towed her toward Pirate.

Pirate reached the bank, with Gideon holding Lori close while hanging onto the stirrup.

"Give her to me," Glenn demanded urgently, then pulled Lori's lifeless body from Gideon's arms.

Gideon was reluctant to let go, not knowing if Lori was dead or alive. But Glenn was insistent. Gideon cringed as he stared at her blue-tinged face and bloodless lips.

The sight of Lori—who usually teemed with spunk and spirit—lying as still as death was enough to provoke Gideon to spew every curse word he knew in one breath and pray for all he was worth with the next.

As Glenn laid Lori on the ground to force water from her lungs, Gideon struggled to his feet. The depressing thought that he'd arrived too late to save Lori tormented him to extremes.

He'd never see those glorious golden eyes twinkling with impish mischief again. He'd never feel the touch of her hand, her lips or her body. He'd never be able to tell her that he was sorry for the misery he'd caused her, sorry he'd taken so long to believe her story, sorry for treating her like a convicted prisoner.

She'd never know she'd burrowed into his heart when he'd tried so hard not to let it happen. She'd never know her memory would haunt him for all eternity and he'd never forget her.

His bleak thoughts trailed off when Glenn's persistent ministrations produced results. His little brother whacked Lori between the shoulder blades repeatedly until she coughed and sputtered for breath.

Hope rose inside him and he prayed he'd have a second chance to make it up to Lori. He dropped down on his knees beside Lori, then swore mightily when he noticed the blood seeping from a wound on the side of her head.

It was no more than a flesh wound. But still...

Gideon twisted sideways to glare murderously at Maggie who was still screeching and flailing against the handcuffs Reece had clamped around her wrists.

"Put a gag on that crazed bitch," he ordered sharply.

"My pleasure." Reece grabbed his kerchief and tied it around the lower half of Maggie's face.

Gideon focused his full attention on Lori then pulled her into his arms. He didn't care if Glenn witnessed the kiss he placed on her colorless lips. Gideon had nearly lost the only woman who ever mattered to him.

By damn, he was going to savor every precious moment—until Clive woke up and ordered Gideon to keep his hands to himself.

"Am I dead?" Lori wheezed without opening her eyes.

"You were, but you're better now," he murmured against her cheek.

He swore he'd never forget the moment when her thick lashes fluttered up and he stared into those captivating amber eyes. His life—one that had meant nothing when he thought she'd drowned—began to matter again. *She* made his existence worthwhile. *She* had become his reason for being.

"There's something I have to tell you," she said hoarsely. "Maggie was Tony's secret lover. She was trying to kill me, not Tony, because she thought I was going to steal him away from her…." Her voice fizzled and she passed out again.

"I'll be damned," Gideon mumbled in astonishment.

"You would've been if you hadn't gotten to Lori when you did," Reece murmured as he dumped Maggie into the wagon bed and secured her. "Another minute would have been too late."

Gideon nodded grimly then looked over at Glenn, who was watching him closely. "I'm the wrong kind of brother," Gideon admitted. "I don't want to give her up, even though I know you want her for yourself."

Glenn grinned wryly as he reached out to trace the curve of Lori's lips. "I must admit she intrigues me, but we knew she was meant for you, even if you couldn't see it for yourself."

Gideon blinked, bemused. *"We?"*

Glenn chuckled in wicked amusement. "Galen, Sarah and I set you up. Sarah gave you a sleeping potion the night I took Lori with me so I could have a head start. Naturally, you came charging after us because you didn't want to let her go. Of course, you hadn't figured that out yet, which is why we had to give you a nudge in the right direction."

While Reece snickered, Gideon stared at his little brother in consternation. "You plotted against me? The *three* of you? This is how you repay me for all I've done for you the past dozen years?"

Glenn nodded his dark head. "Yep, we returned the favor. You're welcome, by the way." He leaned close to add, "Galen swore me to secrecy, in case things didn't work out. Luckily they did, though."

Gideon rolled his eyes in disbelief as Glenn bounded onto the seat so Gideon could hand Lori off to him. Maybe his family wasn't a pain in the ass, after all. Obviously, they knew what he needed better than he knew himself.

Lori woke up, unsure how long she'd been asleep. Her mind was fuzzy and she had a bad taste in her mouth. She strongly suspected Gideon had used Maggie's technique of doctoring food to knock her out and keep her in bed.

When she mustered the energy to sit up, she noticed it was dark outside. Rising, she paused to steady herself, then glanced in the mirror. Her reflection would have spooked a ghost! Her hair lay in corkscrew curls, her eyes were hollow, her lips colorless, and someone had placed a bandage on the side of her head.

She was lucky to be alive and she knew it. Maggie Burgess was a brilliant schemer but she was a lousy shot. She hadn't managed to blow Lori's head off before she sank the canoe.

Depression nearly overwhelmed Lori as she walked down the hall. Gideon, Glenn and Reece might be long gone by now. She wouldn't have the chance to thank any of them for resolving the murder case and saving her from catastrophe. Heavens, they might not even know Maggie had arranged Hubert Burgess's death to clear the way for her plans to sell the ranch and take Tony with her, whether he truly wanted to go or not.

Whatever the case, Maggie had used her wicked charms on Tony and he probably regretted getting mixed up with her. For sure and certain, Maggie had been the death of him.

"Lori! You aren't supposed to be out of bed!"

She glanced down the staircase, relieved to see her father up and about. "You should be lying down yourself. Maggie fed you a strong dose of laudanum, after all."

He shook his head in dismay. "I've never been so humiliated. The woman fooled me completely. I had to apologize to your marshal after Reece and Glenn informed me that Gideon had saved your life when I failed to protect you."

Lori glanced around the store. "Where are they? Did they leave with their prisoner?"

"No, they're waiting until tomorrow morning. They hurried off to man the stage station and serve food to incoming passengers." He grinned. "I don't know which of them plans to do the cooking. That should be interesting. I'd like to see those three men wearing aprons and serving meals."

"I expect all of them can handle kitchen patrol," she contended. "They are exceptionally self-reliant men."

"Warriors one and all," her father admitted reluctantly. "But I am *not* pleased that Gideon brought you here unchaperoned and I still don't know if he acted the perfect gentleman."

We are back to that again, she mused as she veered around her father to grab something to eat that didn't have laudanum in it. "You need to know that I feel the same way about Gideon that you felt about Mama," she confided.

"You can have your pick of suitors," her father insisted. "Find one who can put down roots in one place."

"If it isn't Gideon then it will be no one," she said uncompromisingly. "I'm not settling for less than the best."

"So it's him or no man at all?" her father grumbled. "Dear God, girl, you are just like me. If I couldn't have your mother I preferred to live alone." He studied her closely. "If that's how you feel then I need to have a talk with Gideon."

"No one is going to force him to do anything he doesn't want to do." She scooped up a bowl of ham and beans then plunked down at the table. "So please stay out of this, Papa."

He blew out his breath. "Fine, but—"

His voice fizzled out when Gideon and company strode into the store. She wondered if he could hear her heart breaking. He'd be gone by daylight and she'd never see him again.

And she didn't think she could feel worse.

"Did you send off the stage and feed the passengers without a hitch?" she asked before she munched on her meal.

Gideon nodded his raven head. "They left with fresh horses attached to the coach and full stomachs."

"I don't know what's to become of the stage station," her father mused aloud. "I suppose we could take over the business if we can hire reliable help."

"I sent a note to the stage company," Gideon reported. "They will send replacements immediately."

Lori glanced up to see Gideon staring somberly at her. Then he said, "I'd like to speak privately with you, Lorelei."

She knew by his formal tone that she was about to hear his final fare-thee-well. Lori followed him outside while her father set out food for the other two men.

"My father said you went to extra lengths to save my

life," she murmured as they walked a good distance from the trading post. "Thank you, Gideon. I will always be indebted to you."

She frowned as she watched him halt then pivot to pace restlessly in front of her. She couldn't recall seeing him so ill at ease. He paused to glance at her then shifted from one booted foot to the other. He stared at the air over her head, blew out a breath and began pacing again.

After watching him for another minute, she muttered impatiently. "Just spit it out. I've never known you to beat around proverbial bushes. Honestly, you are the most straightforward man I know. At least you *were* until tonight."

He halted and dragged in an enormous breath that made his chest swell until it looked as if it might pop. "First off, I want to apologize for ever doubting you and for treating you discourteously. I thoroughly regret being a cynic."

She smiled in satisfaction. "Thank you. Considering Maggie's scheming efforts to see me arrested and hanged in a flaming rush, I concede the evidence was stacked against me."

He took a step closer to trail his forefinger over her cheek and trace the curve of her lips. His tender touch nearly broke her heart because he was leaving and she couldn't imagine how she'd survive without him now that she'd fallen so hopelessly in love.

"You scared the living hell out of me during those tormenting minutes while I hurried to find you underwater. I tried to bargain with every white and Indian deity, vowing I'd do anything, if only I could rescue you." He stared solemnly at her. "But the one thing I can't do is give you up, Lori."

She blinked in astonishment when he went down on bended knee. "No!" she croaked in terror then glanced every which way. "Get up, Gideon, before someone shoots you!"

"Someone like your father?" he said, chuckling.

"The last man who proposed to me died." She tugged on his arm but she couldn't haul him to his feet. "I love you too much to lose you—"

She slammed her mouth shut when the words flew from her lips in a rush.

Gideon grinned, his blue eyes sparkling with satisfaction and relief. He remained on bended knee, despite her attempt to pull him up. "Say you love me again, hellion," he insisted.

"You love me," she replied mischievously.

"You're right, sweetheart. I *do* love you," he assured her softly, sincerely. "I promised myself years ago that I'd be extra cautious about women. Dealing with Maggie was another reminder. Not to mention dealing with the vicious, deceitful man who destroyed my mother's life and her children's, as well. I learned not to trust anyone but my family. I convinced myself emotions were misleading and disastrous. But my feelings for you keep growing stronger. Every time I look at you, I wonder how I can possibly survive without you."

Gideon dragged in a hasty breath. Before he lost his nerve he blurted out, "Marry me, Lorelei. Come to Fort Smith with me for the official ceremony. Then we'll build our home on my family's ranch. I'll return to the Osage Police force so I won't be away from you for long periods of time."

Her golden eyes widened again. Her mouth dropped open but no words came out. He was pleased to know that, for once, he'd left this quick-witted, sassy beauty speechless.

"Glenn and Reece are going with us to Fort Smith to

apply as deputy marshals so Judge Parker won't be under-staffed," Gideon continued. "Your father doesn't have to be shorthanded, either, because I can recommend several reliable young men who would enjoy working with him."

Finally, she composed herself and frowned skeptically. "You're not just saying all these wonderful things because you feel sorry for me after I was set up for a murder I didn't commit and then nearly drowned, are you?"

Gideon shook his head. "The very last thing I feel for you is pity. I love you with all my heart, Lorelei. Until you came along to breathe new life into me, I wasn't sure how much of a heart I had left. I need you like I've never needed anything or anyone else in my life—"

She squealed excitedly then flew into his arms—while he was down on one knee. They tumbled across the lawn as she hugged the stuffing out of him and showered him with delighted kisses.

Gideon cherished them, one and all, and he held her close to his heart, feeling whole and alive and complete for the first time in his life.

"Is that a yes?" he asked between steamy kisses.

"Yes, I'll marry you," she assured him. "Because I love you, Gideon Fox. Heart, body and soul. I was afraid you brought me out here to say goodbye, and I knew I'd shrivel up and die when you rode away."

Gideon rolled to his side, taking her with him. He propped himself up on an elbow, then stared into her bewitching face that was surrounded by curly red-gold hair. When he peered into those amber eyes that sparkled with so much inner spirit and shimmered with boundless love, he knew he was staring at his *forever*.

"Say you love me, Gideon, for now and all eternity," she whispered playfully, and then moved provocatively against him, making him ache to express all the incredible feelings and scorching sensations that loving her ignited inside him.

Gideon smiled as he angled his head and kissed her, savored her inviting lips that tasted like heaven. "Better yet, Lorelei, let me show you that you're everything my heart and soul desires."

And he did—thoroughly, tenderly, devotedly—for all the days of their lives....

* * * * *

See below for a sneak peek from our classic Harlequin® Romance® line.

Introducing DADDY BY CHRISTMAS by Patricia Thayer.

MIA caught sight of Jarrett when he walked into the open lobby. It was hard not to notice the man. In a charcoal business suit with a crisp white shirt and striped tie covered by a dark trench coat, he looked more Wall Street than small-town Colorado.

Mia couldn't blame him for keeping his distance. He was probably tired of taking care of her.

Besides, why would a man like Jarrett McKane be interested in her? Why would he want to take on a woman expecting a baby? Yet he'd done so many things for her. He'd been there when she'd needed him most. How could she not care about a man like that?

Heart pounding in her ears, she walked up behind him. Jarrett turned to face her. "Did you get enough sleep last night?"

"Yes, thanks to you," she said, wondering if he'd thought about their kiss. Her gaze went to his mouth, then she quickly glanced away. "And thank you for not bringing up my meltdown."

Jarrett couldn't stop looking at Mia. Blue was definitely her color, bringing out the richness of her eyes.

"What meltdown?" he said, trying hard to focus on what she was saying. "You were just exhausted from lack of sleep and worried about your baby."

He couldn't help remembering how, during the night, he'd kept going in to watch her sleep. How strange was that? "I hope you got enough rest."

She nodded. "Plenty. And you're a good neighbor for

coming to my rescue."

He tensed. Neighbor? *What neighbor kisses you like I did?* "That's me, just the full-service landlord," he said, trying to keep the sarcasm out of his voice. He started to leave, but she put her hand on his arm.

"Jarrett, what I meant was you went beyond helping me." Her eyes searched his face. "I've asked far too much of you."

"Did you hear me complain?"

She shook her head. "You should. I feel like I've taken advantage."

"Like I said, I haven't minded."

"And I'm grateful for everything…"

Grasping her hand on his arm, Jarrett leaned forward. The memory of last night's kiss had him aching for another. "I didn't do it for your gratitude, Mia."

Gorgeous tycoon Jarrett McKane has never believed in Christmas—but he can't help being drawn to soon-to-be-mom Mia Saunders! Christmases past were spent alone…and now Jarrett may just have a fairy-tale ending for all his Christmases future!

*Available December 2010,
only from Harlequin® Romance®.*

HREXP1210

HARLEQUIN®

A Romance

FOR EVERY MOOD™

Spotlight on

Classic

Quintessential, modern love stories
that are romance at its finest.

See the next page
to enjoy a sneak peek from
the Harlequin® Romance series.

Bestselling Harlequin Presents® author

Julia James

brings you her most powerful book yet…

FORBIDDEN OR FOR BEDDING?

The shamed mistress…

Guy de Rochemont's name is a byword for wealth
and power—and now his duty is to wed.

Alexa Harcourt knows she can never be anything
more than *The de Rochemont Mistress*.

But Alexa—the one woman Guy wants—is also
the one woman whose reputation
forbids him to take her as his wife….

**Available from Harlequin Presents
December 2010**

Silhouette® *Desire*

USA TODAY bestselling authors

MAUREEN CHILD

and

SANDRA HYATT

UNDER THE MILLIONAIRE'S MISTLETOE

Just when these leading men thought they had it all figured out, they quickly learn their hearts have made other plans. Two passionate stories about love, longing and the infinite possibilities of kissing under the mistletoe.

Available December wherever you buy books.

Always Powerful, Passionate and Provocative.

SD73069

REQUEST YOUR FREE BOOKS!

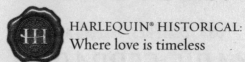

HARLEQUIN® HISTORICAL:
Where love is timeless

2 FREE NOVELS PLUS 2 FREE GIFTS!

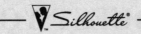

SPECIAL EDITION

USA TODAY BESTSELLING AUTHOR

MARIE FERRARELLA

**BRINGS YOU ANOTHER
HEARTWARMING STORY FROM**

When Lilli McCall disappeared on him
after he proposed, Kullen Manetti swore
never to fall in love again. Eight years later
Lilli is back in his life, threatening to break
down all the walls he's put up to
safeguard his heart.

UNWRAPPING
THE PLAYBOY

*Available December
wherever books are sold.*